I0547572

duality

a novel by neil charles

Copyright © 2016 Neil Charles

All rights reserved.

ISBN: 0692591540
ISBN-13: 978-0692591543

To Petunia

Human beings are born of blood, bound by gravity, eventually to perish... fallible by design... destined.

It is words and actions that present the paradoxical conundrum of fate versus free will.

syncretism

Religion is belief in a supernatural power that has created the universe and endowed humanity with an order of existence. A minimum of seventeen religions each comprise two million followers or more on Earth. The total number of religions is speculative. Their sacred texts offer accounts, legends, and fictions to provide enlightenment and/or direction regarding morals and ethics. The claim of a specific religion as fundamental or superior is of continued debate. Historically, and in the present day, disputes escalate into conflict in the name of religion. However, despite the perceived differences among religions, there are many similarities among their respective tales, which at times are supported by the discovery of artifacts and scientific research.

As example, legends of man communicating with his god include that of Moses and the Ark of Testimony, the Roman messenger of the gods Mercury with his caduceus, and the Chiriqui Indians and their Box of Thunder. Per the Judaic Haggadah, what became known as Aaron's Rod was suggested to have been created by God at night on the Sixth Day of Creation, and then delivered to Adam, the first man, upon his exit from Paradise. It passed through the hands of Adam's progeny, the original earthbound family, where it eventually was bequeathed to Joseph. Stolen after Joseph's death and planted in a garden, no one could remove it until Moses' successful attempt. This last aspect coincidentally parallels the Norse tale of Sigurd removing his father's sword Gram from the tree Barnstokkr to slay a dragon.

Mercury's caduceus, or staff, loosely paralleled the Greek Caduceus of Hermes, a staff entwined by serpents, at times depicted with wings. Mercury was depicted as holding the caduceus in his left hand. The staff offered powers relating to the balance of life and death, with Mercury as the guider of the dead, a protector.

The Indians of Chiriqui (Panama) believed that on top of Mount Volcan they could communicate with their Great Spirit. The Great Spirit would talk to their ancestors through a cloud of thunder using a golden box to reach the Spirit. In comparison Catholicism offers the story of Moses on Mount Sinai, where he constructed The Ark of the Testimony, also known as the Ark of the Covenant, per God's will. The Ark was told to contain Aaron's Rod (coincidentally foretold of in the Haggadah). Aaron, along with his brother Moses utilized staffs from God as shepherd sticks, leading their flocks. The Rods also wielded magical powers, including Moses' parting of the Red Sea, and Aaron's Rod afflicting the unclean with varying illness and plague. Moses' Rod was presumably lost in time. Aaron's Rod was told to eventually be placed in the Ark, which was also lost in time. It is foretold that upon their Savior's return he will retrieve the Rod as evidence of His rule of the wicked, presumably at the apocalypse.

The Box of Thunder, the Ark of the Testimony, Mercury's caduceus, Sigurd's Gram, Aaron's Rod... To go back in time is to get closer to the source of the similarities in these tales. The foundations may be fact, fiction, or a culmination of the two. They would then be subject to mutation from oral tradition and cultural expansion. Eventually lack of tangible proof then births modern day agnosticism and atheism.

How will mankind react if undeniable proof is presented? Will a fundamental religion be realized, sloughing off all false pretense, in effect secularizing the world? Will religions and cultures that do not synch with the truth push back, isolate themselves, or fight against the new reality? Or will that new reality allow for no shadow, but rather force itself upon the earth in an uncompromising manner?

harbinger

The edges are fuzzy in the haze of grasping for a memory. A vast open field lined by tall, ancient trees. Near the middle of the field, a solitary tree devoid of leaves. The fallen leaves brown and crisped, whispering in a humid breeze. Rolling fog on a damp fall morning in the twilight. Eerily quiet… until the screaming.

I remember thinking the blood stained blades of grass reminded me of sweat in my hair from vigorous exercise. Both were the result of a deliberate exertion anticipating a desired result. And when comparing that catalyst of exercise to the cause of the blood, were they really that different? But why was the arm detached? And who or what was that gray, slightly translucent outline over my shoulder as I leaned over the form? And which one of us was screaming? Or were we all?

rude awakening

Early August, Year 1 B.A.

Ron awoke from the nightmare hurtling upwards in his bed. A uniform, panicked scream filled the air, then ceased abruptly. He looked around for the cause of the screaming and found nothing.

His sheets were soaked again; part perspiration, part urine. He focused his eyes on the stark framed photograph of a lonely withered tree across from his bed and concentrated on slowing his breathing. *Third time this week waking up this way* he groggily thought with little amusement, as if this were akin to the repetition of his job on the assembly line.

He looked at his nightstand clock… green chunky numbers illuminated 11:27am on the button again. The same as his last two internal alarms this week. And the two instances last week. And the four the week before. The only thing that's changing is the dream… or nightmare? He's not really sure which.

wrong number?

Mid-September, Year 1 A.A.

The phone on the desk began ringing. The fingers working feverishly at the desktop computer keyboard beside it stopped abruptly, and a half chewed number two pencil dropped beside the phone. The computer monitor displayed a search on *religious artifacts judgment*. The cursor hovered over an article titled 'Fabula of Vetus Voluntas: Vere Artifacts vel Typicus?'. A large, thick hand fell on the phone. The other hand rubbed at weary eyes, then smoothed wavy, dirty blond locks behind his ear as he lifted the phone. "Hello?" In a daze he glanced at the clock in the lower right corner of the screen... 4:24am EST.

At first he heard a rustling noise, then a muffled conversation. A female voice? Then male?

"Hello?"

The muffled voices continued. The female was closer. Half aggravated and half exhausted at the time of the call, he figured someone accidentally dialed him. He was about to hang up when he heard more rustling, then the female voice was coming into clarity "It appears there are quite a few people becoming ill on this fli...".

He pulled the phone away from his ear to check the caller name... Alice. Looking at the clock again on his home computer, he realized where she was calling from.

in the blink of an eye

Mid-September, Year 1 A.A.

Julien looked up at a bird coasting over the field, watching it alight on the breeze with seemingly nowhere to be. He idly wondered if it had flown over to watch their daily pick-up game. Julien had been coming to the pitch during the summer months for as long as he could remember. It was one of the perks of growing up in a smaller town. By midsummer he generally had an understanding as to how the other teens played the game. If he played with any of them during prior summers, the learning curve was all the quicker. This lent itself to stiffer competition as time wore on, and most of the kids honing their skills with time.

"Umm, hello? Care to join those who have been waiting on you to snap out of your botanical musings???"

Julien looked forward, and then had to squint and rub his eyes due to the contrast from the brightness of the clear sky. "Just when I thought they were teaching you something in the off-season, you go and muck-up a perfectly good musing with a reference to plants when I'm looking at a bird."

"Ahh… aloof and full of cow pies."

Julien looked forward to the daily banter of the matches. The ribbing seldom strayed into personal territory. When it did, any number of the participants were quick to sort it out. He blinked his eyes a few times to refocus, then blew a kiss with a grand extension of his hand. He heard light chuckling from the pitch.

He swung the football to and fro over his head between his hands like an old pro, looking left and right. The fielders bore down in their positions. Play time was over. His opening came and Julien sent the ball hurling in the air. He put his head down and took off running down the sideline. Everyone's attention turned to the skyward ball. Then something odd happened.

Julien wasn't sure exactly what was going on due to his focus on running, but he picked his head up when he noticed the regular jockeying for position wasn't occurring. No "I'm on it!", nor customary grunting from stray elbows to the ribs was heard. He looked to where he threw the ball and noticed the players facing him were looking up in the air, but not in the vicinity of where he could have sworn the ball was headed. Then he noticed others closer to him also seemed to be wondering what the fielders were looking at. Had he hit the bird with the ball? What were the odds of that?

The ball hit the ground between several idle boys. Julien had just enough time to hear the loudest sound he would ever hear in his life. The concussive nature of the noise made his ears instantaneously damp with blood, though he had no time to absorb this fact. The ground was hammered roughly fifty meters from him by something enormous he never glimpsed.

Moving at what was later projected as over 500mph, with a debris field of over eight miles in circumference, Julien and his friends would be considered lucky that they were so close to the impact.

memoirs in mediocrity

Mid-August, Year 1 B.A.

Sitting at the dingy kitchen table of his one-bedroom apartment, Ron pulled on his dark brown, scuffed, steel toed boots and tied the laces. Light rain occasionally crashed in rough waves against the sink window with the wind. Walking from the kitchen down the narrow hallway to the hanging hooks behind the front door, he reflected on how he arrived at this point in his life.

The drab beige of every room in his apartment frequently left him in a stoic and pensive mood. His thoughts drifted off to his resume. He graduated in the middle of his high school class with no real ambition in life. Mathematics courses were basically the only ones which held his interest. As a result, those were the classes he excelled in. They also allowed him to skate by relatively unnoticed when his grades lacked in other areas. As a bonus it hadn't hurt that he had an adequate mixture of book smarts and common sense to ensure he got by.

College wasn't a true option, so he never considered it. He may not have known what he wanted out of life, but he knew enough to realize he wasn't interested in a fruitless endeavor where he would be wasting his parents' money and accumulating debt with no true return on investment, whether that be short or long term.

As a result, he struck out and drifted through thirteen

years of meaningless jobs. Initially the goal was to get out on his own, and get by until he determined his true calling, if there was such a thing. This was in the form of migrating from a part time manual labor position to a full time office position with the landscaping service he worked for in high school. That lasted six months and got him into this tiny apartment in a rundown part of the city... The section of the city that time seemingly forgot. It had its run as an up-and-coming beautiful urban neighborhood decades ago, then business expanded elsewhere and the upstanding citizens followed. In recent decades it had become home to both poor and prideful legacies.

He then drifted through several so-called careers. These included, but were not limited to a customer service representative for a delivery service and an office clerk for an accounting firm. His current career, working on an assembly line for the same delivery company he worked for previously, got him closer to not working in an office with the added benefits of insurance coverage and a familiar environment.

Time got away from him during this pensive mood, and he found himself with jacket on and zipped, sitting in his 150,000 plus mile hatchback, affectionately nicknamed The Junker. He turned the key over to fire the ignition. It struck him as odd how the body eases into autopilot for the routine activities at times. The Junker started on the third attempt, partially due to its age, and partially due to the cold weather of a rainy early Autumn evening. Taking a deep breath, Ron ran his hands through his thick mop of brown hair.

He drove the half mile to pick up his friend Mahi for work. Mahi was a grade school friend, and one of the only friends he had. The two were inseparable from the time Mahi was transplanted into Ron's fifth grade class. In hindsight this was due to both of them being outcasts of a sort; Ron being the introvert type that did not seek out friends, and Mahi being the late-comer and only non-white student in their class. Mahi was a talker from the start. And since all the other students weren't comfortable socializing with someone that didn't look like them, he was the only remaining candidate for friendship, and possibly best suited as he would never stop Mahi from ranting. From the start, a current of mutual understanding allowed them to be critical of each other while maintaining respect without judgment. Later they also had similar career aspirations.

Mahi was Hindu. He and his aunt had emigrated from India when Mahi was ten years old. His father was murdered back in his homeland before he was born. He did not know his mother, and his aunt had not given him many details about his family beyond that. When questioned by Mahi, his aunt would only say his life began when they moved here. Mahi has worked for the same delivery company for nine years, and had referred Ron for the customer service job on his original stint with the company.

Ron pulled in front of Mahi's apartment building and honked the horn. Mahi lived in the same neighborhood, but on what's considered the rougher side of the city. Ron was sitting long enough to notice the street was quiet for this time of night, with a smattering of porch, living room, and bedroom lights or televisions remaining on. His mind drifted off with the lull of the windshield wipers. He thought of his plan to meet Lilith at the bar after work. He always looked forward to time spent with her. Even though they worked together, they seldom were able to enjoy more than a passing hello. But even those hellos consistently held a certain kind of tension for him… an electrical current through his body.

Mahi walked up the fractured concrete path along the left side of the apartment building where he resided. His was the basement apartment. He slipped on a wet patch of grass poking through one of the concrete pads and cursed to himself in Hindi. The driver's side window was rolled down and Mahi was close enough that Ron recognized it as a familiar curse... one of several that Mahi would use but never bow to teaching the English translation of as he "won't denigrate the use of language. And besides, I'm not your tourist guide you troglodyte."

Mahi fell into the passenger seat and closed the door. Ron glanced bemusedly at him as he rolled the window up and pulled away into the increasingly rainy night. Mahi appeared to still be composing himself, so Ron decided on prodding him back into dishevelment with "Seatbelt?" in a dull tone that also hinted at knowing what the answer would be. Mahi never wore a seatbelt as "American drivers are slow and cautious compared to Delhi drivers." But he didn't respond to this tried and true question that was the equivalent of putting on a well-worn old comfortable pair of sneakers though. Rather he declared "Angels at Mons".

This wasn't the first, second, or thousandth time Mahi had started a conversation with a series of words that seemingly meant nothing when combined.

Sensing the oncoming verbal volley Ron offered only "Okay."

"Angels at Mons" Mahi repeated.

"Waiting..."

"From our conversation this morning... I forgot."

"That doesn't help. What were you trying to fry my brain with again?"

Mahi replied "Coming home from work, before you kicked me out of this bucket of rust. I was attempting to enlighten you while testing your moral and ethical compass. Or is it compi? Anyway, I need on-going encouragement that I'm having a positive influence on you while also determining if I should continue to drag you through life kicking and screaming on your way toward enlightenment."

"What?"

"Seriously???"

"Okay. Angels at Mons. Was this the World War II battle where the angels appeared in the form of dragons and ate all of the Nazis?"

"Funny, Ronald... Your joke is a thinly veiled attempt at minimizing the fact that you were listening... So to refresh your memory, the British had their backs to the wall in the early days of World War ONE. They were largely outnumbered by the Germans and taking heavy casualties."

"Your point being?"

Mahi continued unabated "And there were numerous reports from the British troops that angels were seen on the battlefield in support of their effort during a key point in the battle. Though it all may have originated as a war time rah-rah story to build British support and troop count that spun into a War of The Worlds-esque event. My point being, as you so rudely interrupted to question, what if it actually happened?"

"I've heard of stranger reports involving large hair-covered bipedal animals walking upright in the wilderness, as well as little grey bipedal beings with bug eyes come to think of .."

"What if there were angels in support of the British troops... if the soldiers saw forms in the sky? Do angels then have a rooting interest in humanity's *good versus evil* struggle?"

"Based on what I was force-fed growing up? Sure, angels would want to see good triumph over evil. Where is this going Mahi?"

Mahi retorted "Why? If you were an angel, wouldn't you be offended by the presence of humans since apparently God wasn't satisfied with JUST you and therefore made humans in His image???"

Ron considered this. "I'd be a fool or far right Christian Republican to think I knew why they intervened. My guess is maybe angels weren't built with the capability for jealously and it never occurred to them to have such a feeling. So maybe they do have a rooting interest for good."

Mahi, unfazed and clinical... "Interesting, but there's a loophole in your logic. The lack of jealously doesn't allow for the angel Lucifer and his followers."

"Touché. Sorry, haven't really studied up on the existential meaning of the Angels at Mons." Ron flexed his hands open at ten and two on the steering wheel. "I don't KNOW." He rolled his eyes, focusing on the road.

In a dreamy, breathy southern accent "Well you've at least proven you are in-fact not a far right Christian Republican. Your 'I don't know' would have been phrased as 'It's God's will'". Reverting to his own tone he continued "Well why weren't Satan's minions there to back up the Germans then?"

"Spread a little thin? There was a lot of hate and attempted domination going around at that time..."

"Interesting theory..." Mahi mumbled while deep in thought as if the response had been a curve ball he had not considered. One of the aspects to appreciate about Mahi's personality beyond this semi-forced philosophical banter was the fact that he would probe not just to prove some point he already had loaded, but to gain more perspective as he truly wanted to know what was behind the curtain. This was definitely a trait they both had in common, but again Mahi was the mule pulling the cart.

Work was a fifteen-mile commute first through the city, then out toward the suburbs via highway into an industrial park. Driving now on the wet highway slowed them down, as the tires on the Junker were about as smooth as an ice cube. Ron knew not to push his luck by rushing when there was no need to rush just to work on the factory line. At most they may have two second shift workers slightly peeved if they're a few minutes late as they are due to relieve them at 11pm.

As if sensing what he was thinking, Mahi put on another familiar pair of old sneakers by asking "When are you getting new tires again? Or tires with any tread for that matter?"

Rcn offered "With as slow as we Americans drive? What's the need? I'm considering taking the tires off to protect them for the spring."

offensive defenseman

August 29, Year 1 A.A.

The crew was small. On this particular dig the family included the Colonel, Anne, and Stanley. Hatim was the equivalent of a cousin, albeit a young one, they were staying with in-country (in Stanley's mind anyway). The Colonel occasionally employed locals to speed up completion of level excavation once he felt relatively certain they'd find nothing else while exposing a small remaining portion of a level on the grid. The boy's businesslike demeanor appealed to Stanley as he himself attempted to maintain that same demeanor in his professional life also.

Stanley had attached his wagon to the Colonel's convoy three years ago. He had been a nomad of sorts over roughly two decades in archeology prior. From a young age he had been precocious with unnerving ambition and a shameless cutthroat attitude in anything competitive. This included graduating at the top of his class in high school. In the process he had earned the nickname Steamroller, not so much for the laborious and efficient work of the machine, but because it flattened anything in its path to attain its goal. He had displayed this attribute in class, and as a bruising defenseman in ice hockey. His stature, six feet five inches tall and two hundred thirty-five pounds, lent to the imposing nature of the nickname, although he did not act on it physically anywhere except on the ice. He took the nickname as a compliment.

He went on to complete three degrees in college, with a Masters in Archeology based on Rome, chased by a Doctorate with a dissertation theme of biblical archeological interpretations. He had always found the Bible intriguing. This was not the result of being raised in a particularly religious household and he had never ascribed to a particular religion at any point in his life, but he knew many religious texts were steeped in a tangible history beyond myth. And he found the discovery of that tangible history to be the underlying current in his professional life. He wasn't looking to prove any religion as truth, but rather wanted to discover what man had created hundreds and thousands of years ago in such blinding belief of their gods. Other than nature, nothing seeming quite as powerful in life to him as did objects standing the test of time propped up on man's beliefs.

Based on his scholastic record and drive, Stanley was able to find work in the field with relative ease coming out of college. It certainly helped that he had tempered his Steamroller reputation in his collegiate years, but what remained was an unrelenting desire to win. This manifested itself in the form of personality clashes throughout his career.

The field of Archeology doesn't necessarily lend itself well to a win at all costs drive. Archeological finds of significance aren't common by nature, and don't happen on any type of schedule. Stanley's loss of interest in the tedium of survey, excavation, and analysis of a dig, coupled with his need for notoriety eventually created friction and abandonment of employment more often than not. With age comes maturity though, and Stanley was no exception. Over the years he eventually came to the painful realization that there were no true shortcuts to the process, and he may not gain that notoriety in his lifetime. And even if he did, he'd have to share it as a team member, as he still had the student loans two decades out of school to ensure that he would be in considerable debt for some time based on his need to be in the field. It was an existence categorized as an employee, not an employer.

So eventually he learned to find his niche. He worked toward signing on as close to excavation as possible (when possible). He signed on with aggressive employers, typically those with stricter deadlines. And he looked for smaller teams to assure more notoriety. One additional aspect of a project that he'd come to seek out was an employer who took somewhat calculated risks.

His current dig with the Colonel met each of these requirements. The Colonel was older, well trained, experienced, and paying for the dig as far as Stanley knew. This meant four things for certain: 1. The Colonel handled the analysis largely himself. 2. The Colonel would be aggressive as he was footing the bill. 3. The Colonel, being older, coupled with paying for the dig, meant he would be looking for a big fish to hang on his wall and could take chances in doing so. 4. The Colonel was a team player and helmed a small team. He'd share the accolades. And there weren't many people to share them with.

But those benefits were currently wearing thin. By Stanley's count, they were 135 days into the dig, very deep into the stratum, and had nothing to show for it. This was turning into a wild goose chase... and a painful one. The Colonel had explained prior to setting out for the excavation that it would be a small crew as the Saudi government was particularly adamant about a monetary donation per crew member, and the Colonel had to choose between money for time, or money for bodies. The positive was the Colonel was hands-on. The negative was very extensive digging by all. As a result, Stanley some time ago had started waking up in the middle of the night sitting up in shoveling position with back pains thinking he was digging. He failed to see the humor in this after the second or third occurrence. He figured he'd stick it out a little longer as putting the feelers out a week ago had brought back no prospects for a new project to sign on to, and Anne being easy on the eyes didn't hurt either. But this project was drawing to a close for him.

Then today happened. It had been a ridiculously hot day in his estimation, and they were into the afternoon, which meant the corner of the grid they were digging in was now exposed to the sun. After lunch, Stanley and Anne had headed back up the hill to continue digging. The Colonel stayed behind as he customarily did this time of day. Apparently age and extremely hot temperatures do not take kindly to the aged. Plus, the square they were working was not exactly comfortable for two people, let alone three.

After roughly an hour of digging and emitting bad grade school level jokes, Anne had stood, arched her back as far as possible to stretch out the kinks, hands on her kidneys, then pinched the front collar of her dusty, sweat-soaked shirt and began fanning it in and out. "I'm out of water, my hat's soaked through, sweat's dripping in my eyes, and I'm boiling. Oh, and I'm fresh out of jokes. Need time to think of more…" she offered with a lethargic but trademark unrelenting smirk.

He looked up at her. "Okay."

"That's what I like about you, Slippy. Your overall lack of response to any of my attempts at humor. It's endearing." She gave him time to respond. There was no rush to anything when you were digging in a desert. She saw he had paused. He was hunched over, head still arched downward, and had begun wagging it back and forth slowly to stretch. For a glimmer of a second she thought she had finally cracked through and he would leak a tiny bit of unprofessionalism like a tire with a small hole.

Then his neck cracked, he dipped his head, and went back to digging. Unflappable, Anne pointed at him in an accusing manner and offered "Hah! You ARE loosening up. Just know you're on the precipice of fun. And I get it. You're afraid the water's frigid. Go ahead... dip a toe or two in first... I'm heading down to base. No worries on me seeing and spreading rumors of you loosening up though. You need anything?"

He looked up at the position of the sun. "I'm figuring it's about 2:30pm. Hatim should be back with water any minute."

As if on-queue, Hatim came into sight at the top of the ramp leading into the pit. Dressed largely in earthen colors (and covered with dusty earth), only the hat and neon green backpack he was wearing stood out. He had journeyed back home mid-morning at the behest of the Colonel, due to the rising temperature and dwindling water supply. The Colonel ran his daily inventory on schedule as his first task that morning, ensured the team was stocked for several hours, verified that Hatim had an adequate supply of water for the 1.5-mile journey home, then sent him on his way with all remaining empty water bottles in Anne's backpack.

A set of small blessings bestowed on the team was courtesy of Hatim's family. First, the Al-Shammari home was tied into the municipal water system. Upon confirming this with Hatim's father during their first meeting in-country, the father had also mentioned that only a little more than half of his neighbors were connected. But even with the connection, Saudi water was not as readily available as in the States. It flowed at an acceptable rate typically two out of every five days. As a result, his family also had scheduled a semi-regular delivery from a contractor that tankers water in from a distant desalination plant. The Colonel gladly contributed to the Al-Shammari family for use of their resources.

Second, Mr. Al-Shammari allowed Hatim to sleep at the camp unless plans dictated otherwise. As it was summer break and the Colonel offered to employ Hatim, his father said the boy was old enough to take on the responsibilities required and he was at the crew's disposal. It had seemed odd that the boy was allowed to stay with them at a younger age, but the Colonel figured playing in their favor was the Al-Shammari's religious beliefs dictating the son was to serve. He also suspected Mr. Shammari felt there was less chance of an altercation with any locals who had no respect for Westerners if his son was there. The boy was young, but he had already displayed intelligence and integrity beyond his years.

"صديقاتي هاي···" Hatim spoke the English language well. His father had been teaching him from a very young age. In turn, Hatim taught Anne and Slippy some words and phrases. This was a phrase Anne knew as "Hey my friends," or maybe "Hello, my friends."

Anne stood stiff and saluted up to Hatim. Hatim returned the gesture. He walked down to their location on the grid, extended his palm, and they took turns high fiving each other casually. Business… then pleasure, their customary greeting. "Watch out, Hatim, he almost smiled."

Hatim's dirt encrusted Pittsburgh Penguins hat was arched. He only dared wear it when they were on-site, well away from the people in his neighborhood. (He was certain would not be so accepting of it.) His face went blank with Anne's comment and his eyebrows rose, further extending the brim of the hat skyward, comically displaying complete surprise on his face. He offered a quiet, awed, well-played, "Did you break him, Ma'am?"

Anne glanced from Hatim to the back of Slippy's head, which tightened briefly, bandana rising on the front of his head. A smile. She knew he had a soft spot for the boy, hence the hat.

"Water, Ma'am?"

Anne strolled up to him. "Thank you, but no thank you, young sir. I'm heading down the mount. أنت رأيت قريبا" With that farewell, she started the trek downhill whistling.

"Sir?"

"No, but thank you, Hatim."

Momentary silence. No rush. "Sir? Can you please explain more in regards to American hockey?"

Slippy held out Anne's hand shovel. "Certainly. Remember, it is actually North American hockey. Seven teams in Canada. Twenty-three teams in the United States." Hatim took the shovel and fell in line digging. Slippy began regaling Hatim with tales of why he felt North American Hockey was the toughest sport around along with possibly rugby.

Several bullet points and back-up references later, Hatim heard a tink noise from the end of his shovel. Slippy stopped talking. He tilted his head to a 45-degree angle, as if attempting to locate the sound through better positioning of his ear. He turned his head to Hatim, who suddenly had the appearance of a statue with his shovel planted in the dirt.

Hatim had unearthed only sandy dirt and rocks since he's been on-crew. This being his first dig, the first few times he had struck something other than dirt he had gotten that immediate exuberant boyish look of kissing a girl for the first time, as if he had just discovered possibly the greatest thing in life. After the initial several instances of discovering rocks though, the luster wore off. But this was different. He had now struck enough objects to recognize the dull bonk of metal striking rock. This noise was off-pitch. It was a metallic tink. And they both heard it.

Slippy leaned over, wrapped his hand around the

exposed spade of the shovel still in Hatim's hand, and removed the shovel from the ground. He then clutched his hand brush and began to slide it gently back and forth over the spot. A silver-white material began to expand with each brush stroke. And an image? "Go gather Anne and the Colonel please."

Hatim came back to life.

sigil

Late-August, Year 1 B.A.

"I don't believe that's legal in this state..." Lilith offered with disdain. She rolled her eyes in the direction of the five fraternity boys at the end of the bar.

"Give the lads credit... After disgusting or scaring off every woman in the bar, including you, they've found a way to entertain themselves outside the norm..." Ron shaded his eyes from the morning sunlight enveloping the college boys from the large windows behind them.

"Oh, I'd call it *norm* for the ankle scratchers." Lilith muttered with further contempt.

"Well they're probably still working out the whole invention of fire thing."

"While burning holes in their pants?"

"Still upset I wasn't jealous at T-Bone's advances?"

In response she simply offered the same smirk that helped lead them initially down a road less travelled some time ago.

Lilith and Ron were on their second round of drinks after the third shift. The bar restaurant across the highway from the plant catered to the plant employees as well as the police officers stationed at the barracks a mile down the road. The latter was the reason it was permitted to serve alcohol at such an early morning hour. And if the former were a bit tired after their shift, crossing a four-lane highway in unfavorable weather with a fifty mile-per-hour speed limit was a quick pick-me-up.

At his persistent look of expectation Lilith finally responded "Nope… unless you think I'm into crew cuts, rugby shirts, and drool?"

"I was going to ask him what store the shirt came from…"

She glanced back down the bar, gave a half amused, half exasperated sigh, and shifted her focus back to stirring her rum and cola. They sat in a comfortable silence for a minute; mirror images slumped over slightly with their elbows resting on the bar. But it was also a silence that may have been due to both of them wondering where the morning was going.

Possibly sensing he was thinking this Lilith gave a shiver as if she just surfaced from being pushed into a cold lake, then in disgust and finality "Junior Bacon." This was their name for the immature children of police officers who were permitted to abuse laws, such as imbibing before legal drinking hours, due to who their parents were. Neither was sure which boy was the son of a local police officer in this particular group, but the fact typically presented itself before long. These individuals often respond unkindly when shut off from the bartender after abusing this perk (as they frequently did).

Something had been on his mind from the prior day clawing away at his brain. The only person other than Mahi that Ron felt would take his thoughts and request for interpretation seriously was Lilith. But that didn't make it any easier to voice after his initial attempt at the topic elsewhere. She was always receptive to his mental wanderings, and seemed to have an intelligent opinion based on any topic he broached. It was really uncanny the way she responded to his ideas. It was as if she had thought about any topic he approached her with for years prior, and had considered every angle. This often included an angle he (and seemingly anyone) would never have thought of.

He spun his barstool around to face the windows at the front of the bar area. Leaning his elbows back on the bar, shoulders pushed upward, the top of his factory shirt collar rested near his lips. Ron tilted his head slightly to the left, folded his lips inwards and pushed the collar back and forth between them. He shook his head while watching the first-shifters drive by heading toward the city, wagging the top of the shirt as he did so. The next stop light was over two miles up, and the cars were already driving slowly due to congestion. In moments like these he realized he was comfortable working the third shift, and even more comfortable having a drink at this time of day rather than sitting in traffic with the same scowl on his face most of the passing drivers had. Ron snickered to himself as he realized maybe this was a small step in his life toward realizing his calling. He laughed again at how ridiculous the minuteness of the comfort was in relation to the seeming grandiosity of a *calling*.

Ron glanced at the shoulders exposed above her black spaghetti-strap top, albeit slightly obscured by shoulder length jet black hair. To his recollection, she always let her hair down immediately upon leaving the factory, along with removing her factory shirt. His eyes then inevitably fell to the beginning of the truncated Catholic biblical script stacked halfway down her left shoulder blade, disappearing into her top. "…the devout are taken away, and no one understands…". He'd pondered the complete verse too many times to count, just as he'd pondered her exposed back beyond numeration. Lilith's clothing choices were always based on functionality and comfort he surmised, hence the spaghetti-strap tops consistently under her work shirt. No matter how cold it was, she was a person who always felt warm. He never took it as an attempt to expose the tattoo.

But it still always managed to make him wonder. He'd only asked her about it once, late in a morning. He questioned the symbolism behind it along with its placement. It seemed odd that the quote started halfway down the shoulder blade, almost out of symmetry on her back. And Ron asked if it hurt as he had no tattoos and was always curious about enduring such pain.

She only offered a deadpan "A sigil… yes it hurt, and you're asking the wrong questions" in response.

He scratched his head at this. Coupled with the quote itself and the fact that she never gave much of a hint at being a religious person, this stuck with him for the past few years since he'd broached the topic in bed that morning.

"So I want to run something by you."

"Must be serious as you stopped breathing a minute or two ago."

"Really?" he blushed.

Without turning her head Lilith offered a role of the eyes and an "Uh, yep."

He caught Lilith looking at herself in the bar-length mirror in front of them. She gave the slightest twitch of a grimace upon inspecting herself. He found this odd as she never struck him as the type to be concerned with her appearance. In fact, that was one of her qualities that attracted him to her. It was a fleeting glance, but it was there, unless he was misreading the situation and he had somehow made her feel self-conscious.

"So I asked Mahi a question yesterday that he responded to only by offering me a sideways glance, and then he changed the topic."

"Wow, did you break him?"

"I didn't see any smoke, but one of his eyes bugged out a bit." He took a long tug on his bottle of beer. Lilith waited patiently. A deep breath, then "Well you know how he is with touting his knowledge of history and religion…"

Lilith rolled her eyes in an exasperated manner and nodded her head in agreement.

"And you know I have my limits with his constant drilling in those areas…"

She offered an additional exasperated eye roll along with a second head nod in agreement.

"So I was reaching one of those points again where I try and outdo him at his own game… which I'm aware I've never been successful at, but this time I apparently stopped him cold. And instead of elation, I felt an odd sense of discomfort between us, like I insulted his dead father or something." He paused, then wrinkled his lips and self-deprecatingly shook his head. "Don't tell him I said that."

She offered a dismissive "Understood and I get your point." The words and her tone were just another dart in the center of the bullseye of his attraction to her.

"So you know one of his favorite topics is religion…"

"Keep going."

"Well in attempting to emulate his thought process for our debates, I asked myself what I know on this topic, what Mahi is going to retort with, and how can I nail any retort to the wall."

"Very noble of you…"

Now it was his turn for an eye roll. Ron turned his barstool sideways to face her, placed an elbow on the bar and extended his forearm in an extended karate chop for emphasis. "Come on, all three of us know Mahi's far more intelligent than me. I've only got him in street smarts, and rarely get to use that as a counterbalance in our relationship. I need to exploit any intellectual advantage I can muster."

He continued "So you know a lot of his life lessons surround the supernatural…"

"Gremlins on airplane wings?"

"Stay with me on this. He was drilling me on something called the Angels at Mons..."

"Ahh, the romantic times of the World Wars..."

"How am I the only one who doesn't know about these things???" he voiced in exasperation. "So you know how my mind works sometimes. It meanders. He scorched my brain with his thoughts on the Angels at Mons to the point that I'm walking around with this running through my mind, which then tailspins in different directions. So I start thinking bigger picture... or earlier picture I guess. I got to thinking about angels being thrown out of heaven..."

Her eyebrows rose just slightly in response. It was miniscule, but there.

Ron already felt a slight tinge of relief that he hadn't made a mistake in raising the topic, and as a result let out a sigh. "I guess my thoughts aren't totally formed yet, so this may seem a little scattershot. His response just left me bewildered."

No wise comments in reply. He definitely had her attention.

"So the angel eviction... not Lucifer, but the *third* from growing up Catholic. I remember the story from the Bible as a certain faction of angels, led by Lucifer, being thrown out of heaven for sinning. This got me to reading passages from the Bible and making an attempt to piece it all together. So let's suppose Lucifer was the first to go... and he did so as he wanted to be God, with his throne above God's stars per the book of Isaiah. Well why did he want to be God? If God created Lucifer and all the angels as perfect and without want, what would have driven him to think he was better? The first ever recorded case of narcissism?"

Ron took a sip from his bottle then continued... "So word gets around that Lucifer's gone, right? Maybe there was a witness. Probably not, I'm guessing, as I could not find any passages relating to it. And one would think that would be a whole different rabbit hole with more than Lucifer being evicted. Angels now start wondering. Maybe they approached God about it, but maybe not. So the first ever cases of fear and paranoia also ensue. *What happened to Lucifer? Why is he gone? Who's next?* Nothing like this has ever happened and it's never occurred to the angels as a possibility. Angels begin to experience what becomes known as panic."

Ron realized he had trailed off with his thoughts as he spoke, but couldn't snap out of it. Everything was fuzzy and gray with black at the edges. He shook his head to refocus, realized he was staring at the floor, and looked up.

Lilith had propped herself upright and turned her stool to face him, drink in hands resting on her closed thighs. Her eyes were steely as they sized him up, with as somber a look as he has ever seen on her face. "Go on."

Holding the neck of his bottle, Ron lifted it out in front of him, twirling it in a circle to size up how much of its contents remained. Cars drove by behind the bottle, perceived by him as hazy moving globules. Zoning back out he offered "And the Book of Revelations refers to a future war in heaven between a dragon and the angels, with the dragon being cast out of heaven after it had drawn in a third of the angels. Well there's no mention of a dragon in creation, so presumably that's a metaphor. I equate a dragon with fire. Lucifer was known as the Morning Star, or the Light Bringer…" He placed his bottle on the bar and held his left hand up in front of his chest. He began wagging his index finger back and forth with each word, back and forth, drawing a connection between them. "Morning Star… star… Light Bringer… light… star… fire. Dragon… Lucifer. I'm thinking that's not a stretch. So Lucifer was resilient. What was he looking to accomplish though? Did he still want to take over heaven? Did he just want to raise hell? Or was his goal to educate the angels and draw them out of heaven?" Then an afterthought... "Was he lonely?"

He went on. "It only brings more questions. I almost feel like writing all of this down as I know I'm not going to recall half of it." Ron felt exasperated. "So let's go back to the start, Lucifer being thrown out of heaven that is. Why? Why would Lucifer be thrown out of heaven in the first place? I don't buy him wanting to be God. I don't have that totally thought out, but I just don't. What if he left?" He paused. "So he was known as the Morning Star. Could that also be a metaphor for him being one of the first angels? And if so, did God confide in him more than other angels? What if God ran His plan for man and woman by Lucifer, and THAT set everything in motion with Lucifer's departure? Suppose God explains His plan and Lucifer questions it from jump-street. And what if it's God who has the first case of narcissism??? Why would Lucifer pooh-pooh the idea? He would have had to have good reason. You don't just question God's judgment if it's not been done before, which I'm presuming it hadn't. And this brings me back to Mahi." Ron finished the last swallow of his beer. His face contorted in the sour reaction of drinking something that is too warm to enjoy.

He motioned to the bartender quickly for another beer, and then returned to Lilith. "Oh, sorry, warm beer caught me by surprise. Guess I got off on a tangent. You ready for another?" She nodded, putting her empty glass on the bar, showing no offense to him not initially doing his gentlemanly duty of asking a lady if she'd like a drink first. "So where was I?"

"Where you started and ended... with Mahi." She was now leaned forward, palms propped on the stool between her legs. Her body language showed she was fully involved in the conversation. Ron was always comforted by the fact that she tuned in completely when he was talking. She wasn't one to be easily distracted and seemed to be one of the few people of that nature.

"So presume Lucifer was one of the first angels, and one that God communicated His ideas to. Lucifer would probably not have been too happy with God voicing that He would be creating man and woman, let alone in His image and giving them free will. This isn't exactly a shocking supposition in today's day and age I assume, but I went one further with Mahi." A deep breath, then "You know the inner voice we had as children?"

"I've heard of it..." was her flat response.

"Well what if that's what put Lucifer over the edge? Think about it. God runs this by him... Not for an opinion, but just to say this is what you have to look forward to. Maybe He even had the idea mankind would be entertainment for the angels. But Lucifer starts adding it up differently. He's thinking 'Why aren't we enough? We sing for you. We praise your name... entertaining you is our existence. What more do you need?'"

He continued. "And maybe God's created other forms of entertainment in the past and it just keeps chipping away at and piling on for Lucifer... something to the effect of 'This is it... You're now making competition for us and giving them more amenities... making them in Your image... giving them a universe to play in... giving them free will... and on top of that setting them up with an inner guiding voice to start out their lives.' At this point he can no longer rationalize his existence being enough and leaves. He isn't evicted at all. I'd be ticked. I'm assuming angels don't need an inner voice as they don't have free will to include the need. And who, or what, would be happy to hear something deemed lower than them has a direct line to the Creator? And the Creator GUIDES them no less."

His thoughts were coming together as he expounded.

"So not only does Lucifer leave, but the angels somehow gain knowledge of this. And maybe they know the dragon is coming, or maybe they don't, but when they see or catch wind of it, many of them have their bags packed because they aren't too happy and want to catch the first bus out of town. They ruled the roost and see creation and Lucifer's departure and do the math that their time as #1 is running down. Existence was good, they sang God's name, played music in His honor, all the good stuff of a party before people get too drunk and something bad happens. And for some reason they don't feel responsible for, all the lights have suddenly been turned on, the music has stopped, and they're feeling exposed and unwelcome. So they're probably thinking 'What the heck?' you know, since Hell didn't exist yet and all..."

"Very funny..." she offered with a cute smirk.

"They're thinking 'Why aren't we enough anymore?', and don't want to wait around to find out what the next upgraded science, sorry, religious project is. The writing is on the walls of heaven. And I would get that. I wonder why there wasn't more of an exodus. Maybe some felt they were still at the top of the ladder and God had experimented in other ways before that never amounted to any threat to their position. Maybe many of the angels didn't know yet about God's play set. Maybe they did and were too scared. Maybe they did and didn't feel a threat... or were too comfortable, particularly since my understanding is there was no Hell, no punishment to that point, so they would not have known the word *consequence*." He scratched his head. "Maybe they were just ignorant."

Lilith picked up her fresh drink, drank it like a shot, and asked the bartender for the check. She turned and said "Hold that thought. Let's get out of here."

And Ron officially began wondering where the morning was going.

Mid-September, Year 1 A.A.

Pascal received the call he knew was coming. He was doing his rounds on the southern edge of town when he heard the explosion and felt the ground shake. He immediately wondered if there had been an earthquake, and looked up in time to see the end of the fireball. The town of Rodez is in Southern France, which is considered a low risk zone for such an event. His rudimentary understanding of earthquakes consisted of a professor once informing him that their area would most likely only ever experience minor tremors due to the on-going collision between the African and European tectonic plates. This was after a truck's engine had exploded in the area and Pascal made the mistake of asking the professor if he thought they were experiencing a quake. Mistake being the operative word, as the professor bent his ear regarding plate tectonics for much more time than he had or wanted to spare.

Pascal had already been driving toward the tower of black smoke on the northern end of town when his dispatcher pinged the car's walkie-talkie. He didn't bother turning off the siren for the call. He gripped the walkie tight to his mouth, depressing the button without hesitation, and starkly asked "Where?" He didn't want to hear the answer. The town was too small and he knew its inhabitants, the Ruthenios, social patterns too well not to know what event was occurring in the area at the time of the explosion.

"Over near the pitch on the north side. I can see it from the window." Sheila notified the National Police Lieutenant hollowly. Even through the mechanical sounding device, it was obvious in her tone that her mind was conjuring the exact same catastrophic result he was. The school aged children would have been playing football under the fireball he witnessed.

He lost time for a second. All noise disappeared. Then he jammed the car brakes on the empty country dirt road. He opened his car door, threw up with a guttural flourish, and sat up, blank again. He wiped his forehead, straightened his hat in the rearview mirror, closed the door and plunged the gas pedal. *Better now than later* he thought. "Dispatch?"

"Yes?"

"Car Seventeen. Can you please…" He released the button on the talkie to gather his thoughts.

Sheila didn't wait. "Call the fire crew and SMUR? Then Commandant next? SAMU? SDAT? I will… and the other officers if you are in agreement. Then I'll call Karine."

"Thank you." He considered everyone she mentioned. Training had clearly kicked in for Sheila. The fire crew is obvious. SMUR will ensure there are physicians on-site quickly via their ambulances. SAMU might be going overboard under normal situations, since fire and SMUR report through SAMU as central control, but protocol for disasters indicates it's a necessary contact. And that was clearly her thought behind SDAT also. His stomach told him this was a disaster also, but anti-terrorism seemed hasty. "Have SMUR grapevine to all other ambulatory support in the surrounding areas. Not SDAT, though. Let that be Peter's call. We don't know if this is an act of terror."

As he drove through town he saw more and more people heading towards the smoke. Everyone looked dazed. Some turned to glance at his passing, mouths agape as if frozen stuck. He realized it had been over a year since anyone in the department needed to run the siren on a patrol car. It was as if the locals, initially perplexed by the explosion and smoke, were only further confounded by another loud noise. Rodez was a small and peaceful town of about 25,000 residents. Most of the people haven't experienced anything close to the last five minutes of their lives except through television.

But that wasn't entirely it. At least not anywhere close to the overarching reason for the Ruthenios to still be so dumbstruck. It was also the charred objects. A young boy was staring, brows furrowed, across the street at what appeared to be a semi-charred sheet of metal broken partially through a second story window. He slowed down to also look. Maybe a car hood? Two blocks closer to the smoke was another large metal panel wedged securely through the front awning and second floor wall of a restaurant. It was shortly after that he saw Veronique, and understood the gravity of the situation.

Veronique was a good friend of his girlfriend, Karine. Pascal had never been able to comfortably befriend her, despite extensive attempts. His long-term dating relationship with Karine was looked down upon by Veronique. He surmised this from her cold demeanor toward him, along with several hints that Karine had inadvertently relayed to him from the women's conversations. Karine was a staunch Catholic and he was not. He'd always been candid with Veronique about his past. She knew he didn't attend any church services with Karine, and was also aware of Karine's acceptance of the arrangement. Veronique, older (by eleven years over Karine, five over him), 'wiser', never allowed him to have the last word any matter in faith, or others in general. She never outright said she didn't approve of their relationship, but Pascal felt Veronique didn't have to vocalize it either. He viewed it as her keeping Karine from stepping off the pedestal of righteousness. Just another small reason for him to turn away from organized religion.

Her looking up at him in utter bafflement currently was therefore completely uncharacteristic. She clung to her shopping bags from the local stores in one hand while poking something burnt and smoking on the ground with her walking cane in the other hand. He brought the car to a stop beside her and looked down at the object. "You need to stop touching that. It's a torso." He began to drive away then leaned out the window again. "Cover it up, and please let no one touch it until I send someone for it." He saw she was still staring blankly in his direction as he made a left turn around the next corner.

The debris became more frequent. Damage to buildings the same. He could only imagine what type of conversation that encounter would result in with Karine. And what discussion of religion? The events of today were already only driving his wedge of disbelief further. The wedge was not just in faith, but also in his relationship with Karine as a result of Veronique's judgment of his lack of faith. Funny how the religious in their piousness often turn their noses up to those of differing beliefs. "Love thy brother," he chuckled. Smoke was beginning to swirl around the streets like fog rolling in from a lake. Driving closer to the source the sky was growing darker despite being midday. And as he rounded the last turn of the thickly-built town, he saw it all open in front of him, and felt the enormous sense of complete helplessness that he'd only felt one other time in his life.

The tower of smoke coming out of the hole seemed as wide as a tornado at the base. Trees in the area were flattened outward from the impact site. It appeared as if all of the windows on buildings facing the field were blown out. Many of the openings on the homes and businesses were occupied with people. Some were rubbing their ears. Others holding towels or clothes to cuts on their bodies. All were looking in the direction of the smoke. Metal was everywhere. And bodies. He was trained not to draw assumptions in his job, but he knew by the sizes of many of the bodies and the athletic gear that many of them were children from the regular summer football games on the field. The parts: limbs, torsos, heads... random combinations. He was seeing more of them as he cruised.

"Lieutenant Pascal?"

He stopped the car, realizing he was now coasting past the site on the outside of the field. Was he thinking of passing it by and leaving?

"LIEUTENANT?"

Pascal looked around and located the source. He had passed the young man in the car and not even seen him. He could have hit him and never realized. But from what he could tell, Romain probably took about the same notice of this. He was standing with his left arm holding himself over his work apron across his waist, right hand raised, fingers slightly ajar in front of his mouth taking in the scene outside the cafe. "Romain? Yes?"

"What... How... How can I help?" Pascal knew Romain from the cafe he frequented. He was in his twenties, shoulder-length hair tousled and blowing across his face in the breeze. They had struck up a casual relationship over the years, and he always gave Pascal the impression of being a stand-up individual.

"Thank you. Please walk toward the crater, but not too close to the fires. If you see anything that smells of petrol get away from it upwind and fast, then notify me. Look in the crater. I need you to look and listen for injured. If someone is injured in the crater, notify me. Do not go in. Then walk an expanding circle around it. If there's anything you can do to help quickly, do it. Don't move any survivors unless they're in danger though. Otherwise notify me asap, then keep walking. Do not touch anything otherwise." After no response, "I'm sorry, can you handle this?"

Romain ran his hands through his hair and tucked it behind his ears with his palms. "Yes. Yes. I'm sorry. I just can't believe this is happening."

"I understand. Now go please. Time may be of the essence."
Romain walked toward the flames, watching the ground to ensure he wasn't stepping on anything, or anyone.

"And Romain?" The young man turned to face him. "If anyone stops you, inform them I've instructed you on what to do, and for them to see me if there are questions."

Pascal knew he was stronger at reacting on instinct, rather than thinking. He now had time to think, and couldn't focus. Was he really considering leaving before? He realized he was completely overwhelmed. He had always wondered if there was a God. Now he was far less certain. He realized the phone in his pocket was buzzing. He removed it, saw it was Karine, and pressed the decline button. The screen changed and he saw she had already called three times. He hadn't noticed the prior attempts. He quickly sent her a text of '1.12.'. This is their long-ago agreed upon syllabic code representation of 'Okay. Call Later.' for just such an occasion. He's only had to use it once in their seven-year relationship. Rodez does not offer much in the way of threatening situations to the National Police. The bulk of his calls are drunks, traffic accidents, domestics, or a combination of the three. He now heard fire sirens.

He looked around. People were edging in from the clearing. He opened the trunk of his cruiser and grasped the bullhorn inside. Wiping the sweat from his upper lip, he depressed the talk button and feedback blared out momentarily, warbled, then ceased. "Citizens... Ruthenios... The National Police needs your assistance at this time. If you are cleared for emergency support services or have any nursing training, or were here during the event, please come to my car. Parents, please take your children..."

antenna for the box of thunder

August 29, Year 1 A.A.

Jabal Aja. Jabal Aja, Norman Versail thought to himself. "How in the hell did I get here? Or better yet, how in the hell did I get to hell?"

Jabal Aja is a granite mountain range to the west and southwest of the province of Ha'il, northwest Saudi Arabia. The different varieties of granite displayed as beautiful ground hues from light-greenish brown, to grayish green, to red. This could be Scottsdale, Arizona he mused… If only you squint hard enough to obscure the huge Saudi flag comprised of electric lights on the side of the mountain. And much like Scottsdale, it's not advisable to go out for a stroll, let alone work outside in August. That's when temperature highs average around 100 degrees.

"Did I mention it's August?" Versail said aloud (to no one in particular) as he glanced up at the old circular thermometer hanging centered on the back wall in the tent. He wiped his sweat laden brow with his handkerchief then absent mindedly returned it to his back pocket. 105 degrees… Just seeing it wore on him. He'd grown accustomed to talking to himself over the years. He supposed the trait was acquired from several of his mentors. It was an expeditious conclusion long ago that Archeologists come across as quite stuffy to those outside of their field, and at times even to those in their field, resulting in becoming your own audience.

It has been a long, hard road to hell he mused with a chuckle. He'd been bitten by the archeology bug as a child digging in his backyard, otherwise known as the Tsegi Canyon in Arizona. His father would often take him exploring in the Canyon as a child, and it wasn't long before he started bringing a shovel due to his father's tall tales of dinosaurs and desert monsters. That bug only burrowed deeper with the discovery of a partial set of Segisaurus bones in his teens. The set being only the second set of Segisaurus bones ever discovered in the area. The dinosaur was a diminutive Jurassic period bipedal theropod. It maxed out at a little over three feet long and fifteen pounds, was nimble, and had three toes at the bottom of each leg. Versail immediately gravitated to it as he was diminutive in size (at just over five feet three inches), light (at one hundred and six pounds), and nimble with nine toes. He'd lost the pinky on his right foot dodging a falling rock as a child.

That find, several collegiate degrees in Archeology and History, and (he thought) the ability at a young age to drone on and on intellectually regarding archeological topics allowed him to dive right into a career that eventually led him to Jabal Aja. He had found employment throughout his career with different crews, resulting in several small finds. None of the finds as significant as the Segisaurus, but enough to keep him tanned, calloused, and well-stocked with ibuprofen for the back pain.

After over thirty-five years in the field, he knew that he was much closer to the end of archeological digs than the middle. A small investment in the technology field two decades back had resulted in a relatively consistent flow of money, with which he was able to eventually stake out on his own, supporting a small crew that evolved into the closest thing he could ever consider a family in such a transient life. The investment also afforded him the relative luxury (relative as he still relied first and foremost on grant money) of playing the archeological lottery, which is to say digging for something semi-mythological (in his mind) based as much on a hunch as any factual information. And this is what brings his crew, his family, to Jabal Aja. The gated community he resides in back in Arizona had nothing on the freedom, tranquility, and sense of wonder of Jabal Aja, and this is what kept him reaching… not to mention the rush.

"Must be getting hot, Colonel. Sounds like you're in the middle of quite the conversation with your paperwork."

Versail startled. Anne guffawed. She had appeared magically behind him between the entrance flaps of the tent. Having a knack for startling him, she took great pride in attempting to do so. She also cracked herself up in doing so… consistently. It was an admirable quality to Versail. "105. No wonder you're chattering like a teenage girl."

"You know me too well, Anne."

Versail was never in the armed forces. His crew lovingly referred to him as the Colonel as he resembled a man from an advertising campaign; white hair, thick black rimmed glasses and a belly. It probably also had something to do with the fact that he looked like fried chicken from so many years in the sun.

Over the years, the most tenured of his crew had names for each other. Anne, aka Alice Malone has worked with the Colonel for the past nine plus years. She technically worked for him, but he felt the duplicitous hours digging in confined, often sunbaked quarters over the years lent itself to a more congenial atmosphere. Not to mention if he treated them as employees, they would have all probably clawed each other's eyes out by now.

He had dubbed her Alice the Annelid a year or two after he first employed her and knew she was going to be with him for the long run. It was almost a rite of passage. Annelids are a group of worms that have been classified as far back as the Cambrian period. They burrow and can regenerate if they're cut in half. They know some other tricks as well, like splitting to form two worms.

Anne and the Colonel had a university in common, where she studied under the same professor that the Colonel first studied and worked under. That professor referred Anne to the Colonel for work. The Colonel was in the field at the time, fully staffed per the capital available to him. Anne, being fresh out of college and desperately not wanting to work in a building (like many archeologists) called him weekly until an opening came available… for five months. Burrowing one might say. Anne was also a twin, hence Alice the Annelid, which evolved into just Anne in time.

Colonel looked down and noticed he had budgetary paperwork in front of him. His back was still to her. "We've been at this dig for what? Four months? You know I abstain from talking budget when we're in the field, at least as long as possible, but we're coming to the fork in the road and I'm pondering which path to take."

Anne sighed. She loved the dig, loved working for the Colonel, and despised these conversations. They always reminded her of the awkward conversations when the passion in a relationship runs dry. And like that uncomfortable feeling of losing someone close, the end of an unsuccessful dig felt like that relationship never coming to fruition. It left the taste of colors being sucked out of the world. She'd come to lean on her relationship with the Colonel. He was a mentor in life as much as in the field, and all he asked in return was for her honesty and back-breaking work.

"Okay, let's have the talk."

Clearance for the dig was no small feat. Considerable lobbying and a donation to the Saudi government were required relating to matters of antiquity, not to mention promise of credit given the government on any noteworthy find. An additional donation and promise of credit was made to the Ha'il Museum. Although monetary, it was fundamentally a different donation. It was a donation in respect for history and the preservation of it. The spending was beginning to take its toll. The Colonel felt more comfortable not looking her in the eyes as he always felt uncomfortable having money and unsuccessful dig conversations individually, let alone both at the same time. "To revisit from before we set out…"

"No foreplay please. Straight to the action."

"Anne…" he offered sternly as he blushed. He was much older than her and felt like a father figure, thus the discomfort in terminology related to carnal relations. He hoped she couldn't hear the blush in his voice as he always attempted to come off as unflappable as possible. That always seemed the right course in his position. "I've only utilized half of our grant money for the start up. This was on agreement with the museum back in the States that I would only utilize the full amount if we found an artifact Not sure if I mentioned this before as I don't like to bog you all down with the financial details, but this allowed me to squeeze more money out of their teat…"

"Colonel! Shut the front flap!"

The Colonel began to blush again, paused in hopes the heat would hide any remaining flush he felt in his cheeks at the double entendre and turned to face her. He tilted his head downward at the optimal angle to give his disapproving eyeball scowl. As he turned, his eyes initially gravitated to the two-inch scar running at a forty-five-degree angle with her hairline on the left side of her forehead. This was a natural reaction from him for two reasons 1. It was an uncommon occurrence, as she either had a hat or bandana on 98% of the time. The other 2%, her hair was down and covering it. 2. She's never explained it beyond brushing it off as a childhood tussle with her twin. This was also uncharacteristic as she generally was a forthcoming person. She had her hair secured behind uplifted sunglasses to wipe her brow. He thought she caught the gaze, so he met her eyes quickly, and matched his eyeball scowl with his voice. "We have a month left on team money before…" He stopped. She looked at him quizzically as she was quickly positioning a dry hat to her head. She then realized why he stopped speaking. They both heard a voice in the distance… young, urgent. It was getting louder and closer.

"أُسـتاذة! أُسـتاذة! أُسـتاذة!"

Anne looked quizzically at the Colonel. "Is he yelling 'Professor'?"

The boy, Hatim, ran into the tent and grabbed the Colonel's arm, pulling him toward the flaps of the tent in an over-exaggerated full body yank that kids could only make look urgent and comical at the same time. The Colonel was slightly taken aback by the uncharacteristic gesture.

The donation to the Ha'il Museum had presented an unexpected perk to the crew. It allowed Mr. Al-Shammari, an assistant curator at the museum, to offer his son as a Hatim-Of-All-Trades of sorts for the crew. Hatim couriered food and weather reports, acted as site steward, and fulfilled other needs from Ha'il to the crew in their group of tents beside Jabal Aja. The Colonel knew they had gotten particularly lucky when the father initially offered his son's name. Hatim was named in honor of Hatim al-Tai, a famous pre-Islamic Christian poet known for his generosity, who also spawned the phrase *more generous than Hatim*.

But Hatim was much more reserved and respectful of the crew as elders than his current demeanor suggested.

Upon arriving at the base tent he would customarily wait outside the entrance flaps after announcing his presence. And if the crew were in the midst of a conversation in the tent, he would wait silently until the conversation ended, or someone noticed him. So the Colonel and Anne both sensed whatever had him worked into this kind of lather required their immediate attention.

The Colonel allowed himself to be led out of the tent, Anne in-tow. The Colonel forgot his sunglasses and sunhat with neck flap. He immediately squinted in the blazing sun and shortly thereafter needed to wipe sweat from his eyes. Hatim released his grip, scurrying ahead of them up the mountain. The boy had the long, loping gait that must be characteristic to lanky pre-teen boys worldwide. He slapped his palms on medium size boulders, pivoting off of them to move quickly up the mountainside. Anne passed the Colonel and the three navigated the trail they've walked daily up to the plateau near the peak of the mount.

Hatim had stopped at the near edge of the plateau, turning and waving them onward and upward. The boy was fast. The Colonel had stopped halfway up, remembering the handkerchief in his back pocket. He pinched it at opposing corners in each hand, wound it in front of him, and tied it around his head. Several minutes later he was near the plateau. Anne, always respectful of any breaking archeological news, waited at the top. She was talking. The Colonel also heard Slippy's deep, baritone voice. "…like nothing I've seen… ever."

The Colonel stopped in his tracks. It is not in Slippy's DNA to make any uncalculated proclamation, even in a joking manner. The man rarely joked. The Colonel closed his eyes, exhaled (he realized he had stopped breathing), and simply stood within himself. He always tempered high hopes of a major find with the harsh reality that 99.99% of humanity never gets the opportunity to discover something truly divine, let alone be second to find something as unique as a collective of Segisaurus bones. But that hair-thin belief in someday being that 0.01% was still tucked deep, deep down in his heart. He was always brutally honest, particularly with and about himself... part of the job that's bled into him he supposed. Or maybe vice versa. Hope had been circling the drain for some time. He didn't close the drain at this moment so much as want to take everything in, just in case.

He opened his eyes and looked around him... the mountain... the tiny tents on the flat below... the symbolism of how small the tents appeared... being so high up on an arduous, arid mountain to climb that presented the possibility of never reaching the peak... Ha'il in the distance... and the silence. No one was talking. Slippy had come to the edge of the plateau and now they were all waiting for the Colonel. Hatim's face displayed eager exasperation. Anne's demeanor was patient with a slight smirk of understanding. Slippy oddly appeared concerned, or confused maybe? Or was it fear in his eyes?

Hatim offered a hand as the Colonel reached the plateau, like he'd done every time he crested this section of the mount since they found it. It was a hand the Colonel never needed, but always took as he found Hatim's unflinching respect for everything and everyone around him very endearing. And he wasn't going to be the one to curb that out of pride or some caveman type belief that a man cannot be helped by a boy.

Slippy had turned his back to them, facing the site. He pointed down into the spiraling excavated pit, toward the far corner portion of the grid they were currently working. The Colonel asked "Is it where we've been this week?" as he peered around Slippy's side.

Slippy only offered "Yes."

"Level 7?"

"Yes."

The Colonel shielded his eyes when he caught a glint of light in front of him. "I thought you lost your watch?"

Slippy turned his head back toward the Colonel far enough to see him squinting at Slippy's arm. "I did. That glint's coming off the artifact."

"What?"

"It's still in situ. And I'm guessing the glint's going to grow."

what happened?

Early November, Year 13 B.A.

It was a menacing look, seemingly more exposed gritted teeth than face. Anger with a purpose, but also anger with quite a bite of hate backing it up. The seditious smile in his eyes sealed that thought. Closer and closer. Faster and faster. Then darkness.

Ron woke up. Fuzzy. He had no clue how long he was out, or even where he was initially. Judging by the bored look on his junior year classmates' faces as they were slowly coming into focus, he surmised he was unconscious awhile. Ron couldn't figure out why they were all in shorts and t-shirts though. They surrounded him, and were all looking down at him for some reason. He was on a scuffed, wooden slatted floor, sitting propped up closer to one of the corners of the room, and he sensed there was someone close behind him.

"...hear me?" It sounded as if the person speaking was fifty feet down a well, shouting upwards toward daylight. Ron remembered teeth like a shark.

"...in gym class, and you hit the..." The voice was going in and out. Hovering, wobbling spots covered everything. Like amoeba under a microscope. Slowly shifting, working. They were in the tone of unprocessed film turned negative after exposure to light.

Ron felt a hand on his back. He turned his head a bit

too fast and everything blurred, spots and faces alike. Ron felt the hand tense and realized he was falling backward. He put his right hand flat on the gymnasium floor and focused on steadying himself against the supporting hand, as if he was a puppet. He let out a long, low groan. His left hand reached for his head slowly, learned from turning his head too quickly. He felt throbbing under his hair follicles, as well as under the skin on his face. It was as if the groan had awoken the throbbing.

"Slow down. Can you hear me Ron?" A now booming soprano fed the pulsing in his head. It was as if someone cranked the volume knob on a stereo quickly mid-song.

He recognized the voice. It took a few additional seconds for the name. Mr. Farina. His gym teacher. Or was it Mr. Corrina?

"Yeeess…"

"Good. Do you know where you are?" the teacher asked in that authoritative, earth-rattling voice.

"Ugghh… too loud."

The teacher lowered his voice as much as a booming voice can be lowered. "Sorry… Do you know what day it is?"

The combination of the bass of his voice and the thrumming of his head were too much. Ron leaned forward and threw up between his outstretched legs. Laughter and gagging sounds of disapproval came from the ring of classmates. He thought to himself that he was going to need a new pair of shorts. Everything went black.

sleight of hand

August 29, Year 1 A.A.

Sitting. All four sat in silence for some time. They looked a little burnt and exhausted after the find. As the artifact was exposed in a corner of the grid, they all sat in a semicircle just staring. Maybe they weren't sitting so much as collapsed at the sight. Being the first to peek into history was always a rush. What is found is never quite what was expected. And therefore the eyes become microscopes drilling down to every speck of surface visible to the point the body becomes exhausted after the initial adrenaline rush and subsequent studying. Hatim believed Slippy was exactly where he had left him when Slippy instructed Hatim to gather the Colonel and Anne.

The artifact rose about two inches out of the ground. Anne, gazing in the direction of it but no longer focused on it, or really anything, spoke first. "Well am I correct in saying we all are wondering the same thing?"

Silence for several moments. "What next?" the Colonel offered quizzically, staring at the artifact as if willing his eyes to burn a hole in it.

"Exactly," Anne offered unflinching.

After the rush, after the studying, then came the "What next?" Continuing the excavation process until completion of exposure was obvious. Documentation, including photography, was a part of the process.

"Well I was… AM prepared with a plan in case of a discovery. But this just seems to change everything." Several more minutes passed. Then "It's 4:17pm. We have roughly five hours of daylight at our disposal. Slippy, please take a break. Can you go down to base to recharge, and then bring up my tool kit? Please ensure the margin trowels, files, and all the brushes are loaded. And please bring my notebook, camera, zip bags, and tape measure." There was no reaction. The Colonel looked up from his watch. "Slippy?"

Slippy was scratching at his backside absentmindedly. He flinched at the Colonel calling his name a second time. "Yes? Camp… kit. Okay." He rose slowly, staring at the artifact as he walked backward toward the exit ramp, tripping over his own feet and falling to the ground before he finally looked away.

Anne waited until Slippy was out of sight, and then giggled, shaking her head. Hatim, bewildered, smirked. The Colonel continued to look worried.

"What do you make of it Colonel?" whispered Hatim after several more minutes of silence.

"I've never seen this specifically depicted. I have some suspicions, but nothing concrete." A pause. "Hatim, Slippy may not have caught everything I asked for. And I forgot to ask him to bring up a resupply of water as we'll all be here longer than expected. Would you mind heading down to ensure he gets everything? He may need a hand also."

Hatim's face displayed suspicion momentarily, eyes sharpened, eyebrows lowered, cheeks puckered. Did he think he was going to miss something? Then it disappeared. "Yes sir." And off he went.

Anne's turn. "Slippy knows what to schlep up the mount in the case of a find. And he's a donkey up here… You know I mean that as a compliment. He doesn't need Hatim's help. Sooooooo?"

"Did you notice Slippy's behavior?"

"Dazed? Scratching? I've had a few long-term boyfriends. I recognize it."

He gave her a look. "Seriously, Anne. That just started. He has more energy than you and I combined. And he's one of the most focused individuals I've seen on the job. Particularly months in after finding nothing. I've never seen him dazed. And the scratching is new."

"What am I missing here? Why send him and Hatim down?"

"I wanted to talk to you alone. I told Hatim the truth when I said I've never seen this before. But I think I have a theory. Slippy's behavior. The sigil..."

"What sigil? The image on the butt end of it? Magical?"

"Yes. Not magical in the vein of a magician performing tricks. Much bigger. My theory involves the supernatural. And if I'm right, Slippy's health is a concern."

Anne was taken aback. She'd never heard the Colonel speak like this. He is not a man whose feet come off the ground when he jumps, or dreams. "What are you talking about? This wasn't what you were hoping to find, is it?" she offered with a touch of nervous humor.

"You grew up hiking right?" He continued at her nod. "If I recall correctly, you hiked year round. Cold weather wasn't daunting for your family?" Another nod. "Well I assume you've looked at a mountain side in January or February and noticed the trees..."

"Where's this going?" The humor was gone when she saw his demeanor hadn't changed from the serious tone.

"Well come January or February, most trees have lost their leaves, right? Only the heartiest are still covered. If I'm right, Slippy is a barren tree, and you, Hatim, and I are probably the exceptions."

habit forming

Early November, Year 13 B.A.

"···too much…" followed by a moan.

"Honey?" It was a female voice… older… an overtone of strength with an inquisitive undertone of fear.

"Let go…" The voice was weak, but not feeble.

The female voice again, this time firmer, but still patient. "Honey?"

"It tingles as if it's still th…"

This time the female voice demanded response. "Ron, I'm here."

He opened his eyes. His eyelids felt spent as if they had just finished a strenuous workout. Ron figured it was from the sliding left and right of his eyeballs during REM sleep. What had he been dreaming? It hurt to think.

"Oh, I'm so glad you're awake!" the female voice offered in a relieved and satisfied tone, as if she was responsible for bringing him back to lucidness. Ron noticed a ringing in his ears as she spoke. Tiles, pockmarked with age, set into white metal framing encompassed his vision. The tiles were yellowed slightly with time, and the pockmarks appeared to stem from the occasional leak from above. Ron realized he was looking up. Suddenly he felt pressure on his hand, and realized someone was holding it. *They must have been holding it for some time* he thought as he felt a warm stickiness.

"Can you hear me Hon?" The ringing came again, and continued for a few seconds after she ceased speaking. He turned his head quickly to the right to determine the source of the voice. Too quick, his head ached. No one was there, only a door. It was white everywhere.

"Over here." The voice was clearly tense with worry, but also tinged with that firm willfulness, as if she was a buoy in the night, flashing out to bring him home from the fog and unrelenting darkness.

Ron turned his head back to the left and the world swam. He belched, tasted acid, and closed his eyes. Ron stifled the bile he felt rising from his stomach with a hard swallow, gripping the hand that was steadying him. He also found a horizontal metal bar with his right hand, and gripped its coolness tightly.

"Oh Dear, take your time. They said you might show symptoms when you woke up. Oh, why did this have to happen? You don't deserve…"

Eyes still closed, he cut her off. "Who are you?" His head began thumping. He winced.

She blinked as if she felt the thump also, then offered a flat response of "What?" After a few moments she took in a stressed, realizing inhale. "It's me, your mother."

He opened his eyes again. A woman sat before him. She had dark brown hair. It was pulled back in a neat bun. The wrinkles of hard years and middle age were around her eyes and mouth. She'd clearly been there a long time, as she appeared slightly disheveled and as if she hadn't gotten adequate sleep in a long time. She wore a yellow blouse. It's silky, loose, too long sleeve extended beyond her wrist, brushing against his left hand as she held it. Gold rings and a gold necklace were tucked into her blouse.

A knock, then a door opened. A woman in a white coat and khakis, also with dark brown hair but pulled back into a pony tail… slightly younger than his mother. "Good afternoon. My name is Doctor Brown." She held her hand out in a confident businesslike manner to his mother. "You look like you've been awake for a very long time. Am I correct you are Ronald's mother?"

"You are correct." It was curt, official with speed. "What is happening with him? I've been sitting here for hours with only nurses coming in checking on his signs. No one has any answers. He doesn't know who I am. When's he going to be better? How soon can we get him out of here? What…"

The doctor interrupted. "Ma'am, I can appreciate your concern and I'll answer your questions to the best of my abilities under the circumstances. Can you please first clarify what you mean when you said Ronald doesn't know who you are?"

"What needs clarified? Ron doesn't know WHO I AM." She drew out the words at the end of her statement.

The doctor intoned "I apologize, Ma'am. I only asked for clarification as it applies to the situation. You are the first person who has spoken with Ron since he awoke, and therefore the first person to gauge what we're dealing with on a cranial level."

"Cranial level? What are you talking about? My son is not a situation. I was told by the school secretary he passed out in Gym class. What's wrong with his brain???"

"I was not implying he is a situation. Ma'am, I was informed Doctor Stevens met with you earlier to confirm a CT scan was completed shortly after your son was brought in. Are you familiar with or did he explain what a CT scan is?"

She exhaled, and her shoulders fell slightly forward. "I remember a doctor some time ago and he did mention tests… I guess I wasn't able to concentrate on all of his jargon."

"I can appreciate this is probably all overwhelming,

and Doctor Stevens can be somewhat clinical. CT is an abbreviation for Cranial Computerized Tomography scan. It's a standard test administered at the presiding Doctor's discretion. In laymen's terms it's a brain scan to produce two-dimensional images of the skull and brain. Having reviewed your son's file, Doctor Stevens had decided to have the test administered as your son's gym teacher reported memory loss, vomiting and unconsciousness after the incident. These factors, coupled with Ron's head potentially striking the floor, the bruise on his forehead, and his remaining unconsciousness since the incident made him a straightforward candidate for the CT. Questions so far?"

"No." She softened slightly. "Thank you for making this easier to understand."

"You're welcome. Do you know how he came about the bruise on his forehead?"

"No. I thought that was part of his fall." Her eyes fogged as she looked at a wall, accessing her memory. "He didn't have that lump yesterday." Her defenses arose again. "Why has it taken hours for you to get the test results? My son has been unconscious. This is serious."

"Regarding the bruise, the gym teacher reported when he first turned around to see your son during class, your son was falling backward. The teacher was uncertain if Ron hit the back of his head on the floor. The teacher also did not see any blow to the front of his head. The boy closest to your son when he fell also stated he did not see Ron hit the front of his head." She paused. "To your question on turnaround time for the CT, a radiologist needed to review the results and a discussion needed to occur regarding those results prior to my coming in. Also, Ron was stable and to be candid, while your son has been stable our Emergency Room has been taxed today with numerous patients... everything from gunshots to strange singes to pregnancy complications..." The doctor hesitated, appeared to realize she was offering too much information, and composed herself.

The doctor finally looked at Ron. "Good morning. Or should I say evening at this point. I suppose since you've had some rest, and judging by your expression, you are probably wondering what exactly is happening here. We should include you in the conversation. Not to mention the fact that we are discussing you." The doctor offered a small smirk, the first sign of non-clinical life from her other than referring to him as Ron rather than Ronald as she did when she came into the room. She appeared happy to shift focus to working toward a resolution, rather than a recap. "What's your name?"

"His name is…"

A curt and polite "Ma'am, would you mind allowing him to answer my questions for the next several minutes?"

His mother appeared bothered, and then her face relaxed when she realized what the Doctor was doing.

The next twenty minutes passed with questions and tests relating to memory, Ron's ability to concentrate, his vision and hearing, balance, as well as other physical aspects The Doctor then circled back. "Do you know why you have a bruise on your forehead?"

"No. My entire head aches. I didn't realize anything in particular was bruised."

"How about Gym class, can you tell me about that?"

"I remember we were going to play indoor football… And getting dressed for Gym… But…" A quizzical, uplift to his tone… "Not much after that?"

The doctor continued to stare at Ron flatly several seconds longer, blinked, then glanced at his mother, inhaling to compose herself. "Based on the incident, your prolonged unconsciousness, and the results of the questions I've just asked, your son…" she turned back to him, "…You have what's referred to as a Grade Three concussion. Different hospitals adhere to different criteria to grade a concussion, but what's conclusive here is straightforward. Your head was definitely impacted once, but more likely twice. You vomited. You were unconscious for an extended timeframe. You have amnesia relative to the incident for over eight hours now. You are experiencing dizziness."

Ron rubbed at his forehead as if the information was an additional impact to it, wincing as his left thumb brushed over the bruise. "Okay…" he offered slowly. "What does this mean?"

"Before we get to that I want to talk about your past. I reviewed your medical history, which was dotted with what I'd consider nothing of relevance to your current situation. A broken arm related to a fall from a tree, a rolled ankle from basketball. Can you confirm if you've ever had any significant blows to your head? Maybe related to the tree fall? Something that may have resulted in unconsciousness or memory loss?"

He finished rubbing his forehead and brought his other hand up to his face, flat hands rubbing up and down his cheeks and temples. "No. At least nothing I can recall." He then chuckled ironically when he realized the joke he'd walked himself into. He glanced at his mother.

Her face was searching with obvious concern. A barely audible hum could be heard reverberating in her closed mouth. "I don't believe so."

"I ask as Doctor Stevens noted that from his conversation with you, your son had previous instances…"

Ron felt the world begin to spin and was having a hard time concentrating. The doctor's speech began to lag similar to a musician's when a hand adds pressure to a spinning record. "…cern is possible demen…" Then it was only blackness.

harbinger 2

The edges are fuzzy in the haze of grasping for a memory. My parents' basement. But immense to the point walls could not be seen but merely *felt*.

It's dark. Just dark enough to see the immediate surroundings. I am wiping clean the dirty dishes scattered about me on the floor with a dry rag. There are two children present, a boy and a girl. Are they my siblings? Are they my children? What are they doing here? Why are they not visibly afraid of the dark? What are they looking at? I only feel in all of us that there is a healthy respect, quite possibly resulting from fear, for whatever is unseen in the basement with us.

Even in the dream I'm reminded of dreams from my childhood that only make this exponentially eerier... a subconscious déjà vu. Sinking to another subconscious level I remember as a child 'waking' up in my parents' bed in the middle of the night and looking into the large rectangular mirror above the wide dresser on the wall behind their door. The mirror was gold framed, old, and easily wider and taller than the dresser it was above. It was almost too big for the room in the daytime. But the reflection of the room in the mirror at night during my dream was much larger, with dark walls that could be felt but not seen. And there was something else in that mirror. Malice might be a description of the feeling projected from within the it. Foreboding another.

In both dreams there was no escape from that empty, slowly expanding room feeling. Also duplicitous were unseen corners that loomed largely ominous for what they were hiding.

sitting in the waiting room

Mid-September, Year 1 A.A.

The Colonel and Anne had been dropped off at the Ha'il Regional Airport by Mr. Al-Shammari and Hatim mid-evening. Handshakes were in order, first from Mr. Al-Shammari. The group exchanged grateful niceties, which Mr. Al-Shammari returned in earnest. The Colonel had suspected Mr. Al-Shammari was initially jaded by generalized media representations of Americans upon their arrival, and that the man had misjudged them before they opened their mouths. That presupposition had seemed to melt away based on the heartfelt goodbyes, quite possibly due in part to their professional handling of being custing unnecessarily from his country.

When his father backed away from the foreigners (the main reason for the change of heart), Hatim lunged at the Colonel, hugging him tightly. The government officials and police officers from the other two vehicles looked anxious but waited and gave the appearance of not taking notice. Hatim quickly released the Colonel and lunged at Anne in a repeated gesture. The gestures were such a surprise (and such strong hugs) that it took both recipients aback based on Hatim's business-like demeanor throughout the dig. Upon discussing the hugs later during their initial flight, Anne had mentioned she thought she had caught a brief look of surprise on Mr. Al-Shammari's face as well.

The flight from Ha'il to Jeddah-King Abdulaziz had gone as smooth as could be expected. The anticipated thirty-seven-minute flight in reality was forty-five minutes with some bumps along the way, but relatively unremarkable. Anne's excitement regarding only one connecting flight was dampened first by the fact that they would be spending the night in the airport for a layover before the early morning fourteen-hour flight to Dulles International Airport in Washington D.C. Secondly, they were in economy class seats for the final leg. Their flight back to the States boarded twenty-five minutes late in the morning, with an additional delay for taxiing.

The Colonel and Anne were both good flyers, but came about their approach in different ways. The Colonel never liked flying. His fear was born of the thought it was unnatural for man to be so high in the air. But that stubborn apprehension tempered with age as he came to the understanding that his life was going to pass one way or another, so why not close your eyes and get around quicker. He still did have some hang-ups though. He sat in the aisle seat... as far away from the window as possible.

Anne's happy-go-lucky attitude lent itself to her approach toward flying. Every flight for her was like a first for a wide-eyed child. She wanted to sit in the empty window seat, but always suspected the Colonel's fear and sat in the middle seat to accompany him more closely.

Both found themselves nervous on this particular flight though. After their post-discovery encounter with the Saudi government, the government felt it best to stow the artifact on the same flights with the Colonel and Anne in what was an unstated but blatant fact: The Saudi's feared it and wanted it off their land as soon as possible. This was also evidenced by the pair of government employees who had transported the artifact in the motorcade with them being on their flights.

The Colonel and Anne were not forewarned of the arrangements, and did not determine the extent of the agents' shadowing of the artifact, and possibly them, until they were boarding the connecting flight. That flight was a single engine jumper on which the agents were the only other passengers. They sat several rows back. This was no doubt controlled by the government. The agents never made an attempt to speak to them. They also were not afforded the appropriate separation from the agents to discuss the situation until the flight to the States. On the flight to the States the agents were eight rows behind them on the opposite side of the plane on what appeared a mostly booked flight. The current situation was clearly not under the same control.

The two did not speak until just after takeoff, 9:37am AST.

"Well I can officially add government escort to my list of accomplishments in life..." Anne whispered as she leaned in toward the Colonel's ear, followed by a nervous giggle.

The Colonel intentionally kept his eyes and head facing forward. He leaned slightly toward her. "Yes... cannot say I was expecting this. Actually, I suppose I hadn't gotten as far as expectations for the commute home since this is all happening so quickly and we're a bit off-the-grid here."

She spoke quickly and quietly, eyes searching in front of her as she spoke, downloading seemingly everything on her mind at once. "Did you know the agents would be on the flights? What about the artifact? Why would the government steal the artifact from us then send it with us?" She didn't allow him to answer. "I'm interpreting the artifact being with us as the government wanting it out of their hands A-S-A-P. But once it is loaded and the plane departs for America, why have agents on the plane?"

"All valid questions. I suppose based on the physical reaction for any number of government officials who would have originally been exposed to the artifact, it makes sense they wanted a controlled and expedited environment for the connecting flight. I'll also go one further in speculating cost is nothing to them when weighing money against the magnitude of potential concerns with keeping the artifact. But I am very curious as to how they vetted the flight crew and agents for the flight…" He scratched at his chin.

Anne's eyes fell out of focus, face slack almost in wonder of the words coming out of her mouth. "I'm thinking they exposed people in-house to it, or at least had it in the same area as the individuals for a timeframe to gauge response. Imagine how odd that experience must have been for these people. 'Please hang out with this object that resembles nothing you've ever seen in your life for an hour or two. If you start to have health problems, we'll get you out of here. Oh, and don't touch it and you can never speak of this to anyone…ever. Otherwise, enjoy the downtime and we'll get back to you soon.'"

Suddenly she became aware of her surroundings, and heard coughing. She purposely paused, then looked around in an attempt to appear casual. An elderly white woman was coughing into a handkerchief across the aisle two rows in front of her. As she glanced behind them, she noticed a few individuals scratching. A teenaged Saudi boy crossed his arms across his chest and itched at his triceps, digging deeply through his long-sleeve shirt. His face was in clear discomfort beyond a casual itch. An Italian businessman blotted the sweat on his forehead with a tissue. His face looked blotchy. She turned back and nervously looked at the headrest in front of her.

"I'd imagine when you work for any government with some clearance, it's probably status quo to not be given pertinent information on assignments at times, not to mention be presented with scenarios that seemingly don't make sense. It may not have created much suspicion among those involved."

Arne suddenly felt a near overwhelming amount of unease due to the conversation and what she was seeing around her. "There's no way they could have vetted everyone on this plane to ensure they can be in close proximity to the artifact. How do we know they even vetted the flight crew?" she offered in a hushed, hissing, accusatory manner.

byzantine empress

Late November, Year 13 B.A.

"You look ridiculous." She shook her head condescendingly.

"Thank you as always for your support."

"I mean it. Sunglasses indoors. And your face…"

"What's wrong with my face???"

"I mean, you're just so… UUHHHGGGly."

"You know I didn't hurt my face in Gym class, right?"

"I know. The ugly has always been there." Then, just for added measure, "I've always warned you to be glad I'm your only sibling. It could be worse."

They were sitting at a two-person table in the mall's cafeteria. Isabella was nibbling at a hot dog and fries. Ron was picking at a bowl of chicken soup, sliding bites of chicken up the side and out of the bowl with his spoon. Small, slow bites. He knew she added that last admonition whenever she'd stepped too far. So he let it slide. They sat eating in silence for a few minutes. She shook her head in disgust at a teenager that walked by with more piercings in his head than original holes he was born with in his body.

Isabella started the conversation back up, staring at him with a deadpan look he'd seen a million times before. "So seriously, I haven't seen you in a while… Is it a new look, or do you really need them?"

"The sunglasses? Need them. The headaches come on pretty quick in any type of bright light... Believe me... how I look to other people is not lost on me, Izzy."

Isabella, being two years Ron's senior, was a sophomore in college. It was Thanksgiving week and she had driven the hour plus commute home late from university the night before. She had asked him out to lunch that morning. Ron had an idea she came back late and asked him out due (at least in part) to her strained relationship with their mother and wanting to avoid her. He also hadn't talked to her in person since summer, and thought it might be nice to catch up. Plus, Ron hadn't left the house in two weeks since the incident, and needed some distance from his mother as well. So they had that in common.

"How's college? You feeling worldly yet?"

"It's tough..." she offered. "...but it feels right. I think you getting away from home for college will do you some good too. Any prospects yet?"

"I don't know..." A long pause. She wasn't interrupting it. He felt her stare and the sudden uncomfortable nature of the silence, so he offered "I'm not sure college is for me." Ron didn't want to say it, but she had some kind of mind control over him where he was always honest and forthcoming with her.

"What?"

"I was dreading this conversation, but I don't think college is for me, Izzy. I don't have it all figured out like you."

"Just because I know what I want to do in life doesn't mean you have to. I've learned a lot at college about myself and others just being out on my own."

He exhaled. Not out of frustration, just due to the weight of the conversation. "I want to be out on my own. I have no intention of staying with Mom longer than necessary. Believe it or not, she's just as strict with me as she was with you. I can't help but think things would be diff…"

"Doubtful. And I wasn't implying you wanted to stay at home."

"Regardless. I'm planning on talking to Steve at the landscaping service about an inside job." He looked at her expectantly.

And this time, Ron could see just a bit of discomfort on her face. And then he could almost see the matronly look leave her face. "Well I'm glad to hear you're lining something up. Tell Mom yet?" She leaned forward staring at him, and he felt uncomfortable for a moment.

Then he realized she was checking her lipstick in his sunglasses. Isabella must have been satisfied and wrapping up the topic. He gave her a look that answered the question to the negative.

"Your funeral. Make sure I'm on the list." With this she changed topics. "How's The Poison Mistress?"

"Mary Anne and I broke up. That's rude of you to ask."

"What? Wait, huh?" She looked dumbfounded.

"Mom told you that Mary Anne and I broke up three weeks ago, right? I heard you two…"

She held up a hand for him to stop. At the same time the dumbfounded look on her face changed to one of, surprisingly and rarely seen, sympathetic sorrow. "She didn't. I'm…" He could tell it still pained her to say "…sorry."

"Sure…"

"You know she and I never got along. But I'm sorry for you." She paused. "I know a broken heart hurts." Isabella had referred to Mary Anne as The Poison Mistress ever since they were first introduced. It was some reference to a woman back in the nineteenth century that poisoned her husband and kids. Isabella had always felt Mary Anne was bad for Ron and implied she knew his friends didn't like her either. Isabella and Ron each had a few friends with siblings in common. He never confronted any of his friends at her implication, but always suspected one of his friends had to have said something to one of their older siblings that knew her. Izzy only dealt in facts.

He didn't say anything for a moment. She didn't let the silence fester. "What do you mean Mom told me?"

Ron replayed the snippets of conversation he heard from the kitchen that morning while he was sitting in the living room. Izzy and his mother had been talking, and at Izzy's mention of lunch, the conversation turned to whispering, which he knew from past experience meant whatever they were discussing somehow involved him. Ron turned the volume down slightly on the television, and leaned forward on the couch (which was facing, but not in view of, the kitchen). He heard his mother and her sniping at each other. His mother with, "Go easy on him, Isabella...", followed shortly after by Isabella saying, "He's lost a lot of weight since...", and after that his mother again with, "...hasn't gotten over....." The last thing Ron heard was Isabella say with some finality "Okay, I promise to be...", before he figured the conversation was ending and turned the television back up slightly.

"I heard you and Mom in the kitchen this morning. It seemed pretty clear she had told you. I heard you say that I'd lost a lot of weight..."

"You have. But I thought it might have been due to the concussion. I know you haven't been able to eat much."

"I also heard Mom say that I hadn't gotten over Mary Anne."

Isabella thought for a moment. Her head tilted slightly downward, eyes searching back and forth, replaying the earlier conversation in her mind. Her brows and eyes lifted. "Oh, she had said something to the effect that you were still having side effects from the concussion."

He suddenly felt like a fool attacking her. Ron had just realized the other day that he spent roughly all his time since the breakup in his room whenever he wasn't in school, and figured he hadn't been eating much since he couldn't remember the last time he ate a meal with their mother. Ron weighed himself the other day and confirmed he had lost twelve pounds on an already thin frame. He figured part of it was the concussion though. It was wishful thinking. "I'm sorry."

She took a deep breath, smiled unexpectedly, and laughed. "You're the classic example of the tried and true phrase..."

"That being?"

"When it rains, it dumps."

Ron realized that whenever she said to her mother "Okay, I promise to be..." near the conclusion of their conversation that morning, it did not end in her promising to be anything but herself toward him. Years later, he looked back to this conversation as one of the key moments that pulled him out of the depressive slump he was in from his break-up, the concussion, and just being a teenager getting ready for the impending change coming with graduation from high school. It endeared her to him as a young adult, and encapsulated the belief that of all the siblings he could have, Ron was lucky to have her as his only one.

dry erase board

Mid-September, Year 1 A.A.

Anne always considered herself a lifelong girl scout. One of her many life affirming mottos was *always be prepared.* As such, she had previously researched their return flight from Jeddah King-Abdulaziz International Airport to Dulles International Airport. The flight was roughly 6600 miles. The B747-400 airplane the Colonel and Anne were on seated over 400 passengers and flew on a northeastern arch. That arch had them traverse the Red Sea, Egypt, the Ionian Sea, Southern Italy, the Tyrrhenian Sea, France, the Atlantic Ocean, several provinces in Canada, and finally several of the United States. As she slid her index finger across a map tracing the arch, she wished she had an old travel trunk so she could cover it in stickers from this trip alone. Now that she was on the flight, she wished she was anywhere but here above Egypt.

They had sat in silence for some time after their initial volley regarding the situation at hand. She was noticing more and more people with some type of ailment. The situation was no longer a matter of her second-guessing a few passengers boarding the flight with health issues. It was a punch in the stomach voicing the realization that they were in very unsettling, uncharted territory. Even boarding this flight, there was a tinge of paranoia and anger at being shadowed by Saudi government officials. The irony of the situation struck her to the core. Now she was angry at the thought of the Saudi government NOT being in control.

"We have to talk to them." she offered in a curt, *this is the solution* manner.

"I'm sorry, what?" The Colonel came to attention.

"Our chaperones."

He paused. "What's your thought?"

"We need to know what they know. This situation is deteriorating quickly. Did you hear the coughing behind the captain at his take-off announcement? I have to think whoever that is up there did not have that cough before the flight. That means at least one person responsible for our safety is not doing well and is probably going downhill."

"Okay. I don't see what there is to lose in approaching them."

"How can you remain so calm?"

"Honestly, I don't see us as having any control over the situation, much like a flight without one of the most significant finds in the history of mankind being stowed away somewhere underneath us."

"Do you understand the need for more information here?"

He paused. "They may know something we don't that could assist. I just don't know that they're going to offer us anything of substance, or that they're going to take any action based on anything we say."

"I need to ensure you and I are on the same team here. If we can get them to talk, we're probably going to need one of us back there with them, and one of them up here. I can't imagine we'd all be able to congregate back near the bathrooms. That might even work best in our favor if we can separate them." Again, there was no hesitation. This was a done deal.

The Colonel scratched at his cheek, sharply inhaled,

then slowly exhaled. He looked either older or very tired suddenly. "Okay. Let's ensure we're prepared."

Suddenly the plane hitched to the right. A few gasps were heard. Anne's face contorted in fear as she looked out the window on a patchy cirrus cloud sky. The Colonel placed his palm over her hand and gently squeezed. He could feel she was gripping the arm rest tightly. "Felt like a normal bonk to me." He offered in an assuring manner.

"Sorry. I'm dialed up right now."

"I understand. So back to the topic... we need to ensure we're on-point attempting to extrapolate the information we need, and the same information from both of the agents if we have the opportunity to interrogate them separately. First, what do we need to know?"

"We need to know if they know anything about the artifact that we don't. We need to know if the flight crew was vetted for this. We need to know their contingency plan if things go south with the flight crew or many of the passengers. We need to know their plan once we land."

"Okay, how do we want to approach them?" A distant look of rumination bathed both of their faces. "I believe I should approach them..." An uncomfortable pause, "...forgive me, as a male figure of authority."

"No forgiveness necessary. I assumed the same."

He exhaled. The Colonel did not like conflict within his family. Anne smiled at seeing his body unwind from the stress of his statement. The Colonel continued "I don't believe we need to use much tact. When I've snuck a few glances in their direction, I noticed the agent in the khaki suit looked nervous. They have to see what's happening to the passengers, not to mention the older female flight attendant."

"I saw her too. That looks like a boil on her neck. How is this happening so fast?"

"It's like it mirrors close exposure to high amount of

radiation. It's similar to Slippy. It's just that this is the first time we're seeing a larger unbiased sample set. We don't know what was happening under Slippy's clothing. We have many more opportunities to see exposed skin here." He regained his original train of thought. "I suppose I didn't let it sink in, but it is now. The khaki agent's apparent unease is starting to disturb me."

"How so?"

"Well they should know what to expect, correct? So there shouldn't be any surprises. Why in the heck is he nervous?"

"Oh, I'm starting to feel nauseous."

"I'm sorry. It pains me to admit this, particularly in light of our archeological relationship", he didn't want to imply she was a subordinate in any way, "but I'm just not prepared for this." He rubbed his palms up and down on his thighs. "But you're kicking my brain into gear. I'll approach them and ask to speak to the lead, which I'm assuming is the agent in the dark brown suit. Give them control. But I'll suggest the nervous agent come sit with you in the interest of not drawing too much attention. He's tense already. If you come across as knowledgeable, not overly confident, and present yourself as looking to him for guidance, maybe you can extract some info from him. Allow him to feel some control and to confide in you to alleviate his nerves. Try to make him not see you so much as a woman. Just don't rush him."

"How in the hell am I going to not act like a woman???"

"I don't mean to offend. I believe you know where I'm going. Just speak as plainly as possible. The less he feels you're a subordinate, but also not necessarily attempting to take control, the more likely he may confide in you."

"Okay. Sorry, on edge… makes sense. Okay, let's… Wait, what if this doesn't work? What if Brown shuts you down?"

"What have we really lost? They have to know we're aware of them. As far as I can surmise, we'll get one of three results: they'll either talk openly, give us a nugget or two inadvertently, or they'll tell us to buzz off. But if we can separate them, we've doubled the opportunity for info."

"Right, let's do it."

The Colonel grabbed her hand again, clenched, offered her his most convincing smile, took a deep breath, paused, and stood up from his aisle seat. "Talk to you soon."

introducing the known unknown

Mid-September, Year 1 A.A.

"مرحبا." The men looked up. "Do you speak English?"

The Colonel had gotten out of his seat and wheeled around the front of the middle section of seats to walk the far isle toward the agents. He noticed the Khaki suited agent watching him, and when they made eye contact Khaki tilted his eyes and head downward to his magazine. Khaki was in the middle seat on the right side of the plane. The Brown suited agent, seated in the aisle seat, made eye contact then averted his eyes looking out the window casually past Khaki and the older white man sleeping in the window seat.

The Colonel made a bit of a show of pushing his palms into his back and arching his chest backward with a groan after he spoke. *No rush here.*

Since the Colonel had stopped and greeted them, both men now had his attention. There was no response for a moment. Were they sizing him up? Was this a show of control? Did they not plan for this?

"Who are you speaking to?" Brown questioned.

"Either of you gentlemen." The Colonel kept it neutral and polite.

There was silence a few more moments. "I do." It was Brown again.

"Thank you." The Colonel took his time. He felt

slightly more at ease as Window Seat was asleep, but was also cognizant of not offering any words that could set off alarms for anyone within earshot. He leaned in to what he felt was a respectful distance. "I was hoping to have a few words with you after we saw each other on our last flight." He attempted to project a relaxed, friendly demeanor for the agents, and anyone else who might hear.

Again silence. Khaki continued to gaze at him and clearly was uncomfortable. Brown looked like a lion in his prime coming out of a doze, kneading his paws in the dirt, deciding whether the animal in front of him was prey or not. The Colonel could easily conclude Brown was in charge here.

"Yes." Brown tilted his head slightly in Khaki's direction then cocked his head toward the back of the plane. Khaki slowly looked at Brown. If there was some message conveyed in that look, the Colonel missed it.

Khaki offered a thick, slow "Excuse me" and began to stand. Brown stood slowly and moved into the row while the Colonel backed up to afford the necessary space. Khaki looked again at the Colonel in a blank manner as he slid into the aisle, then turned toward the back of the plane. From far away, the Colonel had thought Khaki was filled out and seemingly tall for a Saudi. Up close, the man was much stockier and exuded the impression that he could handle his weight. He was also older than originally presumed.

The Colonel originally thought he was probably middle to late-thirties. This man was clearly well into his forties. His forehead was so many wavy stress lines. He had dark circles under his eyes. His black hair had gray strands throughout. And there was extensive scarring on the bottom of his right earlobe as well as on his lower cheek running parallel to his right jaw bone. It was as if a knife started where an ear piercing would be, and ran a wavy line off the ear and onto his lower check almost to the chin. The stitch job was bad. Probably not a result of hospital work.

"You can sit in my seat after your trip to the bathroom if you please" he offered. Khaki turned slowly and looked at him again with that empty gaze, then continued on his course toward the bathrooms. Did he understand the Colonel? The Colonel couldn't get a read on him, but was starting to think that he had possibly misread the men's purpose on this expedition.

"Please sit" Brown offered with a paced wave of the hand toward Khaki's seat.

"Thank you."

The Colonel lowered himself gently into the middle seat, leaned back, purposely took a deep breath, rubbed his palms on his thighs then exhaled. He wanted Brown to feel in control, and what better way than to appear nervous. There was an added bonus of being landlocked in the middle seat also. It was an easy acting job as there wasn't much acting in it.

While Brown was reseating himself, the Colonel noticed he had a full head of jet black hair, seemingly slightly long for a government official. The man was possibly early thirties, with the beginnings of a weathered look probably from work-related stress and long hours. But his equally black eyes were on high alert. They sat in silence for a few moments. Window Seat snored softly once to break the unease. The Colonel leaned forward to look at him, turned back to Brown and smirked a *look at this guy* smirk. Brown was not amused. More silence.

The Colonel exhaled. "I would like you to first understand why I approached you. My colleague and I originally boarded this flight with the intention of returning home and seeing to it that the artifact made it into the appropriate hands." He went on to correct himself. "That's still our intention you see."

The corner of Brown's eyebrow lifted slightly. This

struck the Colonel as odd but he was focusing on his presentation too strongly to focus on that passing reaction. "But further consideration is necessary due to what is happening around us here, which has in fact been occurring since we unearthed the artifact." He glanced around the plane and gave a moment for the agent to respond. No response came. "We thought it best to approach you as we would like to know your contin…"

"Please take your phone out of your pocket." As Brown spoke, he opened the fold-up tray attached to the seat in front of him.

The Colonel was taken aback, but complied, leaning away from Brown to reach into his pocket for his phone.

"Please shut it off and place it on my tray."

"It is shut down. I'm not sure I…"

"Show me please."

The Colonel pushed the activation button on his phone and nothing happened. "It won't activate unless I hold down the power button." He tilted the phone to point out the other button. "I turned the power off at departure per flight protocol." He was puzzled, but decided to take this as a positive sign that Brown was going to have a candid conversation with him. He further complied by placing the phone on Brown's tray. Odd that the man was that paranoid. *Government employees* he chuckled to himself.

Brown kept his eyes on the Colonel while he placed the phone on the tray. He then picked up the phone and slid it into the magazine pouch on the seat in front of him. "Tell me more of your artifact."

The Colonel found this odd. The agent should already know about the artifact, so why was he inquiring about it? He must be dodging any question the Colonel might ask. It appeared Brown did not want to release any information. This may be a lost cause. He thought about what information was relevant to release per their situation to prove the Colonel knew what he was talking about and expedite their conversation in case Khaki wanted his seat back. "We believe it's very old. And we know it has an adverse reaction on certain people. We assume the Saudi government wanted it moved off of their land in an expeditious manner."

Brown seemed to consider this. "And why do you believe the Saudi government wishes this artifact be removed so quickly from its land?" Again the odd inflection on *artifact*, as if he didn't agree with the Colonel's labeling of it.

"As I'm sure you're aware, I've been in the archeological field for close to four decades. I've never experienced nor read of a country not wanting to claim an archeological find as its own. That is striking on its own merit. We can only assume this is due to physical ailments arising from close contact with the artifact."

Something definitely changed. Brown no longer had a stern and uninterested demeanor. He looked as if he was piecing something together based on this info. His eyes squinted. He appeared to be remembering something. What was going on here? "I want to ensure I understand you. Archeology, as in digging?"

The Colonel was now completely confused, and his face must have shown it, as Brown had for the first time turned to study the Colonel since he sat down. Why was he confirming what *Archeology* was? The Colonel glanced ahead as the coughing from several individuals crept back from the periphery of his hearing again. He glanced back toward Brown and Khaki was in the aisle beside them.

He startled as he had not heard any noise indicating Khaki's approach. Khaki leaned down to Brown's ear and whispered something quickly and quietly in their native tongue in Brown's right ear. The Colonel caught "on-point" and possibly "not trust". Khaki then straightened, glanced at the Colonel, and walked back toward the bathrooms, and shortly after came out on the other side of the center section and casually walked toward Anne. Brown swiveled his body upward and put his poker face back on.

The Colonel started to feel as if he had misread who was in charge here and adrenaline began coursing through his body again.

misinterpretation

Early September, Year 1 A.A.

The crowd filed out of the bar and into the cold autumn
night. The bar district in the city was bustling as always on
a Thursday night. Most were smiling and talking to each
other in raised tones due to the decibel level of the rock
concert. Occasionally a passerby would look oddly at the
concert goers, then shake their heads laughing when they
realized why the patrons were screaming their
conversations with each other. This circumstance always
made Ron chuckle to himself at the thought that this was
what a convention for hearing aids must sound like. Or
maybe an old folks home for the non-napping afternoon
crowd. Several of the young crowd members were
bumping and jumping into each other and smiling during
the exodus, as if the concert was still on-going.

"Ugh, bottom feeders." Mahi, head tilted downward,
shook his head disgustedly to himself.

"What?" The response was an elevated voice.

Mahi lifted his head and raised his tone. "Bottom
feeders I said." He was still shaking his head.

"WHAT?" as Ron pantomimed an elderly man that's
hard of hearing, hand cupped to his ear with a stooped
back.

Mahi saw the smirk on his face and punched him in
the shoulder.

"AHH!" He feigned pain while clutching his shoulder. "Luckily you hit with the power of a seven-year-old."

"Must be a tough seven-year-old since you're still rubbing your shoulder."

"Just finishing the massage… you started…" Ron's hands gravitated to rubbing his ears due to the dulled but piercing ringing noise rattling in his head from the show. What was he saying? "You still hung up on that kid bumping into you before the show?"

"You clearly didn't hear what he said after. And it wasn't a bump. He leaned his shoulder into mine hard as he passed. He then said, 'Excuse you, Captain Chutney' as he and his small-minded friends walked off laughing."

He laughed, still rubbing. "You clearly have the mental capacity of a seven-year-old to get ticked at that. They were teenagers… And that was confirmed by the ridiculousness of the bump complimenting the best grade school insult he could muster."

"It was racist."

"From some dumb inbred who through his actions AND words proved he probably flunked out of the fifth grade."

"You wouldn't understand."

"You're probably right. Not many racist epithets tossed toward whitey. But I also won't lower my brain capacity to getting worked up into a lather over some moron. And besides, you know you've been accepted into the white man's club," Ron offered as he stiffened his posture upright, one thumb pointed at his own chest, the other hand giving a thumbs-up. He offered a Cheshire grin, brushed imaginary dust off of his chest, and over-confidently extended his arm to receive a handshake, aping a businessman. He then quickly flinched at the punch he knew was coming.

Mahi leaned into it due partly to the flinch, and partly

to the alcohol coursing through his system. He almost toppled them both over as a result. Mahi burst out laughing.

He glanced at Mahi, and then toward the parking lot they were heading for. "The best I can figure it is as follows…" he offered as he straightened Mahi by clutching his shoulders, swiveling his friend's course from the parking lot across the street where they parked, toward the businesses down the street. "We need food."

"That's a profound thought."

"Wait, there's more…" Ron released Mahi's shoulders as he stopped walking. Mahi played the part of a wind up walking toy set in a different direction. "Spouting racist jokes falls right in line with spouting religion to me." He stopped, raising a fist, lifting his index finger. "The receiver of the info… Mahi?"

Mahi had kept walking. He stopped, turned around, snickered, and back-tracked to his friend.

"As I was saying…" Fist raised, Mahi raised a finger at each contention, and clutched each finger with his other hand at the contentions. "… the receiver of the info either:

"A. Agrees.

"B. Disagrees vocally.

"C. Disagrees, and is in an inferior or vulnerable position, or sees no point in vocalizing, where they stay relatively silent by not responding either way, giving the impression they agree through their silence or want to avoid conflict, thereby galvanizing the racist's views and/or position unintentionally.

"His cronies fall in A or C. If it was B, they would have stopped him, probably in an instance long before tonight, and therefore not been his racist brethren. If they agree, they're just as worthless as him. If they disagree and don't say anything as they feel inferior, they're cowards, probably leeches and should be ashamed of themselves for not enlightening their friend and slapping him back into the *shut your face and learn up* line. And if they're C and see no point in vocalizing otherwise, then they can only blame themselves for their lethargy in morals and ethics as also relates to being friends.

"And as the non-clansman recipient of his humor …" Ron drug out the last while air quoting, "…you my friend might as well slot yourself in C, except with no regrets."

Mahi retorted, fist in air. "I should have said something. I'm no better as a C not knowing this dog. They need to know that what they're doing is perpetuating the ignorance of the human race."

"And if you did that, then what? He's clearly with the group of delinquent troglodytes that all scratch their behinds to the same tune, so what is anything you say going to change?"

"It'll make them think twice next time. And let them know they'll be challenged for their insolence."

"I suppose there's some truth to that…" Ron noticed the fatherly, knowing smile on Mahi's face. He raised his hand and index finger again. "Buuuutttt…" Mahi's face went slack. "…they more likely would have:

"A. Become even more mouthy, like a rooster puffing its chest out while crowing in the morning, while all you want it to do is shut up as you wonder why you bought the thing in the first place.

"B. Would have just continued on their merry way to dumb down society one intersection at a time, gathering lint as they found those that agree with their racism.

"C. Oooorrrrrrr, picked a fight with CAPTAIN CHUTNEY!!!"

Another punch to the shoulder outside of the diner. Mahi held the entrance door open for him, extending and waving his other arm in an exaggerated bowing version of a doorman offering entrance to his establishment.

Ron returned the bow to Mahi, and walked through the door. Mahi promptly hit him in the back with the door as he walked through. "You need to think bigger picture, my friend. If verbalization won't do, you cannot sit inactive… action will have to do."

introducing the unknown known

Mid-September, Year 1 A.A.

"May I sit?"

Anne startled as she was lost in thought and hadn't even noticed the Khaki-suited agent standing to her left. His voice was quiet and booming at the same time. She had just seen him head toward the bathrooms as the Colonel took his seat, but didn't think he would be at her side so fast. Counting her blessings that she had already finished dialing, she was just finishing sliding her phone under the fold-down tray when he arrived. She pulled her hand back out and nervously bumped the magazine hanging off the tray. He was bigger than she originally thought. "Yes… Please…" she offered and tilted her hand, palm up, toward the Colonel's seat.

"May I sit near the window?"

Anne paused, uncertain if he saw the phone or wanted the window seat for another reason. Standing up, she slid the magazine under the tray to clutch and hide the phone against her leg while making a lane for him. Khaki brushed past into the seat, which groaned from the large man hefting his weight downward. Anne was reminded quickly of how she underestimated his size. He was built like a felled ancient tree where the ample trunk began sprouting limbs again.

"Thank you." He sat facing forward, not so much as

glancing at Anne.

She found this odd and began to feel uncomfortable with the passing silence. She felt as if she was already not sticking to their plan. But him sitting beside her was a definite indication that the agents knew that she and the Colonel were aware of them and not intimidated, which she took as a good sign.

Khaki then stifled a burp. Anne offered "Can I offer you an antacid?"

"Thank you but no. My stomach becomes queasy after flight departures, but passes."

There was more silence. Anne shifted in her seat. "It appears there are quite a few people becoming ill on this flight" she offered as blandly as she could.

"That would appear so. Does not seem like a normal circumstance to me." It was deadpan. As if he had mentioned there was a fly buzzing around and he couldn't be bothered with it.

"I agree. Do you know of airlines landing flights prematurely in the case of mass illness?"

He did not answer immediately. "I am sure there is such a policy, particularly with a cross-continent flight."

She felt immediate relief, but he wasn't offering anything specific. Anne knew they were running out of time, but she was also afraid if she got too personal or pushed him, he could shut down. She needed to stick to the plan, but also wanted to flush out any information quickly. "I heard coughing in the background of the pilot's departure announcement. And two of the attendants appear to be suffering from some type of boils or rash. I wonder if the crew was vetted for our luggage?"

There was another pause. She had the feeling they were playing a chess game in a big cardboard box, and the box was on fire. He wasn't answering. Did he not know? Or did he know they weren't screened? Did he just not want to give away information? *Ugh... men with power* she thought, *the start of so many problems*. She laughed at the thought in a time like this. How the mind compartmentalizes.

"Can I provide information about the artifact we're travelling with? I'd like to ensure you understand what we're up against."

"That won't be necessary Ms. Malone," he said as he turned to face her.

She froze. Then she figured herself foolish as they had to know her name. Then she realized that wasn't why she startled.

The male steward cleared his throat at the front of first class, and held the com in front of his face. "Hello passengers. The flight crew would like to say thank you for your patience in our fielding of all of your questions and requests. We regret to inform you that we have passed out all available blankets, and we have run out of ginger ale." Several groans were heard amidst the continued chorus of coughing. "In light of the situation, we do suggest taking turns accessing your overhead luggage if you require a coat or additional clothing for those feeling a chill." He attempted to pass off a forced smile in light of the situation and offered a cheery "The Captain has also turned on the *free non-alcoholic drinks light* for the remainder of the flight."

A worn cheer arose. Several versions of "Wow," and "I've never heard of that," were heard.

"We do request all passengers be considerate of other passengers regarding number of drink requests."

story time

Mid-September, Year 1 A.A.

The game plan was relatively out the window as far as the Colonel was concerned. He concluded Khaki was in charge. Brown didn't have all the details judging by his line of questioning. Khaki clearly wasn't completely trusting with his and Brown's conversation based on what he'd overheard. And the Colonel wasn't comfortable with Khaki approaching Anne. More and more people appeared to be ailing per the announcement from the steward.

One of the seemingly unaffected stewardesses was making rounds with two tissue boxes, holding her arms out in a manner that reminded him of a religious statue of a mortal touched with supernatural compassion reaching out to the masses.

The Colonel figured the announcement was his best angle to undo whatever government pep-talk Khaki had given Brown. "Forgive me if I'm forward, but based on that announcement, I fear we have a mutual growing concern. Ms. Malone and I were part of a small crew on an archeological dig outside of Ha'il when we found the artifact that's being transported with us today…" He went on to explain the story of how they'd arrived at their current situation. He couldn't be certain of what Brown knew, so he laid all of the facts out as he knew them. As the Colonel spoke, Brown's body slowly unwound to its original slightly slumped position before Khaki had made his return appearance. The Colonel took this to indicate he'd brought him back around. "So might I be so forward to ask if you have any additional information regarding the artifact?" The Colonel still attempted to project patience. He wasn't certain that he should tip his cards indicating that he had heard pieces of the agents' conversation. He may need that unknown perk at some point.

Brown's eyes were searching again, and his face began to appear as if it was being pulled downward with the harrowing realization of what was happening. He glanced in the direction of Khaki and Anne sheepishly, ensuring he wasn't being watched no doubt, then began to speak almost in a whisper. "I was placed in a room with a dozen other men. Our host was a black man with a shaved head, in a deep black suit, black shirt, black tie and wearing black shoes. He wore a gold ring on each of his pinky fingers. His facial features were unremarkable, unmemorable. His accent and demeanor were not. His accent was southern American. And he was rigid. Not specifically military rigid, but a militaristic rigidity probably crossbred with martial arts training." Brown's head tilted slightly, and he looked lost in thought. It appeared he could not picture the Host's face. "He gave instruction to relax, talk amongst ourselves, and someone would be in periodically to remove us from the room one at a time. There was a mirrored wall and a camera in a corner of the room near the ceiling. Other than the door, nothing else stood out initially except a crate on the floor in the middle of the room. It was conspicuously nailed shut with far too many nails at each wooden seam, and every nail head was pounded into the wood so the surface was smooth. Not a single nail protruded. It was clear someone did not want this crate opened. There were no markings on it except indented half-moons around many of the nails, as if whoever closed the box pounded the hammer into the nails as hard or deliberately as possible. Or they were in a rush..."

"I apologize for the interruption, but can you clarify why the door stood out?"

"Yes. The door was a dull gray. It appeared made of lead. And it was thick... at least half a meter. It was so heavy it was opened and closed mechanically."

Brown glanced at the Colonel, as if expecting a response. The Colonel didn't offer any, partly as he did not want to interrupt, partly as he inferred the reason for the lead.

"As would be expected, there was silence for several minutes as the men, myself included, scanned the room. Military training..." Brown shrugged dismissively, "Then one of the men snickered. He was large and had the look of a mercenary. 'Another psychological test...' he offered while he shook his head in an incredulous manner. He had the sharp facial features of a bird, which leant to his sarcastic nature."

Brown continued. "The men began talking, offering brief, vague pieces of information relative to their positions in the government. It was initially the standard game of cards any of these tests represented. Everyone held their cards to their chest. We were all officers of some fashion. No one appeared to be new to the service, but no one had an extended tenure either. The similarities did not end there. I would estimate none of the men were younger than thirty years of age. I saw and heard no indications of commitment to a woman. As far as I could surmise, we were all disposable.

"We discussed the box. No one knew what it contained. Several men attempted to move it without success. Upon placing his hand on the box, one man who often displayed a wide smile stated he could feel it vibrating.

Of the additional men that placed their hands on the box, no one else attested to feeling it vibrate. As time wore on, it became evident several of the other men distrusted further statements from the smiling man. Another man, the shortest of the group, sat on the box. Some stood. Others sat against a wall as time wore on.

"About half an hour into the test the short man began showing signs of affliction. He began scratching his ribs with a puzzled look on his face, as if he hadn't had quite that itch ever, or he couldn't understand why he was itchy. Thirty-nine minutes in gears were heard humming in the wall of the door, the door opened, and our host appeared. He lifted his arm, hand arched back leaning at a 45-degree angle with fingers extended in the direction of the afflicted man, palm up. He closed his fingers into a fist just once, directing the afflicted man to approach him. I remember thinking this gesture was a gesture of ultimate control. It was powerful with not a morsel of wasted movement and no room left for doubt. As the afflicted man arose from his seat on the box and approached, the host turned his body sideways, arm and fist still extended, but now in the direction of the door beyond him. He opened his extended hand toward the exit. The afflicted man suddenly appeared feeble in the light of such power, and sulked from the room while continuing to scratch. The host followed him through the door and out of sight, not looking back. The gears were heard again and the door closed."

"The emerging casualness of the men in the room abruptly ended. The room was silent for some time. I am certain the men's reactions were the same as mine… replaying what had just happened in their minds and all that happened before it in an attempt to understand the test and wondering how they could pass it. Some grew superstitious of the box and would not approach it after the short afflicted man was removed. As time wore on, it became evident we had no control over who would pass, and it did not matter who had come in physical contact with the box."

"One by one the men were removed over the following twenty-seven hours by the host. Several showed signs of some affliction, similar to your associate Mr. Melek."

The Colonel was taken aback. He hadn't mentioned Slippy's name at any point. At least that he recalled.

"I was one of the last three men in the room... But most curious of all were the last two men to be removed prior to us..."

The Colonel was lost in thought. Brown must have seen it, as he stopped talking. Something struck the Colonel. "You said initially the room..." He couldn't finish his sentence as Brown's information was circling in his head like water being flushed down a toilet.

"I'm sorry I do not follow."

He pulled the question back into focus. "You said initially the box was the only aspect of the room other than the door that stood out. Was there something additional?"

"Oh, yes..." Brown inhaled deeply, collected himself, and a wry smile materialized. "Have you ever been left to your thoughts in the same room for hours on end?" He did not wait for a response. "This may be maddening for a civilian. It's worse for a trained officer who knows he's being tested without being given details. I took notice of everything, down to counting the sum of cinder blocks on the walls, and then the blocks per each wall. And that's when I noticed the mortar was fresh. I asked myself *Why would a room in a seemingly old building have a freshly mortared interior room?*"

The Colonel shook his head and shrugged his shoulders. It was easy enough to convey the appearance of bewilderment as he was truly baffled by this.

"When I was eventually removed from the room I slowed down in the doorway and scanned the perimeter of it. As far as I could ascertain, the walls behind the cement were also lead based from what I saw... as was the ceiling." Brown looked down, scornful smile still present, and blew air out of his nostrils. His head rocked back as he did so. He shifted his body in his seat toward the Colonel for the first time and looked in the Colonel's eyes. The shift and silence of the moment were exacerbated by the creaking of Brown's seat under his weight. "If the door, walls, and ceiling of a room are lead sir, what might one deduce the floor is made of?"

The Colonel's face went slack at the realization. Dumbfounded he offered "You were in a lead box designed to contain the artifact." He couldn't imagine the resources and manpower necessary to achieve such a feat, but he understood why. Decades of archeological training and field work left him well versed in the elements. Lead has a higher density. It offers poor electrical conductivity, shields from radiation, and deadens sound transmission.

you're the passenger

Mid-September, Year 1 A.A.

Anne couldn't help feel unnerved by Khaki's countenance. How did she not notice the right side of his face? The scarring, coupled with his size and demeanor, was frightening. She was only slightly comforted by the facts that she was in a public setting and the flight was heading back to the States, so this situation would be behind her within hours. Then she heard the in-flight announcement. This was becoming too much to bear. She was unnerved, growing impatient and felt so small and helpless. She needed to take back control, but hadn't the slightest clue how.

Khaki clearly saw her discomfort and apparently reveled in these types of situations. "Can I offer *you* an antacid?"

She wanted to smack him… hard. Anne attempted to buckle down any expression of anger from her face as soon as she felt her blood beginning to boil, and hoped he hadn't seen any conveyance of her true feelings. She shifted in her seat as she spoke so her knees were toward him to face him better. *Do not show fear or subordination.* "No, thank you… I'm relieved you have knowledge of the artifact. Can I ask what you or your government believes it is?"

He took his time answering. She had the clear

impression he had already thought out what questions she (or the Colonel) might ask. "What I think is not of consequence. And as it relates to my government there are only theories. The facts are what your team has probably deduced already. Relative Dating is not possible. Stratigraphy is ruled out as no other artifacts were found in the area to allow for terminus post quem…"

Anne felt her eyebrows raise and quickly retracted them. She almost completely underestimated this man by looks alone. She always felt she was above judgment before people opened their mouths, but suddenly found she was disappointed in herself, if only briefly.

He continued. "Being that it can be assumed there is not another of these artifacts in the world, Seriation can also be ruled out. The object is not biological in nature, so methods such as amino acid dating cannot be utilized. Radiocarbon dating provided no results from any possible fuel used in the smelting process, if there was one. No other testing method would be valid. Also, there are no written markers on the object to assist. Which leaves the most obvious and least useful remaining clues…"

"The fingerprints from the hand imprints, and the symbol", she offered absentmindedly. Clearing her mind from the trance of his words and knowledge, she began to chide herself then thought better. There was no longer anything to hide here. It took her back to thinking how it was possible for handprints to be impressed in the metal, or whatever the material was. Any time she pondered of the artifact, she cringed at the idea of how damaged a person's hands had to have been after gripping red hot metal to make detailed imprints such as those. They couldn't have been faked in her estimation. They were just too detailed and realistic to be an artistic rendering. She found herself wringing her hands, and reached into her clutch for moisturizer at the visualization of the damage the impressions must have inflicted. "Has your government run the prints?"

"For what purpose?"

"To determine if they belong to anyone in their records?"

"You honestly believe they belong to an existing person?"

"I don't know... I just think it could rule out..."

He cut her off. "Then you are operating from the standpoint of ruling out the possibility of a fake. Or that it was recently produced."

"Of course."

Khaki leaned back. His seat creaked under his weight. He seemed to be considering something. "In the time we have remaining, I'd like to tell you a story..."

Anne found this an odd phrase. They haven't even reached the near side of the Atlantic yet. *Translation error on his part* she thought.

"I grew up on boats. And at a young age I worked on fishing boats. One particular captain I crewed for operated under the premise *Money Is King*. This often led to questionable decisions as related to fishing trips, namely in the manner of shipping out or continuing to fish in unsavory or worsening conditions, particularly when money was tight. This made for uncomfortable situations amongst the crew for a host of reasons, but as most fisherman are poor where I came from, the crew generally accepted the risks as their families needed what scant money could be made, even under the best of conditions." He paused. "May I ask if you've ever been deep out in an ocean?"

The question chilled her to the bone. She had always felt deep waters were ominous, and full of potential terrors, to the point of even avoiding horror movies involving boats. "No."

"Then I will paint a specific picture for you to visualize."

She quickly added "But I can appreciate the magnitude and power of an ocean…" in hopes wherever he was going with this wasn't too graphic. She noticed his mouth twitch briefly. Was he taking pleasure in this? She saw he was missing a molar on the upper near side of his mouth.

"Oceans are giving, and can be quite unforgiving. The sea near my birth home is as beautiful as it is ominous. It offers very warm waters to fish and swim in. And it offers dangers such as unpredictable currents, rogue waves, tiger sharks, stonefish, and a host of…"

"I'm sorry, stonefish?"

He considered this. "Though dissimilar, you might compare warnings of being weary of it to your jellyfish. It is venomous, with spines on its back that lift when threatened. The spines are sturdy to the point they can penetrate the bottom of a shoe if stepped on. The pain is comparable to being hit very hard with something solid, such as a tree branch or a metal rod. The pain slowly moves through the body, and as it moves it feels as if you are being struck repeatedly in the areas it's coursing through, to the point the afflicted often ask to have the infected limb removed. Problems such as kidney pains and other ailments can last for years."

Why did I ask? Anne thought. She felt herself whisper "How's it treated?"

"I've heard of several methods. I can attest that boiling water can destroy the venom if quickly applied to the afflicted area." At the cringe he saw on her face he offered "The individual is grateful for the treatment. The new pain is largely overridden by the swelling and the coursing pain of the venom."

"That sounds awful."

"It is. And there is much that can go wrong when on a fishing expedition. When I was nineteen, that particular captain took us out at the end of the season for one last attempt at a haul. The season had been particularly bad for several reasons."

She imagined he was referring to being stung by a stonefish.

"We departed so late that there were very few boats seen during our journey. And those few were seen within sight of land. This was no doubt also due to the projection of a major storm blowing in from the ocean later in the week. The season had been relatively tame as relates to the weather. No major storms. Fishermen can be particularly superstitious regarding trends such as this. None of the crew was enthused at the prospects of this trip due to what may come. And seeing ships as competition in the water is nowhere near as disconcerting as seeing no ships in the water when weather projections are ominous." He scratched at his cheek. "One thing I learned from a young age is that a nervous crew will quickly be strained in the event of adversity.

"The fishing the first few days was abysmal. Tensions rose amongst the men. Fights broke out. Gear was broken. The captain's angry and condescending tone was heightened beyond any prior expedition with him. Closer to a week in I was jabbed in the forearm with a stonefish's spines when I was pushed over from behind into a receiving table during a scuffle. Fortunately, there was no doubt what I was struck with and I was treated with scalding hot water being poured over my arm in an expeditious manner."

He pulled his jacket and shirt sleeve back several inches. He allowed her sickened gaze to linger. The hair on the top of his arm halted in an erratic, wavy line above the wrist, where it was married to scarred, smooth skin. He slid the sleeves back down without any perceivable reaction to her visible response.

"I can only assume I passed out from the stress and traumas, then was put to bed… When I awoke I was in the ocean with a life vest on. Today I look at the sting as no small blessing since I was put to bed in that vest. My skin was burning from the water soaking my bandaged, burned, stung arm. It was night. I heard a brief gurgling sound that must have been human. As I spun in the water I located a small life raft. Other than that, only wreckage. It was as if the boat was pulverized. Everyone was gone. It was beginning to rain. The warm water was of great benefit, but the ominous sea swallowed everyone and nearly everything I came with. I gathered all of the wreckage I thought salvageable. Another blessing included fishing line still attached to half of a deep sea fishing pole."

His eyes were lost in a blank stare, possibly visualizing the scene at the time, or maybe it was just his mental state. Anne had no idea where this was going.

Khaki continued. "As I've said, fishermen are superstitious. For many this includes even considering the possibility of a shipwreck. In reality, it's something you can never put out of mind, like attempting to un-see, or never recall something catastrophic. It creeps into your mind and at times is difficult to suppress once again. I had always said to myself that I could handle being lost at sea better than most as I was raised in the sea. To a point I was correct. But in hindsight I know there is no way to be fully prepared.

"What I would have you understand is being lost at sea is the equivalent of a bleak, continuous disaster. You're fighting the tangible in the form of limited supples, large waves, and since the ocean is clear you can see fish such as sharks from a long way off. You're also fighting the intangible in that the ocean is generally very quiet, with hot weather in the day, cold in the night, there are no landmark signs of life above water to be seen, and it is easy to lose hope of finding land or being rescued. I had no compass, and no inkling of where I was due to not knowing how long I was asleep, or where the storm had pushed me.

After a pause, he asked "Do you follow what I am telling you?"

"I'm not sure. But what happened to you? Obviously you're here today…"

"I lost myself in despair after what was probably a week, and only pulled myself together by pouring my mind into the miniscule prioritizing of tasks necessary to live. Your mind is your greatest enemy. That situation left me knowing my place in the world, what I was capable of, and what was out of my control. And that is the realization that is necessary now."

Anne was seeking the answer to his riddle. "We'll I've definitely attempted to determine what the artifact is. Are you saying that we just may never find out?"

"No. Apply the inversion of my story to your original question." He paused to let his suggestion marinate. *"What does the Saudi Government believe the artifact is?* The artifact is the sea to them, based on initial testing, sacred texts, and the illnesses befalling large portions of those in close proximity with it. This includes many within the government. With the artifact on land, we cannot control its gravity. We are susceptible to its bidding."

She felt like she now knew a proverbial bogeyman was behind the door being opened here, and her chest was tightening at the anticipation. There were too many questions.

Khaki continued. "The Saudis never expected this. They understand what they see with their eyes, and they seek to control it, no matter what it may be. Their journey with the artifact began attempting to understand it to exploit it in my estimation. But they quickly grew both impatient, and more importantly, scared. Much like my time lost at sea, once they understood the situation was out of their control, they made their decision. But they did not learn, their reaction was one of fear. This is why the end of my time at sea is not of consequence here. They were scared largely because of their intangible lack of control, which is a very bad way for the Saudis. Even the tangible around them began to feel ominous and threatening. They didn't know if someone set this upon them, or if someone would claim it, unleashing further death. They did not embrace their situation. They wanted the artifact as far away from them as possible, rather than further attempting a deeper understanding and acceptance of their new place in the world. Their plan will buy them time, but it is folly."

"Wait, death? People are dying?"

"Yes, the government tested keeping individuals within certain proximity of it once they concluded it was making people ill. If the ill subject was not removed from the area, they wasted away at an accelerated rate and expired."

"Jesus…"

"Ahh, yes, your God. You might want to ask him about that."

She picked up on the flippancy of this statement. But maybe there was more there. "Sacred texts? What sacred texts?"

stealth bomber

Early September, Year 1 A.A.

"···just like that…"

He cut her off. "And I'm supposed to *unconcentrate*, is that even…"

"It'll prove itself. But I'm not certain my underwear over your head will facilitate the effect any more quickly."

She was lying on her back in the center of the bed. Her left arm was arched up to support the back of her head on the stacked pillows. The index finger of her right hand was in the half-empty beer bottle resting upright at her side. She had a comfort in her own skin about her that he had never seen in a girl.

The room was darkened from blackout shades. A lava lamp was the only source of light. The purple lava lazily formed, broke apart, and reformed as it rose and fell, casting ever-changing shadows around the room. Ron was sitting on the lower corner of the bed near her legs. Her underwear partially obscured his left eye. "Well okay." Ron nodded at the beer. She arched an eyebrow, lazily grasped it, and took a swig. She angled the top of the bottle toward him. He finished it and clanked it against its empty brethren on the nightstand near the lamp.

Rolling his eyes, Ron inhaled sharply, stood beside the bed, arched his arms in a letter Y, wagged his fingers back and forth, and bowed as far over as he could in a grandiose gesture with arms still extended. She took the opportunity to lean forward, hook a finger in the open leg of her underwear, and pop it off of his head. As he arose Ron gave a mock dejected face. She in turn flung her underwear at his chest in the fashion of firing a rubber band with her hands.

Ron didn't attempt to catch them, rather letting them fall down his body. He cleared his throat extensively in jest, entwined the fingers of his hands and, extending his arms in front of him, turned his hands inside out to crack most of the knuckles while walking to the foot of the bed.

"Today..." she offered with a retaliatory mock exhale, rolling her eyes.

"Okay." He squinted, then opened his eyes wide. "Relax."

Ron inhaled, exhaled. A minute or more passed. He could not allow his eyes to lose focus. "Nothing..."

"I'm not in a rush," she offered flatly.

He blinked, taking his time looking up, down, then up again at her body. "I'm glad you're not."

"Would you get it together?" She offered another eye roll.

"Okay." He inhaled slowly, exhaled deeply, and relaxed. Ron was staring at her... attempting to see her wholly as she suggested. His eyes slowly unfocused. It wasn't long before his mind started to wander. *Did I leave my car door unlocked outside?* It was funny how the mind worked... he was right where he wanted to be and began thinking of the most ridiculous and mundane things.

Her body began to creep toward obscurity. It began to remind him of zoning out in a classroom, or driving too late at night when the dark road becomes a blur and the car staggers across lane lines. Ron found himself sinking to a further depth. Her form blurred from light skin tones to grey, and he felt that tiredness swallow him further, as if he and his vehicle were being pulled to an unknown end... his foot on the gas pedal was irrelevant. Lilith's body became increasingly fuzzy and shuddered.

Ron lost track of time as she became translucent to the point the yellow sheets around her were a sickly yellowed grey, slightly visible through her form, almost as if seeing the sea through and behind a jellyfish. Then the oddest thing happened, although his mind didn't process it at first. The grey expanded outward on either side, almost in strips, where her neck, biceps, and ankles would be located. The expanded forms near the neck and ankles presented themselves as diamond shapes, *or sharp shards of glass angled upward if my eyes were in focus* he thought. But the grey forms by her biceps were what would stay most vividly with him for decades. Those forms blossomed outward and fell back seemingly into the bed. He only surmised into the bed as the forms reappeared out of the sides of the bed in the original grey form of her body as they were no longer over the yellow sheets. The forms twitched independently like... like...

He inhaled quickly as if the ride that was pulling him suddenly came to a screeching halt. His eyes come back into focus. She and the bed came collapsing back into focus. "What was that? Wha, what are..." he asked.

Her face portrayed somberness and what seemed to be hope. "That's for you to figure out."

Ron was breathing heavily. None of this was making sense suddenly. "What do I do with this knowledge once I figure it out?"

"That's also for you to figure out." It was almost a challenge.

His head hurt suddenly, possibly from leaving his eyes out of focus for so long. Maybe from pulling them back into focus too quickly? He didn't know. Ron suddenly heard a ringing in his ears that was initially quiet, and increased in volume gradually. He felt his legs go weak, fell to a knee and caught the floor with his hands. As he toppled over he thought he knew what her tattoo meant, or at least as it related to her, and the last thing he heard was her voice coming from a tunnel above him. She called his name and it sounded like a velvet hurricane.

the past's future

Early September, Year 1 A.A.

"I think you've had too much alcohol. You're not a violent man". Ron sat down with Mahi at the booth. The diner was standard inner-city in every way. It had been around seemingly forever, offered low-grade cuisine, was adorned with dingy, torn seat cushions in many of the booths, and served predominantly liquid and or chemically induced patrons. Ron always felt comfortable here as he and his friends frequented the diner when inebriated after some event. There was also the vibe of no judgment that he seldom felt in other public settings.

Mahi sat with his back against the inside wall of their booth, right elbow resting on the table while he thumbed a beat on the lacquered surface. He shook his head after the disinterested waitress left the table. The restaurant was also always populated with the prototypical sullen late-shift wait staff.

"Your lack of concern over those characters has me worried." Mahi slurred just enough to be noticed on 'cern'.

"I've stated my case. No one wins regardless of outcome in my opinion."

"I don't believe you understand my point…" Mahi ran his hands side-by-side up and down his face. He inhaled deeply as he did so, chest shuddering with the intake of breath, straightening his posture in unison. He dropped his hands, opening his eyes as wide as possible, to the point where he was also raising his eyebrows. He smiled, exhaled, and slumped back over, hands now in his lap. "I want to tell you a story. And I want you to listen, and not say anything until the end."

Ron did as he was told, only he jutted his lower jaw out to tilt the straw he was chewing on upward in an affirmative gesture while raising his eyebrows in anticipation. A facial *go ahead*....

Mahi misread the look slightly. "Don't be moody. I'm not demanding utter silence, just that you HEAR what I'm saying."

"You have my attention. Learn me, Master."

Mahi's eyes narrowed, studying his student's face for possible sarcasm. He concluded he saw none. He picked up his coffee, focused on it and sipped. Setting it back down carefully his face became sharply intent. "When I was younger I knew of a very powerful man. This man had much land and influence over people. He was visited by a well-known prefect that had access to an elite political group that the powerful man felt he was owed access to. Upon seeing the prefect arrive at his home, the powerful man felt his ascension to the ranks of the elite had arrived.

Intent again on his mug, Mahi took a longer drink of coffee. "His arrogance led him to welcome the prefect in a very dismissive manner. Imagine if upper management at work sent a Human Resources manager to your house and you didn't get off the couch to shake their hand, or offer them a drink or a seat as you now felt some new level of entitlement... felt on the same level of management as them solely based on the assumption of that representative coming to your house. Well the H.R. manager wouldn't appreciate that very much, correct? And the discourtesy could lead to the insight that the host was discourteous based on some preconceived notion that has not been bestowed upon them.

"Needless to say, the prefect departed in anger. The powerful man soon realized his folly. He attempted to locate the prefect to apologize for his arrogance, but the prefect would not grace the man with his presence. Nor would the prefect make himself known to the elite group as they had sent him to the powerful man. There was considerable fallout from the series of events. Word travelled of his disrespect, and he began to lose favor with those around him. The elite group had also become more vulnerable to competing interests as they lost the services of both the prefect and the powerful man."

"I know I agreed to not interrupt your story, but can I ask you one question?"

Mahi rolled his eyes. "Aside from the one you are asking now, you deaf dog?" Mahi actually had a bit of a scowl on his face. He then gave a half smirk as he narrowed his eyes. "Yes."

Ron was taken aback slightly by this reaction, but chalked it up to alcohol and continued on. "This was your experience from prior to coming to America? From your younger days?"

"You could say that."

He found this response odd from Mahi, but didn't know why. Ron wasn't going to interrupt again though, at Mahi's prior request. Not to mention he always found Mahi's stories and thoughts intriguing. He didn't want Mahi to lose the thread as he seemed half in the bag.

"May I continue?" Mahi sternly questioned, as if to a child. He received a timid nod only in response, so he picked up where he had left off. "So as I was saying…" Emphasis on that last word. "The powerful man had lost curry from the prefect, the elite, and his constituents. The elite had lost curry from the prefect, no longer valued the services of the powerful man, and as a result were more vulnerable to outside forces. So the elite then recruited a replacement for the powerful man. This did not go over well with the man, and was exacerbated by the fact that his replacement had filled his role exceptionally in the eyes of the elite.

"The powerful man also suspected his replacement's background and motives, and as a result he descended into what could be considered madness. The result was a failed attempt to bait the replacement into indiscretion. As a result of the failure, he then murdered the replacement."

Ron wondered where Mahi's story was going and what any of this meant.

"The powerful man's land and influence continued to suffer from his indiscretions, as did the people of his land. The family of the deceased replacement then conjured an enemy to avenge the murder."

How intoxicated was Mahi? Ron wondered to himself. *Maybe Mahi had been watching too many movies lately? Conjuring enemies?* Mahi is always good for a story, and typically they're based in reality even when they involve murder, but this one seemed to be derailing just a bit.

"The elites could no longer stand by knowing that the situation was spiraling far out of control. They struck a deal with the henchman to not destroy the powerful man. The powerful man was also persuaded to end the hostilities. Time passed and when the situation was thought concluded, the powerful man attacked and killed the henchman in a brutal battle. The powerful man then disappeared in presumed shame at his decent into madness."

They sat in silence for several moments. Ron had become enrapt in the story and attempting to figure out what Mahi was talking about to the point that he had blocked out the noise of the restaurant, which was just dialing back up in his ears. He was wondering why Mahi had offered such an elaborate story in relation to neither of them addressing the racist young men at the concert.

When Ron felt confident the story was complete (Mahi was staring into his coffee cup), he asked "Can I ask how the powerful man killed the henchman?"

"What?" Mahi came to life, grabbed a creamer from the cup the waitress left with his coffee, opened it and drained it into his coffee as he spoke. "Oh, the powerful man amputated the henchman's right arm, cut his belly open, then drown him with the ocean." He made a circular stirring motion with his arm, mug in hand, coffee and creamer swirling slowly.

Ron's mouth dropped open slightly at this nonchalant closure by Mahi. *Drown him with the ocean?* He considered Mahi must be spinning what possibly started with facts into fiction. "Sounds like the powerful man came from a good family," Ron said sarcastically. "A little scary not only drowning someone, but cutting their arm off and stomach open first," was all he could offer.

"You could say that. Oddly, his brother also had one arm…" Mahi trailed off.

They sat in silence for a few minutes, and Ron blankly stared at the table, eyes darting horizontally attempting to ascertain what he was to glean from this story, coming up with blanks. Mahi casual looked around at the patrons of the restaurant and the framed pictures on the walls.

Ron took a deep breath, preparing to speak. "Okay." Mahi stirred again at his word, lost in his coffee. "I believe I've pieced together at least part of what you're driving at with your story. Actions have consequences, sometimes major and unforeseen." He let it hang there.

No verbal or visual clues from Mahi. Mahi clearly wanted him to expand.

"Inaction also has consequence. If the powerful man had only made the decision to simply greet the prefect respectfully and hear him out, not really doing anything but being polite, the result would probably have been vastly different."

Mahi winked and tipped his coffee mug at him. "It's a good lesson, and one worth remembering." He held up his right hand, palm facing forward with middle finger extended upward, other fingers curled under his thumb. His equivalent of the American index finger, *Eureka!*

"And I appreciate your use of the word *consequence*... It only gains a negative connotation based on man's use. The fact that I took no action against the racist could have a larger ripple effect. What if in his confidence they now come across another non-white? What if he pushes it further than just an ignorant remark? What if there is physical violence and the subject could not defend themselves as well as me?"

"Okay, I officially feel a lot worse now."

"That was not my intent... Only to educate. Do you feel you will make the proper decision when your time comes?"

What an odd question, Ron thought. "I think anyone likes to believe they'll make the right decision, but there are just so many factors. You attempt to prepare or reinforce yourself for certain scenarios you've already experienced, or that you've heard or read about. But there's just no way to know for certain."

"That's not true. It boils down to fear regardless of the scenario. I obviously feared being beat up and that was why I didn't respond. I've been in similar scenarios before and have always reacted in a similar manner. I know my flaw and haven't learned from it."

"That's not true, I've seen you stand up for yourself bef..."

"Wrong..." Mahi sighed. "You've seen me respond in certain scenarios... Where fear was not a motivating factor."

Ron tried to recall prior instances he'd seen firsthand

or heard Mahi or another friend describe.

Mahi continued. "If you tell yourself you will fear no man, no physical or mental reprisal, and then act in that galvanization, you can then sleep with no fear of nightmares."

The waitress arrived with their food. She set/dropped the plates down and raised an eyebrow at Ron, then turned to Mahi with the same "*Well?*" face. He and Mahi looked at each other, aloof, and at the same time he offered "Ah, thank you?" Mahi offered "Looks great?" She shook her head and walked away.

the problem of dirty hands

Mid-September, Year 1 A.A.

The airplane hitched slightly, causing many of the ill passengers to moan. The number of voices was startlingly plentiful to Anne. Khaki looked at his watch, then out the window. Anne found this curious as there were still hours remaining on the flight. She also surmised it wasn't a nervous tick. The man exuded confidence. *Why was he looking at his watch?*

"What we are taught as children forms our initial religious beliefs. As the mind develops, our thirst for knowledge, or lack of drive, further molds the pursuit of knowledge in the form of religion and history. This thirst, or laziness, further galvanizes or alters our religious beliefs. Religious, atheistic, and agnostic beliefs beget a certain amount of accepted history… namely for the lazy or biased. Those beliefs also beget principles." He began holding up fingers with each of his next points. "Worldly educators, life experience, having an open mind, and drive are the fundamental basis of spiritual evolution.

He continued. "A doctrine I hold sacred is to see more than just black and white in the world. And this is key in relation to religion and history. There is much to learn in cross-referencing religions and cultures. What I have come to find is there is quite a bit of gray the more one researches, like most things in life. For instance, are you familiar with the Ngbe-Bugle Indians of Chiriqui?"

"No." Anne's mind was in full spin.

"Have you ever heard the term Box of Thunder?" When she shook her head briefly, he continued. "Quite ominous sounding, the Box of Thunder, yes? The Indians of Chiriqui believed that on top of the mountain of Volcan in northwest Chiriqui, Panama, they could communicate with their Great Spirit. The Spirit would talk to their ancestors through a cloud of thunder using a golden box to reach the Spirit. This belief was supported by ancient maps of petroglyphs depicted on rocks dating back to around 600BC." He paused to allow her to absorb what he was saying. "Does any of this sound familiar?"

Another head shake from Anne.

"Then I assume you have also not heard of the Mesopotamian deity of the underworld, Ningishzida?" He smirked at the same response from Anne. "Ningishzida is translated as Lord of The Good Tree. This is the earliest symbol of snakes twining an axial rod. And this was millennium earlier than Moses' staff...."

Anne's mouth dropped. It hit her like a ton of bricks.

He went on. "Mercury in Roman iconography carried a similar caduceus. His wand offered powers relating to the balance of life and death."

"Aaron's Rod," Anne whispered. "And the Box of Thunder is the Ark..." She covered her mouth with her hand. It never occurred to her, or the Colonel or Slippy for that matter as far as she was aware. She knew the Colonel had suspicions, but he had never vocally conceptualized them for her to be sure. But hadn't the Colonel mentioned that she, Hatim, and he were exceptions?

"Quite right." His smile was sinister, accented by the missing tooth. "Your God instructed Moses on Mount Sinai that he was to construct an Ark."

"And Aaron's Rod was in the Ark of the Covenant

with the Commandments..."

"Yes, which the Philistines stole. And their people became ill, and died from plague for their thievery."

Anne looked around, seeing people with boils, sunken cheeks, several appeared passed out and barely breathing. *Were some of the passengers dead?* Dozens were coughing.

Khaki went on "The plague included boils, hemorrhoids, and rats. Somewhat surprisingly the Philistines kept the Ark for seven months before being happy to return it to the Israelites. Custody of the Ark was then documented until the Babylonians destroyed Solomon's Temple. And this was around the time the petroglyph maps date back to in Chiriqui."

Anne began feeling dizzy. The oncoming gravity of the situation was all too much.

"The only other documentation of it is a Greek text, suggesting the Babylonians took the Ark along with other holy treasures and carried them away from Babylon. Babylon being located where modern day Iraq lies. So if the Ark or its contents survived to this day, but there's no documentation of the location of the artifacts, one may postulate that such sacred objects provided for Israelite's protection might be tucked away somewhere not terribly far from where they were last reported ..."

She cut him off. "My God, it's Aaron's Rod..."

"...or, separated, sending the Ark off to distant Panama in the instance someone might learn of it and track it, and kept what might be deemed to matter most close, but in a different direction..." He let that sink in. "Tell me of Aaron's Rod..." he suggested, as if he was a teacher validating his student has read her assignment from the prior class.

"Aaron's Rod... Moses' brother Aaron. It was told to have wondrous power. A weapon really. The common interpretation or foundation is that both Moses and Aaron had shepherds sticks. It's not really a leap that they represented power or authority over a flock or group. In Moses' case, both his literal flock and the Israelites. It's what he parted the Red Sea with. There was something else there, but I cannot recall... something with food or drink." She pondered, but Khaki did not, or would not, interrupt. "Aaron's Rod was a different story. There was a magic one-upsmanship between him and some pharaohs I believe. Something with multiple shepherds' rods being laid together, all of them becoming serpents, and Aaron's Rod eating the other serpents?"

"And are you familiar with the Rod's significance in the Haggadah?"

"No."

"The Haggadah stipulates the Rod served multiple masters, including Adam, Abraham, and was used by David to defeat Goliath. It eventually disappeared with the Ark, but the text suggests that the Rod will be returned to the Savior as evidence of his rule over the wicked." He seemed satisfied, then added "I've researched a great deal after my initial encounter with it."

"Wait... Adam? As in the first man?"

"The Rod was suggested to have been created by God at night on the Sixth Day, and then delivered to Adam upon his exit from Paradise."

"It's all the same artifact... And it's... real?"

"It has many names. And historians will doubtless disagree on what it should be called and what it truly represents, based on their knowledge of religion and history. What will not be argued is the result, which you have seen previously, the Saudis have seen, and we are seeing today. They all probably have aspects of it correct."

"What does this mean? The handprints are for someone who is alive today?" She rubbed at her temples, thinking there was some other realization she was missing from the artifact... something that should be obvious.

"Quite possibly… or of those in the future. Why the imprints are at both ends and different is not clear either." He paused and rolled his wrist until a pop was released. "Let me return to an earlier question. You had asked what the Saudi Government theorized the artifact is. The King is Muslim and holds the Qur'an sacred. It speaks of Aaron extensively, including mention of the Prophet Muhammad seeing him in heaven. He is therefore held in high regard. The Qur'an further confirms the Ark will be returned to Israel and that it contained relics of Aaron."

He continued. "The King was so taken by the effects of the artifact that he consulted the Ulema." Khaki noticed Anne seemed confused. "They are the group of Islamic religious leaders. The Ulema had formerly held sway with prior Kings of Saudi Arabia for decades. The current King has been distancing himself from them since he first came to power, which is therefore of considerable significance that he would now seek their guidance. The Ulema includes several worldly scholars, one of which recited from the Catholic Bible's Book of Isaiah for the King. The quote indicated …*the devout are taken away, and no one understands the righteous are taken away to be spared evil.* Can you guess how he responded to this?"

Anne lost her former train of thought. She disliked his guessing game in light of the current situation. She shook her head.

"He threw the Ulema out of his chambers. His next action resulted in where we are now. He is clearly scared of it. One can assume he believes the object is ending the lives of the devout, and since he was not ill from being in close proximity with it, he would not go to heaven, nor be spared evil."

"Wait, what?" She caught her voice rising in urgency, then whispered "I thought the sinners were dying?"

"This is his interpretation. One of the Ulema said the King alluded to as much before they were forced to leave.

He wants the artifact to disappear... He no longer views it as a weapon, if he even did at first. He sees it as an omen in line with your horsemen of the apocalypse. My conclusion cannot be disputed as we are here today."

"What do you think?"

"Of the King's interpretation? If one is to believe the artifact is Aaron's Rod, Mercury's caduceus, whatever incarnation you prefer, then there are only two ways to interpret it based on what has been occurring to those in its presence... The dead and dying are the damned. Or they are the saved. Human beings are self-centered by nature. It is in our DNA. The sick will believe themselves as saved in light of this knowledge. The healthy will view themselves the same. Quite the conundrum, particularly when considering someone will yield its power to cleanse the earth."

Anne hadn't gotten this far down the rabbit hole in her mind yet. He didn't have to paint a clearer picture. The Rod will divide the world, and destruction will follow. Ironic that a tool of God could bring such violence, but really how ironic was it based on all of the death already wrought on Earth in the name of religion? She realized she has never been so wholly frightened in her life.

She felt desperate. "I have to ask..." Anne knew this was a sign of weakness but she no longer understood. "Why are you being so forthcoming with me?"

"I have been trained to be a good judge of character. You strike me as honest and brave."

The plane hitched again and a loud mechanical winding down sound was heard. The passengers, including Anne, looked around. Exasperated sighs and screeches were heard from throughout the plane, initially with the seats in front of the engines. The panic quickly spread. She turned back to Khaki, whose head was bouncing between his watch and the earth outside of the plane. He checked his watch then craned his neck to look down toward the ground, then back to his watch again.

"What's happening? Why do you keep checking your watch?" Panic was growing inside of her. She brushed her hair back from her forehead, realized she was exposing her scar, and pulled a lock back down. *Vanity in a time like this* she thought.

"I'd like to answer your former question." He stopped.

He glanced past her. Anne followed his glance. A tall, clean cut man in a black suit was walking past them. Chiseled face, lean, possibly Italian. Anne noticed an ear piece. The man moved quietly and looked very grave. A sheen of sweat covering his face. She turned back to Khaki, who had angled his body in her direction, with his hand on the back of her seat. He appeared to be weighing something in his mind.

"I have the impression you possess an open mind in regards to the religious or spiritual, and that speaks volumes regarding a person's potential over most any other statements or reactions."

She was touched by this. No one had ever said anything as nice as this to her in her life.

"To your last question. You also were on the team to discover the artifact. You deserve the truth. My King has decided the artifact needed to be removed from this continent. In fact, to a removed area of the globe."

"But he had to know this could end in disaster if the wrong people, such as the pilots, fell ill." She also figured she now understood the handprints on the artifact, and this was tantamount to the world.

"He planned for that. That is why we are on this particular flight. You see the government tested people remaining within proximity of the Rod well after showing initial signs of illness. The eventual mortality rate of afflicted is 100%. The plan is that if the plane is to crash, it will crash in the Pacific Ocean. That way the Rod will be hidden away again, delaying the seemingly inevitable for mankind."

Anne couldn't believe what she was hearing. "You're going to kill us all...." She lived in denial that people could actually murder hundreds of innocent people, no matter for what cause.

He looked forward. "I am not going to kill us all. I am here to ensure if it is going to happen, it will not be stopped."

He glanced forward and saw the Italian suited man leaning over, speaking to another suited chiseled man several rows forward. The second man, possibly African, rose casually, glanced back in the direction of Brown, then clearly toward Khaki, and turned to follow the Italian through the closed curtains toward the next forward section. Khaki looked toward the passengers to Anne's left. The closest, a young woman in her twenties, was asleep with her hands across her stomach. Or maybe dead. He could not see the faces of anyone beyond her. He heard moaning from immediately behind them but could not see faces through their seats.

"I am going..." Anne began with a stern, but still quiet voice, as if attempting to find the force necessary.

He cut her off, raising his voice for the first time, slightly, but with enough force that it stopped her cold. "Would you like a magazine?"
He was holding one out in front of her with his hand. She was dumbfounded at this question. As she looked down the last words she heard were a sincere "Forgive Me." Then there was darkness.

Khaki had brought his other fist, index finger knuckle extended in a Phoenix's Eye, swiftly into Anne's temple. As he connected he dropped the magazine in her lap, and reached across her to cup her far bicep, holding her from rocking swiftly with the blow.

He grabbed her right shoulder with his left hand, and

shifted her quickly slackening body as if he were helping her get comfortable. He offered a "There you go. Try and relax." in case anyone was listening. He brushed her hair back from her face, and slid his thumb slowly across her scar, figuring she had seen true pain in her life also. Then, tilting her seat back, he ensured her head was not going to allow her body to slump forward, then slid his fingers down over her eyelids. He offered a silent prayer for her soul. Glancing around to ensure no one had witnessed the act, he stood up casually, and began to follow the suited men toward the front of the plane. He stopped short, turned, picked the magazine up from Anne's lap. He offered her a satisfied look, which might be misconstrued as someone looking longingly at a loved one.

The reality was Khaki was satisfied she would not be able to disrupt the plan. He turned in pursuit of the two men. Tucking the magazine under his armpit, Khaki buttoned his jacket as he walked. He thought to himself that Anne's death was much quicker and peaceful compared to the fate that was looming over Earth.

assessment

Mid-September, Year 1 A.A.

In the few hours since the event, the crater area had been gradually circled off with police and emergency vehicles (as they arrived), creating a crash site barrier from the public and scant media. Only fire trucks were inside the loose ring, with hoses snaking throughout the area. The fires were extinguished but the smoke was still substantial from the event. Fire personnel clad in chemical-protective disposable coveralls continued to douse the smoldering piles. Two helicopters circled the scene. After the initial search for survivors was completed all personnel (except response crews) in the area were pulled back. No survivors were found in the field.

Based on what he had witnessed, Pascal surmised the passengers of the crash were largely (if not as an entire group) blown apart and scattered. The complete bodies appeared to be locals who were far enough away to not have been obliterated by the impact, but close enough to be felled by the concussive blast, fire, and debris.

Pascal had overseen the early stages of the operation until his Commandant had arrived on-scene. He had then begun documenting names of all individuals who were on-site at his arrival and segregating them into support and witness groups for interview. Dozens of authorized response personnel were currently combing what was now deemed the Control Zone, now cordoned off in quadrants. These included fire, rescue, military, medical, health, and environmental representatives, and possibly others Pascal was not aware of. Photography of the area was on-going, along with cataloging of findings and bagging of bodies and body parts. The town was further sectioned into secondary quadrants which authorized personnel were also working. This was referred to as Control Zone Two.

Pascal's Commandant walked away from the SMUR head toward Pascal, rubbing the back of his neck along the way. Before today he had the weathered look of a man with white hair in his late fifties that had spent decades doing hard labor outdoors, and already looked even more world-weary less than three hours post-event. The two had not spoken since the Commandant's arrival when Pascal had initially updated him on all aspects of the situation and the Commandant took control.

"Commandant Dupin."

"Stick with Peter if we're not in front of anyone, Pascal."

"Do we have any intel?"

"Yes. But first I want to say thank you. What you've established here in regards to control of the situation and support of rescue has been commendable…"

"There's been no rescue sir."

"I realize that, but given the fact that this is not a situation we're readily trained for, you've provided a top notch example of execution. It hasn't been completely by the book necessarily… I'm referring to your citizen rescue team… but I wouldn't have done it better."

"Thank you. I feel like there's a but…"

"There's not. We'll be questioned on that last aspect, but due to the circumstances, namely the size of our force compared to the scope of the event, I'll be backing your decision making completely. I want you to remain on point for the duration." Peter shifted his eyes to the crater. Pascal seemed to pick up something in that glance. "We're in for the long haul here for the next several days or longer."

Pascal felt nothing toward Peter's appreciation or suggestion of extensive work in the near future. He valued Peter's input, but felt he'd only done what was necessary. He also felt that this wasn't a situation where he could make a difference in someone's life. Everyone in the immediate area at the time of impact was dead.

Peter continued "The intel is as follows, and this is under wraps for now as it hasn't been released to the press… According to the BEA, early returns from national and international airlines indicate this most likely was a larger airliner coming out of Jeddah-King Abdulaziz in Saudi Arabia with a destination of Washington D.C. in The United States. It's the only flight any of the airlines do not have account of that was due to fly through this region of the country. There is early speculation of possible terrorist involvement. No speculation of mechanical failure due to the weather being favorable and no reported air traffic concerns from that plane, or any plane for that matter, prior to the event. The BEA's stressing avoidance of interpretations or speculation naturally. Several countries may already be involved as my understanding is the more assistance the more likely expedited resolution. The scope of this is already spinning well beyond our control, which quite frankly, I'm glad for. We're just not equipped for this."

"What of the first responders' illnesses? I've been seeing people scratching and doubled over being helped out of here. Did you see the woman vomiting violently?"

"No, but seeing body parts scattered could have done that to her. There's just no way to tell specifically right now where the origination point of the concern is. The sick reportedly were not all searching the same area.

My guess is there are pockets of fluid throughout the area creating hazardous fumes that are getting these people ill. You can see how many people on-site are unaffected. I think our hope is the breeze and water from the fire trucks are washing away those probable concerns."

"Commandant? Commandant?", came a voice from behind them.
Peter scanned the area for the voice, then turned back to Pascal. "Can you track down HMRT? It's in our best interest to confirm if they have a lock on any hazardous materials in the area and are working toward neutralizing them."

evinced nescience

Mid-September, Year 1 A.A.

"May I ask what happened after the test?" The Colonel still had a look of utter surprise on his face from Brown's indication that he was in a lead box with the artifact.

Brown hesitated, possibly considering his words, then offered "I and the two other remaining individuals in the test were separated. It was later explained to me that I would be chaperoning a package headed for the United States on connecting flights. I assume the other agents were given the same information."

"Is your partner one of the other two men?"

"Yes."

"Have you discussed any of this with him?"

That assumption by Brown was clearly a slip. Brown had stopped talking at the Colonel's follow-up question. He gave the Colonel an angered look, which said *do not trifle with me.*

The Colonel wondered *was Brown upset with himself for being forthcoming? Or not considering the need to discuss the situation ahead of time with Khaki? Or because he perceived I knew more than him? Was this a control issue?* "I apologize if I overstepped my bounds. What I mean to ask is if your government is aware of the seeming power of the artifact."

"The King is in control of this situation."

The Colonel now knew Brown did not understand the power of the artifact and quite possibly the extent of what was happening on the plane. "Does your King know what the artifact is?"

"That is not for me to know."

"Is the flight crew aware of what is in their cargo hold? Is there a back-up plan in the instance the flight crew or a substantial number of the passengers are ailing?"

"The situation is under control."

My God, the Colonel thought, *he doesn't know. And he has no idea what we're up against.* He decided it was time to be completely candid. "I want to ensure you appreciate the gravity of the situation. Please look around at the passengers."

Brown did not move and only stared at the Colonel.

The Colonel didn't have time for this. Lowering his voice, he leaned in toward Brown's ear. "Good sir, at least half of the people on this airplane are ill. And the illnesses seem to be worsening. See the woman two passengers to our right? Her skin has a green pallor and is glistening. She appears unconscious rather than sleeping. Did you hear the announcement? Please look around you. This is not the time for pride. This flight is probably not making it to America, I..."

"Stop speaking." Brown's voice momentarily raised volume. "I am not ignorant to the situation and will not tolerate your insolence."

The Colonel offered a hissing whispered retort. "This is not insolence. It's our lives and the lives of hundreds of people on this flight." He gritted his teeth at the end of his declaration. He refused to turn a blind eye to what seemed inevitable.

Brown, composing himself and without hesitation, countered... "Are you familiar with the Ichneumon Eumerus, Mr. Versail?"

"What?" The Colonel was taken aback at Brown

knowing his name, then realized this was no surprise. The man was clearly attempting to take back control of a spiraling situation with misdirection of some sort. The Colonel could not clear his head though to focus on what Brown was asking him.

The airplane hitched slightly, causing many of the ill passengers to moan. The Colonel clutched the arms of his seat to steady himself, then released and flexed his hands in a show of tension. He was not surprised by the audible response of the ailing to the unexpected movement, and when he looked at Brown, he saw no discernible resemblance of nervousness or fear.

Some time passed with neither man saying anything. The Colonel racked his brain attempting to conjure up a memory regarding the Ichneumon Eumerus, but he was blanking. He suddenly felt an itch on his arm, and remembered something. "A wasp? Or a bee?"

"A wasp. And are you familiar with its mating method?"

"No, but I fail to see the relevance…"

The plane hitched again and a loud mechanical winding down sound was heard. The passengers, including the Colonel, looked around. Exasperated sighs and screeches were heard, loudest initially with the seats up in front of the engines. The panic quickly spread.

"This situation is salvageable, but I fear we will not live through the day if we do not act!" the Colonel pronounced. "We need to work as a team as we both know pieces of this situation and it is our duty to act in our knowledge."

Brown wasn't even looking at him. The Colonel's blood began to boil. He hadn't felt this way in years, maybe decades. He opened his mouth to lay into Brown and stopped talking when he saw Brown's face. He had the appearance of a student that had studied all night for an exam who was now blanking with the exam in front of him. The Colonel followed his gaze toward a tall, clean-cut man in a black suit walking toward the front of the section. The man was probably Italian, and appeared fit. The man moved quietly and looked very grave. He also had a sheen of sweat covering his face. The Colonel turned back to Brown, who appeared to be weighing something in his mind.

The Colonel's focus shifted from the Italian to Brown. "What is it? Do you know that man?"

"What? No."

Just then, Brown and the Colonel glanced forward and saw the Italian suited man leaning over, speaking to another suited, chiseled man several rows forward. The latter man was probably African.

"Sir, I'm not certain how else to convey to you that the situation at hand…" the Colonel began.

The man Italian was speaking to rose casually and glanced back in the direction of Brown and the Colonel. Brown kept the gaze. The Colonel turned away, uncertain why, then turned back. The African had shifted his focus toward Khaki and Anne's direction briefly, and turned to follow the Italian through the closed curtains toward the next forward section.

Brown suddenly appeared very uncertain, as if mulling a critical decision over. He leaned forward and reached into the magazine pouch. He clicked the power button on the Colonel's phone to ensure it was still off. Satisfied, he handed the phone to the Colonel and flatly stated "Please return to your seat."

The Colonel turned toward Brown. "Wait, who are those men? What is happening here?" He glanced forward again. "Why is your partner following them?"

Brown cocked his head forward quickly, too quickly. In a rushed, forceful tone he urged "That is privileged information. Please return to your seat and say nothing to those around you. You will only make the situation worse." Brown began to stand.

Both men noticed the plane's forward section lowering and Brown clutched the top of the seat in front of him to steady himself. They were beginning to descend quickly. Just then, they both heard raised voices from the front of the plane, but couldn't hear the words.

"Return to your seat now, Mr. Versail." Brown stepped out into the aisle, closer to the front of the plane, forcing the Colonel to walk toward the back of the plane to circle back to his seat.

As the Colonel began to walk toward the back of the plane, the Ichneumon Eumerus' mating method dawned on him. He stopped in his tracks. It was coming into focus, but what did it mean? He turned back toward Brown's seat, opened his mouth, and noticed the man was disappearing into the forward section of the plane.

beginning of the end of the beginning

Mid-September, Year 1 A.A.

Khaki walked through the next two economy sections, pacing himself to avoid detection from the two men he was following. He used the magazine as a prop, scanning pages as he walked casually. He knew where the men were headed. He was not going to lose them.

The plane continued to angle downward as if in decent. It was enough for Khaki to bear down with the front of his feet to steady himself. Moaning, uneasy murmurings and slight panic at the continued descent was voiced throughout the section. Khaki heard discussions of why there has been no announcement from the cockpit regarding the recent change in trajectory. Khaki glanced around at the passengers as he walked. He noticed several people that appeared to be dead. Fortunately, enough people were sleeping, sick, or concerned with what was happening for total panic not to set in. This made his path easy to navigate while relatively unnoticed.

Khaki reached the front of the second forward economy seating section and glanced up the stairwell. No one was visible. He ascended the stairs. As he did, Brown came through the opening at the rear of the same section. Brown's unease was visible on his face as he scanned the area. Seeing multiple sections of the ill was breaking down his defenses.

Khaki heard a slightly louder commotion from the Upper Deck as he ascended the stairwell. He paused not quite at the top of the steps for the necessary reconnaissance. He could see a stewardess attempting to calm several passengers down, offering "…are with the United State government and are simply checking with the pilots on the change in trajectory." She was holding on to the seats on either side of the aisle to steady herself as the pitch of the plane appeared to be continually increasing. She walked back toward him and the galley. Beyond her he saw two pairs of suited legs near the cockpit.

The colors matched those of the agents, although from his viewpoint he could not see the upper halves of their bodies. Knocking could be heard followed by "Captain or copilot, please look through your peephole at my badge. We need to have a brief discussion…"

Khaki knew the time was here. He was tasked with allowing the flight to take its destined course, whether United States or into the ocean, he would not know which. He looked at his watch again, realizing they were still not over the ocean. Based on the changing descent of the plane he surmised the eventuality of the flight crew was already playing out earlier than planned. The members were incapacitated in some manner. The U.S. agents should not be able to gain access to the cockpit. *Should not.* The aircraft was far away from his homeland. The time had come and this was now *best-case scenario.* He rolled the magazine as tightly as possible into its spine, then gripped it hard at an end in his hand and ascended the remaining steps.

The stewardess was back in the galley near the stairwell as he crested it. She looked him up and down expectantly as she readied her cart for a beverage and snack round. He pointed the magazine toward the front of the section and offered a deadpan "With those gentlemen…", tilting his head toward the agents.

She leaned in and whispered "We haven't gotten a response from anyone in the cockpit in some time. And we shouldn't be descending. I don't know if everyone's asleep up there or what's going on. Please be as casual as possible. We can't afford chaos up here with so many people sick. I'm working on keeping the passengers calm" she offered as she looked down at the cart.

He leaned in and matched her volume and tone. "I'll dispatch them quickly." He began to walk to the front of the section, then turned back as he saw the African, who was closer to him, turn away from the cockpit to scan the section. "Please continue with your duties" Khaki suggested while glancing at her cart. He took his time turning to face the front of the plane again. The African had turned his attention back to the closed cockpit door with the Italian agent in front of him. The Italian continued knocking while he held his badge up, intermittently raising and lowering it so anyone inside could confirm the identification picture matched his face. He sporadically duplicated these efforts for the globe camera near a corner of the ceiling.

Khaki moved swiftly and quietly. As he approached the agents, time slowed down for him acting as the aggressor. But time moved excruciatingly fast for everyone else who witnessed the chain of events as they were all unmistakably passengers of the situation.

The African sensed something and turned back to see Khaki roughly fifteen feet from him and approaching. Leaning his head back toward the front of the plane as he unbuttoned and reached into his suit jacket with his right hand, he offered a deadpan "Mario, six o'clock."

The stewardess began her round at the rear of the section, offering beverages and snacks to the right, then left sides of the last row. As she did so Brown crested the steps looking at her back and the cart, forward view obstructed from seeing anything fully in front of her.

Mario slid his id into his suit jacket pocket while he turned his head away from the cockpit. His left hand rose again to knock while his right reached into his jacket. Sensing his partner's tone and hearing his words, training had kicked in. He focused on Khaki as he peered over the back of the African's left shoulder. Quietly and emotionlessly he directed "Possible Saudi officer, Robert. Identify us. Only subdue if he engages. Signal me if unfriendly." Mario kept his hand in his jacket, turned back toward the cockpit, and continued knocking and speaking in the same tone to convey no change in demeanor to anyone watching, or anyone on the flight crew that may be listening or watching.

Brown peered around the stewardess and saw his partner advancing on the cockpit. He also verified the two suited men were between his partner and the cockpit, and that the Italian was knocking on the door. What he then glimpsed scared him. His partner tightened his grip on the magazine. Brown unbuttoned his suit jacket and began to advance.

"United States Government Agent sir... Please stop and identify yourself" Robert offered as he raised his hand in a halting motion. He also brought his other hand slowly back out of his suit... empty.

Khaki lifted his empty hand and waved politely, but continued to close the distance between them casually without speaking.

Robert saw Khaki gripping the rolled magazine tightly, gave a two count for any type of response, and assessed that it was time to pull his gun. The advancing man was not stopping or talking. He opened the flap of his suit, and drew the gun out to his side facing downward. The man did not stop. Robert raised the gun. "Engaging, Mario."

Several passengers nearest the action gasped.

Brown could not see the gun, but knew the African

was talking to his partner, that his partner wasn't stopping, and that he was hearing gasps. Brown closed on the stewardess and her cart, which was now three rows in from the back of the section. "Excuse me, Madam."

The stewardess started to turn back towards Brown.

The plane hitched violently and began a much steeper descent. Passengers began screaming. Moaning also increased as several ill passengers felt their seatbelts cut into their stomachs with the motion. Some flew face or chest first limply into the seats in front of them. In the front row of the back half of the section, an elderly man in a plaid designer shirt and brown slacks fell forward onto the floor in front of the emergency exit.

Robert's gun hand lifted toward the ceiling with the unexpected and violent motion. He reached back with his other hand to steady himself on something as his shoulders fell back onto Mario, flattening him to the door as he was reaching for his gun. Both men groaned.

Khaki saw his opening, and using momentum to his advantage leaned forward into his last two steps to meet Robert. As he did so he reached out with his right arm to pin Robert's left, and brought the baton shaped magazine in flush and vertically to the center of his own stomach. He then pistoned it up into the underside of Robert's chin, driving the man's head back into Mario's head. Both men groaned again as blood and chips of teeth flew from Robert's mouth with his lower jaw being hammered shut into the upper jaw. Khaki head-butted Robert as momentum felled him into the man.

The plane's nose was now angled in a steep decline. This brought the cart hurtling into Khaki's back, followed by the stewardess who was still holding onto it. Drinks flew back off the cart onto the stewardess and surrounding passengers as if in zero gravity. As the cart sandwiched the three men further into the cockpit door, bones were heard cracking, and the stewardess's body conformed into an L shape over the cart, smashing her face into the top of it. Immediately unconscious, her limp body then pitched over the cart with the momentum, smashing her head and body into Khaki. More bones were heard breaking... whose bones they were was not known. Only further moaning was heard from the pile.

Brown fell forward, arms flailing, attempting to make purchase, but merely smacking into seats and the backs of passenger's heads as he passed. He landed head first on the cart and pile of bodies, denting in the cart. His momentum flipped him sideways forcefully over onto the pile of bodies.

Every conscious person in the section was now screaming. Several unbelted passengers smashed into the seats in front of them were pushing off the forward seats or reaching back to grab their own seats. Others, folded forward while strapped into their seats, or laying prone on the floor, weren't moving. Crying and moaning were prevalent also.

The plane began to nosedive with no further word from the cockpit. Having just crested the stairwell to the back of the section, The Colonel was pitched into the rear of the row of seats on the rear right side, jarring the occupants' seat-belted bodies forward again into the seats in front of them, or folding them into their laps from his impact. He too was moaning and still crying after finding Anne dead in her seat. The Colonel would not get a chance to confront Khaki, whose skull was now buried under the stewardess's body.

further research necessary

Mid-September, Year 1 A.A.

Support Zone. Dusk had settled in over the scene of the crash. It had been nearly half a day since impact, and industrial lighting rigs had been set up throughout the area, throwing false shadows in every direction. As he scanned the area, Pascal felt he was on the periphery of some great irony between the shadows and his conversation with the Hazmat Technical Advisor. He was relieved that equilibrium was sorted as someone higher up made the call that no new personnel were allowed in the Control Zone, and those ill in Control Zone Two were removed from the area completely. No new individuals appeared to be pulled out of the Control Zone for unexpected illness. The long day had settled in for the dozens working on-site.

The Support Zone consisted of a group of three tents (one large, one medium, one small) erected just outside the vehicular barrier separating the Control Zones. The command post for the operation was located under the small tent, which consisted of several makeshift tables constructed of wood and screws obtained from a nearby construction job. The medium tent was deemed the hospital. The hospital is generally reserved for the large tent in response events, but due to the only townspeople needing medical attention being comprised of those with cuts, bumps, bruises, and concussions from the force of the explosion and flying debris, there was not a large call for medical attention after the ill were removed.

The large tent was littered with supplies and refreshments for the working crews. Pascal walked from the large tent with a bottle of water toward the small tent, passing over artificial shadows from people and objects as he did so. He approached Peter, who was bent over a makeshift table with other ranking officials, deep in discussion. Pascal patiently waited. Peter wrapped up his conversation, and the man and woman he was in discussion with departed.

"Lieutenant…"

"I have an update Commandant."

Peter glanced in the direction of the two departing officials, then back at Pascal. "Talk to me Pascal."

"I've had a lengthy discussion with the Hazmat Technical Advisor. HMRT's assessment of the scene as relates to possible chemicals or gases resulting in the on-going illnesses of the response teams has come up negative thus far."

Peter's eyebrows rose.

Pascal sighed uneasily at the gravity of what he was saying and the reaction. "They've combed the area thoroughly several times due to the obvious concerns. Their chemical weapons detectors are coming up negative for anything beyond fluids expected to be found in an airliner."

"Are they saying whatever the concern was is gone? Or what are they theorizing the source is?"

"They're not."

"I don't understand."

"That makes two of us. They have nothing. Airplane fuel will not cause the reactions they're seeing. The Advisor confirmed they've seen individuals with the following…" He pulled his notebook from his chest pocket and flipped a few pages. "… vomiting, exhaustion, hemorrhoids, boils…"

"Hemorrhoids? Boils???"

"I had the same reaction. She insisted several of the afflicted had sudden hemorrhoids and/or boils when they had no history of them. She went on to say that the grouping of symptoms isn't adding up to any known chemical exposure she's familiar with. She refused to even guess when I pushed. It doesn't compute for her. She even used that phrase… *doesn't compute.*"

Peter then leaned in and whispered something that Pascal had not heard him ask in his fifteen years working under the Commandant. "What do we do here? I'm nervous for those working in the CZ. Hell, I'm nervous for Rodez. What if this is a radiation exposure of some sort and we're all going to be affected? We don't even know if it's contained or over. And there's what, a few dozen affected already? And dozens more not showing or reporting symptoms."

"Thirty-seven affected so far."

"Probably more than a third of those that have been in the CZ!" he whispered. "We've got to keep a lid on this. I'm certain some of the details will leak to the media …"

"We may be able to minimize that. We're obviously already on the news globally, with the response teams being seen actively working the scene. That will provide some sense of control in itself. My concern is…"

"The roids and boils getting out…" Peter finished. "HMRT won't release any information…"

Pascal finished his sentence, "…and I've recommended they strongly stress those afflicted not speak to the media, or even to retain them if possible without causing further unease. I've also rounded up several of the officers and asked them to work the list and gently persuade them to not speak to anyone. And the

Hazmat Advisor will notify our point person of new cases."

"Thank you." Peter took a sip of his fresh coffee. His glasses steamed slightly. "I have an update from the BEA. Based on a preliminary scan of the passenger list, no passenger jumps out as a possible motive for terrorism… quite the opposite. An American soldier, two CIA agents, and two Saudi Arabian police officers were on the flight, so there was some form of police presence. The remaining passengers all appear civilian without any known extreme political or spiritual leanings thus far." He removed his glasses and wiped them with a handkerchief from his breast pocket. His face was in stern concentration and wrinkled like an English Bulldog.

Both men were silent for a time and looked bewildered. Two firemen approached the large tent, helmets tipped back on their heads, both rolling down their protective suits to their waists, walking from a shift change that was continuing to soak the largest smoldering piles in the CZ. Both were covered in sweat and soot. The larger man was wiping his forehead against his bicep as he spoke. "…doesn't make sense though George. How's there not even a smudge?" He grabbed a water bottle, opened it, and poured it over his upturned face, opening his mouth to begin drinking the second half of the bottle.

George stopped chugging from his first water bottle. "I'm not saying I understand it; I'm merely stating there has to be an explanation. Could it have been bonded with some protective agent?"

"Against that blast and the excessive heat? Look at every other piece of metal in the area. Bent from the crash, blackened, some partially melted."

Peter looked up at Pascal. "Did you hear that?" He tipped his head in the direction of the firemen.

"Partially, yes."

"I learned a long time ago that there will be times

where clues to a mystery may walk right into your field of vision and you don't see it." Peter turned and walked toward the firemen. "Gentlemen, can you please point me in the direction of the object you're discussing?"

George grabbed a fresh water bottle and the firemen walked Peter and Pascal to what was originally the primary fire. They circled it toward the east. George offered "This is a guess, but based on the scatter of the plane debris, and the fact that whatever that is that's partially sticking out of the ground, I think that it was stowed in the back underside of the plane."

"Based on the general direction of the body parts and luggage?" Peter offered.

"Yes sir. I'm thinking the plane came down at a slight back leaning angle, so everyone and everything on the upper half was driven into the ground or catapulted in a western direction... the original path of the flight. The larger luggage and contents of the underside seem to be closest to the crash or easterly."

"And what do you both think THAT is?" Peter pointed in the direction of the pristine raised object in the middle of the large crater, partially masked by the smoke continuing to billow from the burnt wreckage, but unmistakable as its appearance was clean silver framed against the backdrop of the charred and blackened area. The roughly three feet protruding from the ground had some slight alternating twist, or bend to it, but that appeared by design rather than from the impact.

The other fireman chimed in. "Not a clue, but someone does since it was on the plane."

George pursed his lips, raised his eyebrows, and gave a tilted nod and shoulder shrug indicating *that's about right*.

"Thank you gentlemen. Your work and input are appreciated. Please get back to your break." Peter turned to Pascal, waited a beat until the firemen were out of earshot, then whispered "We need to get someone in-touch with the United States CIA and Saudi Arabian governments asap. This situation just grew exponentially."

"Commandant Dupin... Commandant Dupin!" Peter and Pascal turned to see a fellow officer approach quickly, almost attempting to restrain herself. "Dispatch reports you need to contact Director-General immediately."

Peter and Pascal both offered the same dumbfounded expression. Peter mumbled "I'm sorry? Director-General?"

"Yes." She exhaled. "Yes. As you can imagine, Dispatch urged that you expedite the call. Dispatcher..." She looked around before continuing. "Sheila said Director-General has critical information for you as relates to the event, and that he couldn't reach you by phone."

Peter's hand darted into his pocket and he clicked the activation button on his phone. It had been ringing consistently since the crash and he had been attempting to answer as many calls as possible. He allowed numbers he did not have programmed to funnel to voicemail so he could screen them before responding. He accessed his voicemail, found three new messages and played them. He held up a hand to the two officers for silence. His face reddened in obvious embarrassment as he listened to the first message. He looked and saw the latter calls were not from the same number and deactivated the phone.

"It must have come in late. The voicemail's showing being over an hour old. I checked the phone fifteen minutes ago and there was nothing." Mystified, he seemed to be justifying missing the call to himself. He snapped back to the present. "Pascal, hold that last thought." He turned to the other officer. "Please let Sheila know I'm calling the Director-General immediately. Thank you."

With that, the officer offered a clipped and nervous "Yes sir", turned heel, and departed.

Peter returned the call to the head of France's

National Police force, signaling Pascal to wait as he walked several feet away for privacy. Pascal could not hear much, but did note Peter's tone and demeanor alternating from formal greeting, to apology, silent nervousness, weariness (he wrung the back of his neck several times with the palm of his free hand), and finally confident reassurance as he came back to Pascal at the end of the call. "Yes sir, I will update you within the next twenty minutes. And I will program your number into my phone immediately. Thank you Director-General."

Pascal was wide-eyed. "What?"

Peter exhaled deeply as he straightened his upper body after what had to be at least a partial scolding in Pascal's estimation. "We won't need to reach out to the United States and Saudi Arabian forces. They've both already been in touch with the Director-General."

Pascal opened his mouth but nothing came out.

Peter seemed to be considering how much to say. "We're too far along for me not to brief you completely Pascal…"

Pascal wasn't sure if Peter meant too far along as relates to the event, personally, or both.

"You know this needs to stay between us… I'd assume you, like I, have never spoken to the Director-General. I've only been in his presence at larger scale meetings and events. I don't know how he presents himself out of the spotlight…."

Pascal nodded agreement, then "What?" He couldn't handle the suspense.

"He sounded stressed when he led in saying he was not at liberty to provide complete intel. What he offered was that he had been contacted by high ranking government officials from both countries. The representatives each acknowledged there was an object of extreme interest on the flight, with the Americans stressing it must be recovered with extreme discretion.

The Americans are arranging for it to be picked up as quickly as possible. He gave instruction that I am to contact him every twenty minutes without fail for status updates and he is to be notified immediately once the object is procured. What's odd to me is he sounded nervous."

"Did you confirm we have visual on it?" Pascal didn't need to ask if Director-General provided a description. He knew they were discussing one and the same.

"Yes. To which he sounded slightly relieved. He confirmed only Hazmat is to approach and remove the object, and that it is to be immediately and discretely transported to the station, secured in the safe, armed guards on the ready inside the doorway to the basement and throughout the building, with no one allowed access to the basement, or that side of the building above it. The guards are to be removed and quarantined in another building if health concern."

Pascal's eyes widened throughout the relayed instruction. "What the hell is it Peter?"

"He did not say. I don't know if he knew. I'm not sure why, but I feel like there was something about our conversation..." Peter paused as he was replaying the conversation in his mind. "At least one of the officials knew people would become ill when in proximity with the object. I didn't ask for clarification as I didn't feel it was my place to do so."

"So it clearly came from Saudi Arabia and was being transported to the United States. Why the hell was it on a commercial airbus? The Saudis had to know people would become ill, and I'm guessing the Americans did also. What are we up against here?"

"I'll take that as a rhetorical question, Pascal."

"Of course... sorry, I'm dumbfounded."

"Between you and I, me too... He said the object is to be shipped to the States, and mentioned we are only to release it with guidance from him and him alone. The police station is to be guarded by all non-essential personnel, with Marshall Law enforced as necessary. He suggested…"

Pascal cut him off. "WHAT? Marshall Law enforced as necessary???"

"Correct. He fears if there is a group responsible for the crash, they could be after the object. He also suggested scheduling an officer's only event review to act as decoy. This wouldn't be a stretch from standard briefing procedures. We will just need to hold two meetings to ensure the Control Zone is patrolled consistently. Also, the Americans require two lists of all individuals that entered the CZ: those afflicted and those unaffected. Contact information is also necessary."

"Peter, I'm becoming less comfortable here. These are our people. I know I'm here to take orders but I'd like to voice my opinions if permitted?" Peter only nodded as if he didn't want to interrupt. "I'm not keen on exposing the Ruthenios to anything beyond what they're already experiencing. There is nothing pleasant about this. We've lost at least a dozen children, maybe twenty. And that's only the people we believe were at the site. The town is badly damaged. There are body parts still being located. A lot of psychiatric support is going to be necessary. And we don't even know what we're up against. I get the feeling the Americans are going to swoop in, take the object and leave while providing as little intel as possible. Can we at least be provided with information on what the object is? Some assurance of support? We have to have some leverage here. We need something to show our town that we're in control and working through regaining some normalcy here…. And are we to hold the black boxes for review once the Americans are here?"

"That's it… That's what I was grasping at. There was no mention of the need for the black boxes." Both men offered puzzled looks toward each other. "Everything you're saying is reasonable." Peter glanced at his watch. "I'm almost due to reach back out to the Director-General. I'll cover the bases and see where that lands us. I'd imagine he'll be expecting questions from us. He's probably asked a few of his own since we last spoke."

diagnosis

Mid-September, Year 1 A.A.

Slippy hung up the phone close to two hours after he had answered it. He sat back and stared into space, unable to grasp everything he just heard. His home computer screen displayed graphic pictures of boils and carbuncles. He ran his hands back through his hair. Roughly an hour and twenty minutes into the call he thought he heard the man speaking to Anne offer an almost soothing "There you go. Try and relax." Then he no longer heard Anne or the man; only moaning and coughing were heard in the background for some time. This was followed by whom was almost certainly the Colonel pleading "Oh Anne… Anne… Anne please…" in the background, followed by more moaning, coughing, and eventually extremely loud screaming before the call died.

Everything in front of him was a blur. He gripped his pencil. *What the hell just happened?* No answer came. He voiced it in a combination of anger, paranoia, and fear. "What the hell JUST happened!?!" The only answer this time was in the form of a tinge of pain from his side at the heave of his body with his exertion. He dialed Anne's number back, receiving only voicemail. He tried again with the same result, dropping the phone with a thud and a bounce on the desk.

His mind raced. "Colonel…" he whispered.

Fumbling for the phone he dialed the Colonel's number... with the same result.

He was replaying what he had heard in his mind. "Notebook", he exhaled. His eyes came into focus and he looked down at the uneven panicked writing on the pages as he flipped. He had been recording what he heard throughout the call and noting random thoughts. Not all of it was legible. At the bottom of the second page he had capitalized and circled the word AIRLINE. Knowing their airline, he frantically keyed in the airline's website on the internet browser. He found the flight tracker, and having flown back home from Saudi Arabia about a week prior, it took no time narrowing down their flight from Jeddah-King Abdulaziz on the list. There weren't many flights of the same destination and he knew they departed around the same time of day he had.

Slippy had become ill the same day they unearthed the artifact. He almost immediately began feeling symptoms when it was unearthed. Originally he had chalked this up to coincidence, but the more his mind replayed the scenario of their discovery with his strange symptoms after the find, and the phone call he just heard, he began to believe there were no coincidences anymore.

Slippy found their flight on the tracker and breathed a small sigh of relief as their arrival time was listed roughly on track with when they departed. He quickly rationalized there would be no way this information could be current if something happened... too soon. Then he began considering the worst. He turned on the television and began frantically scanning the major news networks. Nothing. He paged through his notes. He was having a hard time focusing. "What should I do? Think, think. There's no indication of a crash. Who was Anne talking to? Where was the Colonel the whole time?" Slippy figured Anne knew what she was doing. She had called him on purpose. She knew what she was walking into... at least to an extent.

He was attempting to determine his next step. 'Should I go to the Government? What if something happened and they decide to bury this?' He glimpsed the boils and carbuncles on his computer screen and remembered what he was researching when he was distracted by the phone call. He slowly lifted his shirt and pulled back the large bandage as the throbbing of his body reintroduced itself, comparing the carbuncles on his lower right side to the boils on the screen. His loose shorts were also unzipped and open at the waist, exposing his boxers. His boxers were pushed down to his pubic area. The reddish groupings of boils emerging from his shorts were not receding since they originally formed. From all of the definitions and descriptions he'd found, his particular case was extraordinary. They were roughly double in width and height than what he'd read about and seen. And normally carbuncles form on the back of a man's neck. His were on his side and all over his crotch. He had to stifle moaning when he touched the drainage points that ached so painfully.

What scared him more was that he did not meet any of the criteria for someone afflicted with carbuncles: no diabetes, alcoholism, drug use, exposure to greasy substances, family history, etc. They didn't seem to be showing signs of near eruption, nor were they receding. He'd been applying hot compresses and antibiotic creams religiously since the day he arrived back home in the States, but there was no marked improvement. The fact that he had hemorrhoids for the first time in his life was also stressful. The cream for that wasn't working either.

Religiously he snickered to himself. "Religious... Religion." He had a lot of time to think in pain since the discovery, and much like a wounded animal, his focus became that of survival only. The phone call was a distraction to him. His fear for Anne and the Colonel's safety was now an afterthought, part of his Steamroller reputation. His mind raced with ideas of self-preservation when he determined what the artifact was on his flight back to the States. He wondered why he hadn't realized it on-site, but chalked it up to Aaron's Rod possibly being skimmed over in his schooling. He now knew what the artifact was at his core. And what it represented to him was the fact of God, and the ensuing fact of his own death. The rest of the world didn't matter. He merely feared only for his survival.

He was having a hard time focusing. *God as reality. How much of the Bible was true? Where was the artifact? Did the plane crash? Am I going to die soon?* His eyes teared up again at the fragility of his existence and how small he felt. *Why did I deserve this?* He got over that last feeble plea quickly. He was alive. Distance from the Rod seemed to have slowed the symptoms. Slowed... but not stopped. He gathered himself. He knew he wasn't weak. He knows everyone dies. But this is something he can control.

For several hours he went over his notes. He replayed the phone call in his head. He ran searches for information on the computer. Thought back to the discovery. Thought of opportunities in his life he passed up... Situations he wished he handled differently. Longed for the short time ago before the discovery. He couldn't keep it all straight. And worst of all every pained throb that came from the afflicted parts of his body kept reminding him of his mortality and of God.

The news talk show on the television was interrupted with news of an on-going story. He had forgotten to monitor the television! He turned up the volume.

"... Jim, we've just now received confirmation that the airplane crash earlier this morning is in Rodez, France. As you can see on our map, Rodez is located in the southern portion of the country. What you're seeing on the video feeds from a short time ago is the crash site at what I'm told was a soccer field a short time…" The video was initially from a helicopter view of the site, wreckage in every direction. The screen then switched over to a feed from what appeared to be a news conference on the ground. A police officer was speaking to gathered media (*not enough reporters and cameras* from what Slippy figured) while the reporter on the broadcast continued to speak of what little details they had so far.

Slippy knew what plane it was and saw the badge of the police officer meeting with the media. The gears in his head turned. He now knew he had two choices. *Fight or flight.* Knowledge was power and he determined his only chance for survival in this situation was to get to the Rodez police and wield his knowledge toward his own end. Other than running, it was the only means of saving his life. He opened a new browser window on his computer and began searching for listings of the Rodez police department.

grift

Mid-September, Year 1 A.A.

Pascal hung up his phone, holding it in both hands, arms extended in front of his eyes with his wrists over the steering wheel of his parked cruiser. The night was young and he appreciated the anonymity of the shadowy darkness in his car, even if it was still parked in its original position from much earlier in the day (with personnel around him seemingly everywhere). His body felt as if he'd been awake more than twenty-four hours, even though he was only midway through a double-shift. He exhaled, set the phone down on top of the dash, and sat back. He picked up his fresh coffee and sipped.

This was his first opportunity to sit down for a few minutes since the beginning of the ordeal. But rather than sit in relative peace, he had called Karine. He assured her he was fine. They had a small argument over a call she had received from Veronique. Apparently the latter felt he had been completely insensitive to her situation when he saw her near a dead body earlier. He began to correct Karine that it was only a torso, then decided against it realizing how tiring this day and the endless disputes over Veronique had become. He simply clarified that he was responding to the initial call and couldn't stop to assist Veronique. He also assured Karine that he had help sent for Veronique as soon as it was possible. Pascal had to stop himself from thinking the call was a mistake. He wanted to be comforted by Karine, told everything was going to be alright. But he knew going in that Veronique would have called her and somehow made him a bad guy.

An additional byproduct of the women's conversation was Karine's imagination running wild. Maybe he was desensitized by all he had seen today, but she painted a much dire picture based on her earlier conversation and the media coverage. In his mind all of the action was over. It was only reaction now. He told himself that he still did the right thing in calling her. He wasn't certain if he was trying to convince himself.

"Car Seventeen report..." his police radio cracked.

He was startled out of his thoughts, spilling his coffee slightly on his pants in the process. It was Sheila calling. He grabbed for a napkin and brushed his pants as he answered on his walkie. "Car Seventeen reporting."

"Seventeen please call station at this time." Her tone and lack of referring to him by his title or name was more formal. Pascal surmised many more ears were now on the airwaves due to the significance of the situation. He might have considered this odd if it wasn't for the day he was having. He scanned the interior the car, then remembered the phone was on the dash. He quickly rang the station.

"Dispatch."

"Lieutenant Seventeen reporting..." Pascal offered, immediately realizing he referred to himself by title and car number by accident. He wasn't ready for the formalness of this situation.

Sheila didn't miss a beat. "Lieutenant, I've received a civilian call of interest relating to your current case. He was able to confirm two of the deceased on-board the airbus and stated he worked with them. He has been screened and his information checks out. He stated he has information critical to the crash. Prepared for relay of information?"

What the hell is this? he thought. Sheila was still being formal on a closed line. He pulled his pen and notepad from his breast pocket, angling his phone between his ear and shoulder as he readied the pen. "Relay." Sheila stated the name and number, which immediately struck him as odd. "What country is this phone code Dispatch?"

"United States, Lieutenant."

He jotted down a few notes, thanked Sheila, and hung up. He tossed the phone back up on the dash, and glanced at the notes on the pad resting on his thigh, scratching the center of his furrowed brow as he did so. Pascal looked up and around in the field for Peter. He found Peter several yards away standing alone and on his phone. He looked confident, but Pascal swore he noticed Peter swallow hard. Pascal impulsively decided not to wait, but wasn't certain why. He dialed the number provided, continuing to glance out the window in Peter's direction.

There was a long pause. He thought the line disconnected and went as far as checking his phone to confirm the line was still open. He then heard an unfamiliar ring tone and pattern. The phone rang several times and was answered with a fumbling noise and deep, breathy "Hello?"

"Hello, I'm calling for Stanley Melek. My name is Lieutenant Pascal..."

"I know who you are. Thank you for calling back so soon."

Pascal took note of the phone fumble and interruption as odd. He then realized neither he nor Mr. Melek was speaking. Odd again. "My deepest sympathies for the untimely loss of your coworkers today. I was informed you have information regarding the airbus crash? May I inquire how you have specific knowledge as to the origin of the crash?"

"I want to talk about the cargo."

"Okay. Please enlighten me."

"I figure the American government has already been in contact with you?"

Pascal remained silent for a few seconds. Mr. Melek was not going to let him off the hook without reply. "There are many aspects of this case that I cannot discuss, such as who our government may have been in contact with regarding this tragedy."

"It's not so tragic once you understand the gravity of the situation. In fact, it may be a blessing. And the fact that I know the American government has reached out to you should provide any further verification you need that my call is legitimate."

This chilled Pascal to the bone. This man sounded lucid, intelligent, and offered no sadness toward the situation, particularly in a circumstance where two of his close colleagues were killed.

"How can I be of assistance, Mr. Melek?"

"I'm calling to be of assistance to you, Lieutenant."

The hairs rose on Pascal's arms.

Slippy continued. "I don't know if you've recovered it yet, but has the American government asked for the artifact? And have they explained why they want it?"

"Again, Mr. Melek, I'm not at liberty…"

"I'm betting they're not providing you with much info. I'm also betting they have serious interest in obtaining it as quickly as possible. Are there sick people near the crash, Lieutenant?"

"Where are you gathering such information from, sir?"

Slippy knew he had the Lieutenant's attention. His gamble had paid off and all he had to do was reel him in. "Your government should consider if it's best to hand over a weapon of such magnitude to another country who very well may utilize it as a weapon of mass destruction."

"I'll ask you again before I terminate the call, Mr.

Melek, where are you obtaining such information?"

"The artifact has not been in the American government's possession previously. I know this to be a fact. Surely that will allow some lawful action on your country's part to retain the artifact in its own best interest."

"Please enlighten me on what the artifact is, Mr. Melek."

"Thank you for your time, sir. I wish you and your people peace." He hung up.

What an odd way to end a call, Pascal wondered. *Maybe he was a crazy.* But there was too much truth in the screening and the conversation. Pascal looked up. Peter was walking his way, backlit by the artificial light, with a shaded, aggravated look on his face. Pascal stepped out of the car.

"Peter, I…"

Peter cut him off. "I just hung up with the Director-General. The Americans' Secretary of State has already circled back with him. The Secretary confirmed he was not only reaching out on behalf of the Department of State, but also on behalf of the F.B.I., C.I.A., and a host of other government departments that share concern for our town and the object. They are apparently a step ahead of us. Before I could voice our concerns, the D-G said the Secretary offered their best psychiatric support experienced in such situations. They've also offered support for the clean-up, our full inclusion in the review of the black boxes, as well as shared intel on the object."

"Did the Secretary offer any intel on the object?"

"He alluded to the possibility of some unknown space elements based on research from prior space programs."

"Sounds like he's throwing out a line and hoping we'll bite."

"I heard something in the D-G's tone when he

relayed that info to indicate he's in agreement with us there."

"Peter, I realize we're getting this second-hand, but doesn't it feel like we're being belittled by a big brother here? I'm thinking they're not expecting anything of relevance on the black boxes. And it would appear they're offering select info on the object, if any true info at all. I really think we need to push back here. We're exposed and going to be left with too many open ends here."

"I already did. And I asked him for his thoughts on why the Secretary of State would feel compelled to include he was calling on behalf of other government agencies also. Why bother offering that when you're the Secretary of State calling? It struck me as a scare tactic. I suggested the D-G offer a slew of concerns that result in the detention of the object until further research is complete."

"And?"

"He thanked me for the input and suggestion, and informed me he had already informed the Secretary of State that France would be retaining the artifact until such time it felt all concerns regarding the object are answered... namely when there's confidence that the population has not been exposed to a weapon, Earthly or otherwise, and that the current health effects are known to be past or at least subsiding. He cited radioactive and otherwise weaponized objects and substances are strictly forbidden on-board commercial aircraft flying through French airspace. He went on to confirm national interest in not releasing an object that may hold the key to recovery of the afflicted. And he mentioned a host of other laws that had been potentially violated here that need researched before this event can be concluded."

"Wow." Pascal felt no sense of second-guessing the decision, but his, Peter's, and the D-G's unity and confidence made him feel no less uneasy about the pushback to a superpower of America's stature and what it might mean.

"I agree with your assessment."

"How'd that conversation end?"

"The D-G said the Secretary was quite upset and guessed the man hadn't heard the word *no* much in his position. The call ended with the Secretary stating a task force is still en-route to our location, and that they will stay in the area until this situation is resolved, which he assured the D-G would happen in the meantime once the Secretary contacts our President."

"So what do we do now?"

"The D-G provided instruction. He has been supportive of our work thus far and our concerns. He has given us authorization to move the object under the cover of night to an undisclosed location that only you, I, and a selected tactical team are to be aware of."

"You mean we're going to HIDE it?"

Peter glanced around at Pascal's startled response to ensure no one was near. "The D-G prefers the word *secure*. We are going to run misdirection with the response effort focusing on another area of the crash, as well as a news conference update to draw off media and other snooping individuals in two different directions from the object's area. While that's underway, we'll have Hazmat extricate and secure the object, leaving it on-site for safer transport. You will then body bag it, leave a second body bag, place the object in your car, and meet me at a safe room in an abandoned mine southeast from here. I will have a tactical team in place to assist in monitoring the area for safety." Peter saw the questioning look on Pascal's face. "The team's not going to see the bag or know what we're doing. They're only going to know there's an undisclosed threat to the mine."

Pascal attempted to sort out these details. He was becoming overwhelmed. "It's not that. Body bags? Abandoned mine? I've never been informed of that location… Why such secrecy overall?"

"I'm told the object is seven feet long. Regarding the mine and secrecy, don't forget the D-G spent more than a decade at DGSE. I believe a prerequisite for working in military intelligence is paranoia, which includes endless levels of secrets and secret locations. I don't believe he trusts anyone with this many open-ended questions and other countries involved. It's obviously safer to keep the object away from the general population. We've proven ideal candidates not only in our mindset but also in our being two of the only government employees to have an idea of just what's going on here. Not to forget we haven't been stricken by the object's effects. We don't know if anyone else is after this, or if other groups will be once word gets out of its potential for destruction."

"People are going to notice we're gone… And that the object is gone."

"I'm not worried about us being gone. We've been working this since the crash. We are turning in for the night. You'll need to take the squad car to the station for a tinted unmarked in the garage, leave your keys in your personal car, and depart for the mine in the unmarked. I'm going to pick up the second bag you're leaving on-site shortly after you and after the conference ends to allow myself to be seen. It's going to be packed with junk metal roughly the same size and weight of the object. I was able to get the object's weight from the cargo manifest and the bag's going to be locked with me having the only key. Whatever the devil that object is, thing's a heavy bugger. I'll then drop my squad car off and secure the bag in the safe. I'll be establishing an armed guard for the second bag. Then I'll drive an unmarked, pick up Maria and drop her back off at the garage. She's going to drive your car home, meet a friend for dinner at that restaurant down the street from you, then her friend will drop her off at the garage to pick up our car. You'll just need to notify

Karine you need a good night's sleep tonight and that you're not to be disturbed, and we're both covered."

"You have this all worked out. There's a real threat here, isn't there?" He exhaled. "And your wife's not going to ask questions?"

"Maria knows the drill by now. I've asked her to do other things in the name of law enforcement in the past. She's glad not to know details. I'll drop you off at home on the way back from the mine."

"Does anyone else know about the object?"

"I'm assured *no* from the D-G. Many people have seen it here, but we're fortunate that no one's really talking about it other than it being odd that any wreckage could be so pristine."

"I know one other person that's seen it and believes he knows what it is."

ouroboros

Mid-September, Year 1 A.A.

Commandant Peter Dupin had driven around the perimeter of the mine for over an hour after his arrival late in the evening. He replayed his conversation with Pascal in his mind dozens of times when he couldn't locate him or reach him by phone. The number rang and went into voicemail the few times he dared call. Peter continually second-guessed the directions he relayed, and kept coming to the same conclusion that he had made no errors in directions and that his mind had just been playing tricks on him. The route was a simplistic one, consisting of only a handful of turns from Rodez to the mine.

He had given up waiting on Pascal and driven the route back to Rodez, then again to the mine. Each way he drove slowly, scanning the sides of the road while attempting to reach Pascal by phone. He eventually buckled and tried the walkie-talkie in the unmarked, offering a generic but specific-enough request for a response from him. If anyone overheard this and questioned him later, he would be able to brush it off as someone breaching their police line as a prank in the middle of the night.

Peter had begun sweating profusely as the overnight hours ticked on. If something happened to Pascal, and more importantly if something happened to that forsaken object, he would probably be finished on the force. He realized only the Director-General, himself, and Pascal were aware of the plan. With Pascal missing, the D-G would place responsibility of any malfeasance on Peter's head. And he couldn't blame the D-G for that. Plus, if Peter even attempted to expose the truth, no one would believe him. Ethically he would never attempt so for two reasons: 1. He believed in their plan for the sake of national, if not global safety. 2. He was not raised nor trained that way, and that extended to his training of subordinates on the force, including Pascal.

He would be linked to the disappearances of the object from the crash site and Pascal no doubt. He just couldn't understand how Pascal could have gotten lost, or just be gone. They were the only two locally that knew of the plan, and it was a relatively simplistic one. The ruse had gone off perfectly as far as he was concerned. He was able to scan the Control Zone as Pascal made the pick-up and was satisfied there were no onlookers or suspicious individuals. It was nighttime and the edge of the CZ was dark though. There was no way to *guarantee* that no one saw. But he reassured himself that he saw no car tail Pascal's vehicle from the site either.

When Peter had returned to Rodez from the mine he had no choice but to drive by Pascal's house. He did not want to be seen at the station or site, even in the middle of the night, but had to attempt to track Pascal's last whereabouts as closely as possible. He found his wife Maria had returned Pascal's car, which meant Pascal had to have left the station for the mine in the unmarked.

Circling back to the mine a second time in the pre-dawn hours he was able to drive as slow as he chose as very few cars were on the road. He was able to count them on one hand and noticed nothing suspicious about any of them. It was closer to the mine that he noticed the odd light over the side of a bridge some twenty-five feet down an embankment. When he stopped his car and reversed over the bridge, it was then that he took stock of the missing section of safety wall on the far side of it... big enough for a car to fit through. He guessed he didn't notice this on his original pass en-route to the mine as the bridge was dark and his mind was elsewhere. Peter backed off of the bridge and parked as close to the wilderness on a nearby emergency pull-off as he could. He sat with the car's engine turned off. Only the dashboard lights illuminated the night. *Should I call for back-up and an ambulance?* He wasn't certain why, but thought he shouldn't yet. He immediately felt awful about himself as a human being, let alone an officer of the law. He had put his own concerns before Pascal's life potentially. But he didn't reverse course.

He grabbed his flashlight from the glove box before departing the vehicle. Glancing back at his parked car as he walked toward the embankment, he was satisfied a passing car would probably not notice the vehicle, similar to him initially not noticing the bridge damage or light down the embankment. Reaching the edge of the bridge, he confirmed it was definitely a car in the stream, upside down with the lights still on. The front end was smashed into the water and the trunk was open into the air nearer to him. The headlights lit up a small section of the relatively shallow stream providing an eerie glow to the lazy downstream flow. Peter stopped breathing, dumbfounded, then clicked on the flashlight and sprang into action. He hurried down the steep hillside, grasping at any shrubbery he could to steady himself in his descent. The glow from his flashlight waved erratically as he did so. Glancing up at the gap in the retaining wall of the bridge as he descended, he attempted to project how the car could have lost control, plunged through the barrier, and rolled to crash into its prone position. It made no sense.

Did Pascal fall asleep at the wheel? He didn't think so. *Did an animal jump out in front of the vehicle causing him to swerve?* Doubtful on a bridge. *What the hell happened?* Pascal had to be moving with some speed based on the crossed lane, the trajectory and the roll.

Peter skidded into the stream while attempting to slow himself down at the bottom of the hill. As he waded out the water came up to the middle of his shin. It was ice cold. He was approaching from what was the right rear side if the car had been upright. Reaching up he grabbed a hold of the bumper to steady himself while looking first into the open trunk, then down into the water below. He scanned the immediate area with his flashlight and only saw some of the heavier contents of the cruiser's trunk submerged that hadn't washed away in the current. He leaned over to look into the car from the upside down right rear door window, but that side of the car was too submerged, crumpled and mud-caked to do so. The car had to have landed on the right side while smashing into the ground, before it came to rest in a more level manner on the hood and front of the roof.

He smelled gasoline. Trying to hurry, he waded against the current up the right side of the car, steadying himself against the underside. Something struck him as odd. He turned back briefly and cast his light toward the section of rear bumper he was just holding. It was dented. He didn't recall any of the unmarkeds having been in accidents recently. Turning back to the front end he heard a distant snapping noise. It came from the hillside toward the far end of the bridge over the driver's side of the car. He quickly raised his light in that direction, but the distance was too great to see whatever animal it was.

Peter turned his attention back to the car. He didn't have time to determine the source of the noise. He trudged around the front end, boots sinking unevenly and requiring effort to remove from the stream base.

"Pascal… Pascal…"

No response. He leaned down to peer in the driver's side window and noticed blood dissipating in the moving water under his flashlight. Falling to a knee, he saw what he feared. Pascal was still belted into the vehicle. The deployed airbag was partially deflated. Upside down, the top of Pascal's head down to the bridge of his broken nose were submerged. Several of his teeth were missing, which seemed odd to Peter due to the airbag having deployed. Odder still was the bruised and bloodied imprint Pascal's necklace had made from mid-throat to behind his ear. He glanced around and saw the body bag was not present. Peter then put together what he was seeing and reached for his gun. He crouched lower to the car for cover, and looked up over the underside of the vehicle.

As he scanned the area around the car he heard a sizzling sound approaching and turned his head just in time to see the orange fireball heading straight for him. He had only moments to form the beginning of a prayer to God before he and the car were on fire.

Up on the hillside, the gold pinky ring attached to the hand clutching the flare gun shimmered in the light of the blaze.

enough chain to cause damage

Mid-October, Year 1 A.A.

Mahi sat sideways in the back corner booth of the restaurant, feet up on the seat cushion, back to the wall. He glanced out at the patrons around him, arm draped over the booth back, toward the singer in the front window. It was the weekend and the bar was relatively busy. Karaoke night was clearly a draw based on the volume of drinkers that saddled up to bastardize their favorite songs. Mahi had talked Ron into going out to someplace new as he was feeling in a rut. They were in the drinking district and walking down the main drag of bars and restaurants when the marketing of substandard singers at the front of this particular bar reeled them in. Taking in the scenery Mahi soaked up the buzz in the air. It felt good to be part of the current of the city.

"This place makes me laugh" Ron chuckled, returning from the bar with another round of beers for them. He slid Mahi's down the table to him and fell into the seat opposite, also sitting sideways with his back to the wall. Ron shook his head with a smile. "Stinks of swank." He picked at the basket of popcorn between them.

"What... bartender do something snooty like say *thank you*? What about this place is upscale? No smoke stains or writing on the walls like our normal hang-outs?"

"I suppose there's less ambiance, yes...."

"You're just not accustomed to being around women who wear make-up and don't have at least one visible tattoo."

"Less ambiance, yes…"

"So what were we talking about? Oh… that article you were reading. Well it's just that if I'm to believe in a blowhard's opinion on glob…" Mahi trailed off, staring toward the direction of the entrance.

A draft passed through the bar when the lobby doors opened. Ron's eyes shifted to follow Mahi's gaze. A man walked in with two women behind him. *So much for chivalry* Ron thought. The newcomers fit into this establishment as much as Mahi and he did, which was to say not much. The trio, all dressed in predominantly dark colors, looked bedraggled, as opposed to the trendy, polished appearance of the bulk of the crowd. They made a beeline to the bar, laughing as they did so.

Mahi turned back to him. "You invite her?"

The third of the trio was Lilith. Ron didn't notice her until she came around the near side of her companion. She was laughing at whatever joke he was cracking while they ordered drinks.

"No… you?"

Mahi gave him a *you should know better* look. Oddly, Mahi and Lilith did not get along. Ron chalked this up to them being too similar in personality: They were both very intelligent and opinionated, particularly in matters surrounding morals and ethics. Ron had always found it amusing that neither seemingly recognized themselves in each other. It wasn't quite narcissism in his opinion, but maybe they felt each other were a threat somehow? Ron never got his head completely around it and never attempted to pin it down further as they were both mature and treated each other civilly. But there was always an undercurrent there… Two aged prize fighters that have never been in the ring together, respecting each other's record but believing they could take the other out.

"We can pull up a chair so everyone can sit."

There it was, respect from Mahi despite his thinly veiled feelings. Ron turned from Mahi and waved a hand in Lilith's direction. Lilith eventually saw him and offered a surprised, warm smile. The smile receded into a more stoic nod after a few seconds. He assumed that was her recognizing Mahi. She grabbed her companion's arm and excused herself from their conversation at the bar.

"Boy, you got it…" Mahi coyly chided.

Ron turned from Lilith back to Mahi. "What?"

"I can feel heat coming off of you suddenly…"

"Shut it… Hey Lilith…"

Lilith approached the table and fell in beside Ron. "Heckle… Jeckle…" She bumped her knee against his under the table and left it there. "What are you two doing HERE?"

"We'd ask the same of you, madam…" Mahi asked coolly.

"Grigori, Mariangela and I were out and about and saw the sign for karaoke… too good to pass up for a laugh."

Ron chimed in. "Same for us. We thought the front window was going to break from the harpy that was screeching when we were walking by."

Silence crept in momentarily. Mahi broke it with another flat question. "What's the story with your friends?"

She turned to Mahi. "No story, just some people that live in the same building as me. Mariangela and I hang out at times. Grigori's new to the building. You haven't met Mari?" She gave Mahi an odd look. Not quite puzzlement.

"While Mahi's angling for a date with Mariangela, I'll excuse myself to break the seal." Ron offered a wide, sly smile at Mahi as Lilith slid back out of the booth to allow him to leave.

Mahi offered a specific hand gesture in bemused response. He watched as Ron departed toward the stairwell to the downstairs bathroom. Mahi then turned, removed his feet from the seat and leaned in toward Lilith as she reseated herself, quietly hissing "What right have you to bring them here?"

She blankly stared at him, taken aback by the underlying accusation, and then snapped back just as quietly "They have every right to be here."

"Based on what?"

"Based on the hierarchy... You know..."

He cut her off. "I know you lost any right of claim to the hierarchy a long time ago, and therefore you will not be able to assuage my fears of either of them attempting to influence him."

"I..."

Mahi raised his voice slightly to a higher pitched whisper. "And if I sense any, ANY attempt at persuasion from either of them, I will strike them both down. In fact, I will strike them down if they are in eyesight sixty seconds from now." His teeth were gritted, ears reddening.

Mariangela and Grigori's heads both snapped to attention in utter, unmistakable fear toward Mahi, despite being at least twenty-five feet away near the karaoke singer belting out a song at the front of the loud bar. Mahi did not acknowledge them, but rather continued to stare at Lilith, his hands stretched out flat on the table. Suddenly Lilith felt a sharp, digging sensation in her right calf. Needle points. Mariangela and Grigori hastily left the bar in such a rush that several patrons around them craned their heads at the swift departure. The karaoke singer even missed a line of her song from being so startled.

Lilith bore down on the flash of pain in her leg as much as possible, but couldn't fully suppress the briefest of grimaces. She hadn't felt such pain in ages. It was

179

immediately familiar nevertheless. And it was a reminder of the darkest time of her existence. A time she swore to herself she'd buried far enough down in her mind to never be accessed. "We... did not..." She made fists on the table in an attempt to bear down further. "...come here for trouble."

"How else should I interpret your foolish actions? You expect me to *believe* you just happened upon us? With them?"

She felt the pain dig in further. "Please..." Sweat began to bead on her forehead.

"I know you felt it when I did. We are NOT to interfere."

"Ple... Please..."

The needle points retracted... slowly. Lilith's body slumped ever so slightly with the withdrawal.

Mahi turned his head in the direction of the stairwell, and his demeanor instantly relaxed as Ron walked toward the table. He raised his voice. "That was quick. Didn't we discuss proper hygiene regarding washing your hands after...?" He trailed off upon noticing Ron had stopped several feet from the table, his face an unfocused gaze in their direction. Mahi was uncertain, but wondered if Ron was looking under the table. Ron *was* far enough away to see the unseeable. Mahi convinced himself that Ron couldn't possibly see what had been occurring, no human could, and chalked up Ron's gaze to prior brain traumas. It wasn't the first time he'd seen that look unannounced.

Ron snapped out of the haze he was in, wondering why he was suddenly thinking of the Angels at Mons. He hoped a migraine wasn't coming on as he briefly saw some blurring of color under their table. He dropped back into the seat beside Lilith. On the periphery of his mind he momentarily associated that blurring with Lilith, but couldn't connect it to something specifically and let it go. He put his hands out across the table near Mahi's nose.

"Smell.." He then noticed Lilith had her head down and was rubbing her leg. "Leg okay?"

"Ahh, just a cramp…" She offered dismissively, head still lowered.

Ron cautiously slid a hand onto her thigh under the table. "Hey, I'll pull up a chair for your friends." He turned around to wave them over, but couldn't locate them.

"No worries, they had to head out… to meet another friend."

"Oh bummer, they should have told their friend to just come here." He smirked. "Does Mahi want to get to know Mari? Or did he scare her off?"

Neither answered immediately. Mahi filled the void without irony. "I scared her off."

"So what'd I miss?"

Mahi again. "Oh, we were just discussing decisions having consequences."

"Ooo, sounds ominous… And shockingly like you Mahi." Ron offered a devilish smile, then realized Mahi wasn't smiling and Lilith's head was still down. His smile faltered "What was it about? You two look like you're at a funeral."

"It's nothing. I just know enough about Mariangela to know I'm not interested in her. No matter… I was just making the point that weighty decisions need the same weighty consideration." Mahi was looking at Lilith, then shifted his focus to Ron. He raised his eyebrows. "What if you're presented with an opportunity? An opportunity to make a difference in the world, and you're empowered with the decision as to which desperately hungry people get cookies, and which do not?"

Ron's smile came back but he took note that Mahi seemed to be changing the subject from whatever he and Lilith had discussed. He decided to play along. "Why not just give a cookie to everyone?"

"Not an option. You have to decide who is worthy

of the cookies."

"What about those that aren't desperately hungry?"

"They've made their decision."

Ron wrinkled his nose and tilted his head at Mahi's response, then glanced at Lilith for her reaction to this odd response. She had stopped rubbing her leg but was leaning on the opposite leg and now taking sheepish sips of her drink. She was listening, but not jumping in for whatever reason. Ron supposed she wasn't in the mood for one of Mahi's heavy discussions.

"Okay, so we're only talking the truly hungry, and I don't have enough cookies for everyone. That's a tough one... I suppose I'd want to come up with some type of test, right? See if they deserve that cookie." Ron thought about this. "Okay, this is weird." He shook his head at the connotation of himself being the jury in such an arbitrary hypothetical. But he knew Mahi didn't suffer fools and didn't waste his own time, so he ruminated on it. "I'd ask them if they feel they deserve the cookie. Put it back on them."

"That smells a little like a copout to me."

Lilith looked at Mahi seemingly per his response.

What was up with her all of the sudden? "Okay, maybe it's a copout. Let me think... hmm... I've got it. I'd ask them about the last time they ate... You know, when was the last time... and what it was they ate. And just observe their response. Hear it, but also *observe* it. I'd like to think I could read who's telling the truth and who's not. Sniff a lie..." Ron suddenly felt too serious. "NO COOKIE FOR YOU!"

Mahi's lips widened in a naked, satisfied smile.

Lilith finally chimed in. "I don't think you're out of the woods yet." She looked at him. "That doesn't answer how hungry they are right now though. Some people get hungrier than others quicker, some slower. Not to mention it's almost using the fact that they previously ate against them."

Mahi's smile drooped.

"Well thanks for throwing that wrench in…" Ron gave Lilith a small elbow to her arm. "You're right though, I don't think it would be as easy as confirming when they last ate… just not always a telltale sign. Come back to me later. I'll have to think on it…"

"I'm sure we will…" Lilith offered. "So who's up for some karaoke?"

wake up call

Late September, Year 1 A.A.

Eyes fluttering horizontally on a pillow. Voices down a tunnel. Men. Serious. Stern. A swooshing sound. He couldn't decipher what they were saying, but had the odd feeling it was regarding him. Were they under water?

Ron opened his eyes sleepily to an odd feeling. *Maybe a dream?* He couldn't remember. Sitting up he looked at the painting opposite his bed of the lone, barren tree…branches reaching out. It felt alive, as if it were reaching out to him. He heard voices outside. It came back to him quickly. This is what he heard while he was dozing. Why did it make him feel so nervous though?

A hard, slow paced triple knock on his front door. He inhaled quickly and turned his head fast, too fast. A vein in his neck pulled and he winced. His body wasn't alert enough for this. Turning slowly and awkwardly toward the clock he noticed it was 11:17am… Too early for one of his friends to be stopping, or his sister or mother. They'd call first. Everyone knew he would be sleeping after work. Or was he at the bar last night? Ron wrenched the sore side of his neck in his hand.

Another hard, deliberate triple knock. As if whoever was outside had all day, and wasn't leaving until the door opened. That was what the knocks indicated. Ron drug himself out of bed, offered a hoarse "One minute", slid on a pair of jeans from a chair in the corner, then pulled on a random long sleeve t-shirt from his dresser. He didn't realize he was wearing all black. He muttered over this intrusion of his sleep. It was probably going to be someone at the wrong apartment door, and now he wouldn't be able to go back to sleep. He'd be grouchy all day.

Two car doors closed in near unison outside as Ron walked toward the bedroom door. He paused, walked over to the window, and noticed two men in black suits, tinted sunglasses, and ear pieces walking around the near side of his building. It dawned on him that they were probably circling his apartment complex. Again a triple knock at the door. No voice, though… no one calling out to him. *What the hell is this?*

Ron backed away from the window. He didn't think the men saw him. Gingerly he walked down the hall toward his front door. The carpet masked the movement of his bare feet well enough. Just then he heard a neighbor's door open in the hall, followed by what had to be the voice of whoever was in front of his door. "Please step back into your apartment sir."

Whichever neighbor it was, they obliged without debate as Ron heard the door close again quickly. There was no response, not even an "Okay" from his neighbor. The situation was growing ominous. Two feet away from the door he began to lean toward the peephole.

"Mr. Cone."

Ron froze. How did the man know he was right there? He didn't recognize the voice. And no one he knew, not even his landlord or boss, referred to him as *Mister*. His eyes searched. *What the hell IS this?* He began to lean forward to the peephole again.

"Mr. Cone, my name is Federal Agent Monger. I am with the Department of Homeland Security. Please look through your peephole for my identification."

He was shocked. Ron's eyes raced horizontally back and forth as he rubbed his sore neck. He slowly looked through the peephole and saw Agent Monger's identification. Military looking. Chiseled features. Close-cropped jet black hair. Otherwise nondescript. The Agent was clearly in no rush. He held the id steadily in place as if his id had been scrutinized a thousand times before.

"Why are you here Officer?"

"Agent, sir... It is United States Government business. And it is private. May I please come in?" Not whispering, but not loud. The tone was firm.

Ron's mind searched. Why did he feel a sense of guilt? He'd done nothing wrong. Did he go to the bar after work last night? No. More lucid now he was certain he just came home and went to bed. *What else was there?* Ron grabbed a ball cap from the hooks near the door and pulled it down tightly to his forehead. After a deep breath he opened the door. "Sorry... You woke me up. And I guess I wasn't expecting to see a Federal Agent at my door today."

"Understood sir. I appreciate your candor."

They were both silent for a moment.

Ron realized the Agent was holding a briefcase. Or maybe it was a piece of luggage... and he was clearly waiting to be invited in. "Before I let you in, I need some piece of information regarding what this is concerning." He was still stupefied. "I haven't made any calls requesting a visit." *Stupid*, he thought.

Agent Monger leaned forward with some discretion and offered "Your fingerprints."

"What?"

"Sir, need I remind you this conversation is a private and confidential matter?" The tone was still patient, but firm. The Agent then opened his stance to the right and tilted his head miniscully up and back toward his neighbor's door.

"Oh... Okay... Please come in." Ron's mind continued its acrobatics. What if the Agent meant to harm him? What could he do? The man's suit coat had one button clasped. *Formal with easy access,* Ron assumed... *He must have a firearm.* Had one of his neighbor's made some ridiculous assumption and called the police on him?

Agent Monger realigned his body to the front door. Neither man spoke or moved again. The Agent slowly lifted his right hand, palm upward at an angle, offering to follow his subject's lead. Ron took the cue and backed down the hallway, eyes on the Agent, and finally turned, leading the man into his kitchen. Ron extended his hand out toward the near chair of the small two seat table. The Agent unbuttoned his coat and sat down, placing the odd looking briefcase at his side. His jacket parted back toward his hips as he did so, exposing the handgun holstered at his right side. He was casual about it. Was the visual purposeful on the Agent's part? Was it meant to intimidate Ron?

"Do you have any idea as to why I am here, Mr. Cone?"

"With all due respect, I believe I've made that clear."

"Yes... I suppose you have."

The malice behind that last reply was palpable. It reminded Ron of someone, or something from his past. The ease of the pace of his verbiage... like he was a natural born predator. It didn't seem to be a trained characteristic.

Agent Monger inhaled slowly and deeply through his nose. His eyes gave the appearance of a shark's during attack. Dead... seeing nothing, feeling nothing. "What is your familiarity with fingerprints, Mr. Cone?"

"I'm sorry?"

"Fingerprints. I assume you know what fingerprints are?"

"Of course. I've... I've just never been asked about

my knowledge of them." Ron tried to clear his mind as this situation was growing increasingly uncomfortable. His eyes scanned left to right and back. "Umm, no one has the same fingerprints?"

"That is correct. Not even identical twins." It came off completely dry. "Did you know the use of fingerprints dates back at least two thousand years?" He paused. When he received no response, "Assyrians and the Chinese used them on legal documents." Another pause from him. "Fingerprints are skin corrugations, or ridges, whose precursors begin to develop in thirteen week old fetuses. In many people, the overall patterns between their hands…" He held his in front of him, palms up, glancing down at them, "…are roughly the same, but could be different on a finger-by-finger basis." He wiggled his fingers sequentially, then turned his hands over, glancing equally at the backs of them, as if admiring a killing machine, before he retracted them. "The patterns only change in size throughout a person's life. They can be scarred with major injury, but will regenerate otherwise if damaged."

"I… did not know most of that."

"Interesting… Where my presence here gets really interesting is the FBI's fingerprint analysis." The Agent studied his face with the mention of the FBI. "Algorithms are programmed in its identification system to correlate the similarity of an input print, or prints, to the multi-millions of fingerprints already stored in the FBI's database. This system includes criminals, suspected criminals, government and military employees, as well as others. Law enforcement officers nationwide also continually submit fingerprints to the file on any serious charge." He paused as the look on Ron's face changed to one of dawning. "Good, I see this is starting to register with you."

"I was arrested in a case of mistaken identity a few

years ago for a murder. I was told my prints would be wiped off the system once they figured out I wasn't who they were looking for."

"They never found him, did they?"

Ron held his eyes to the Agent's. "As far as I remember, no. I only know the facts of my alibi checked out, and the sole witness confirmed I was not who she saw fleeing the scene."

Agent Monger studied him, as if looking for tells of a lie. His demeanor then reverted to the empty gaze again. "I can tell you that prints are to be removed from the database if a suspect is found to be not guilty. For one reason or another... call it wishful thinking... the prints aren't always deleted." Another pause. "To continue, a partial set of prints were input into the system recently. The algorithms compared the ridges, the bifurcations, and their locations to create over ninety similarity points in creating a template for these input prints."

"Bifurcations?"

"Where the lines of your prints split... When the template was cross-referenced with the identification system's database, can you guess whose prints they matched?"

"I don't understand where this is going. What were the input prints from? I have nothing to hide."

"We'll come to that soon. I'd first like to withdraw doubt from your mind. We would probably not be sitting here if the FBI wasn't over 98% accurate in their findings relating to fingerprints. All ninety-one points from the input template matched your thumb and first three fingers of your left hand. With that number of points matching, the percentage of accuracy is just about 100%, rather than 98%."

"What about the pinky?"

"What about it, Mr. Cone?"

"You mentioned the near 100% match of my fingers

to this other set of prints was based on the thumb and first three fingers. Where's the pinky print?"

"That was not made available. Do you follow the national news?"

"I read up on anything that jumps out at me periodically."

"How about lately?"

"Can you be more specific?"

"Items of archeological interest."

Ron's mind went blank. His eyes darted again horizontally. He was attempting to piece together the different tracts of information the Agent was providing, and was failing. "No, nothing recent that I can recall. Can we please end this charade? I'm failing to see where this is going and how it applies to me." The Agent's face remained unchanged. It was unnerving.

"An artifact was discovered in the Middle East about three weeks ago. Something that hasn't seen daylight in potentially close to two thousand years if certain..." an exhale as he offered "...stories... are to be believed. Ringing any bells?"

Ron was becoming annoyed but attempted to hide it. He arched his eyebrows and shook his head.

"The fingerprints of your left hand match one of two sets of prints on the artifact."

"Wait, WHAT? I thought you just said the artifact hasn't been seen in a few thousand years?"

"Correct." He reached down slowly and lifted the suitcase onto the kitchen table with both hands. Placing it flat, he smoothed his hands on the side that was now upright. It appeared thicker than a standard briefcase, and much heavier based on how the Agent hefted it onto the table. Agent Monger's turn to arch his eyebrows. This time not in annoyance, but some type of disdain possibly. He placed his left thumb and right middle finger on the scanners aligned to either side of the oversized handle.

The case offered a tiny positive sounding bleat. He then replaced his hands flat on top of the case and strummed his fingers in a slow, suspenseful beat, for several seconds too long to be remotely comfortable.

"I have a test for you Mr. Cone," he offered with an expectant pause. He then keyed in a code on a small screen embedded under the handle, which resulted in two further positive bleats. Metallic, mechanical swiveling sounds muffled through different areas of the case. The Agent looked up in dumbfounded, pleasant surprise. He opened the case slowly, removed a large rectangular black box with some effort and placed it beside the briefcase. An opening in the side of the box faced Ron. "You don't have to feel nervous about this test. There was nothing to study for."

While Ron stared at the box, the Agent closed the briefcase and then set it on the floor in its original position. It was clearly much lighter after the black box was removed. Agent Monger then returned his attention to the box, centering it in front of him. He touched the box on the side nearest him. The box made a dinging sound, and the top of it, a digital screen, glowed green momentarily in its entirety. After going black again, yellow bars traced the width of the screen in one direction, originating from the end nearest the Agent down to the end closest to Ron. It disappeared, then lit again, this time tracing a yellow barred vertical pattern from right to left. The shape of a left hand could be seen within the quickly flashing patterns.

"Please flatten your left hand and place it into the box."

"What is this?"

"An HPIU... Acronym for Hand Print Identification Unit."

"You already have my fingerprints."

"Correct. The FBI is interested in your handprint

sir."

"Why?"

"Confirmation as to if your handprint matches the handprint points recovered from the artifact… in place of the missing pinky finger print. Please place your left hand flat into the box, fingers spread evenly."

"How can my prints be on an artifact that's a few thousand years old???"

"It may be much older than that."

"WHAT???"

"Sir…"

Ron cut the Agent off. "I'll have no problem supporting an alibi that I haven't been in the Middle East the last few weeks. I haven't touched the item in question to leave prints on it."

"Please place your left hand into the box sir."

"What happens if my hand print matches? Answer me first."

"I owe you no further answers sir. The results of this test will determine what information I provide next. I will not repeat my request."

"I think I need a lawyer."

"Irrelevant. A lawyer will not be able to prevent the FBI from obtaining your handprint in matters of national security."

"National security? You have the wrong person. I'm no threat to the United States."

"That's not for you to decide." Agent Monger slid the box closer to Ron, eyebrows raised in expectation. His physical demeanor had not changed otherwise. No frustration with the delay. All control.

Ron was scared. There was no way around it. He didn't see a way out of this test. But what should he fear? He paid his taxes, never left the country, and minded his own business. "Okay…" Why the urge to run?

There were at least two, if not more agents outside.

They were prepared for a flight risk. But why? They had to know he was not violent, even with the mistaken identity murder charge in his past. His mind began to wander off about profiling and how this must be how some minorities feel every day in America.

Agent Monger cleared his throat and tilted his head down toward the box.

As he watched the Agent, Ron began running his hands on his thighs, drying them off. He lifted his left hand parallel to the box, then glanced at the Agent. Whatever reaction he was looking for, there was none. Sweat was beading on his forehead. Taking a deep breath, Ron slowly inserted his hand into the rectangular box. The box was slightly bigger than his hand. Peripherally he swore it reminded him of something. So black, ominous, almost looming, something never before seen, and yet knowing.

Ron slid his hand into the box to his mid-finger knuckles. The screen illuminated with the yellow bars matching the size and shape of his hand as his fingers moved. Small blue points began appearing all over the x-ray of his hand. He felt claustrophobic, but no physical sensation otherwise. He looked up at Agent Monger, who only raised his eyebrows in the manner of *Well, what did you expect?* At this reaction, Ron exhaled. The tension passed. He slid his hand further into the box down to his wrist, and eventually felt his middle finger bump the back side of the box when he pushed further. The inside walls were warm and vibrating, although neither appeared to be the case from the outside… odd that the box wasn't designed much larger to accommodate for individuals with larger hands.

The blue points multiplied seemingly by the dozens. Quickly at first, then slowing after about a minute, and then finally stopping. Ron's eyes searched back and forth at what had to be at least seventy or eighty points. The screen had the appearance of a galaxy of stars. He almost missed the tiny positive bleat sound as he was focused on the arrival of a pulsing green glow that surrounded the galaxy of his hand. Then his wrist began to hurt.

Ron shoved his chair back with his right hand as if stung. His body, anchored by the weight of his captor, the box, forced the chair (and his body) to slide back further on the right side than the left. His caged left hand slid only slightly. "What the…???"

"Please compose yourself, Mr. Cone." Agent Monger hadn't budged at Ron's attempted retreat, only offered in his continued even pace, "It appears you've passed the test with flying colors."

"Get it off of me." Ron pled as he shoved the palm of his right hand into the top near side of the box, attempting to free his left hand.

Agent Monger was unmoved. He inhaled deeply at a sudden recollection. "When I was briefed on this assignment, I was not impressed. It smacked of what might be referred to as a wild goose chase. And the more I considered it, I kept coming back to another bird at the thought of there being some reality about the situation we now inhibit."

Ron was still panicked but attempting to compose himself. "I need you to remove the box please. It is cutting off the circulation to my hand."

"That's just not going to be possible, Mr. Cone. Think of it… Think of it as an insurance policy. The engineers behind that box may have designed it with a little extra zeal. Too lose an enclosure and you could remove your hand. No, it needed to be tight. It serves its purposes."

Ron furrowed his brow. "And what are those?"

"It's ingenious. It secures your hand to protect it from harm. It acts as a modern day ball and chain to deter a…" He made a forward circle, a flourish, with his extended right hand, palm up "…hasty departure. And just to show off, it also includes a tracking device. Stronger than any other device I'm aware of as it was explained to me. Satellites could track you hundreds of feet deep into a mine." He paused. "Cooperate and it will be removed in time."

"Cooperate? You expect me to cooperate after you've sprung this contraption on me?"

"I'm afraid you don't have a choice." The Agent leaned back slightly. He clearly wasn't concerned with a flight risk, or being attacked. "Well I guess Reism's out the door. This is just too good. To think I'm the first person to be present in the presence of this unquestionable evidence."

"What are you talking about?" Ron was still pushing at the box.

"Oh, right. In reviewing your file and considering the ever slim, but apparently possible current reality, I couldn't help but to think of the ortolan bunting. It's a French bird. And forgive me if I'm being so naïve to think that you haven't heard of it?" When he saw his subject was still attempting to free himself from the box, he took it that he had indeed not heard of the bird. "Well the bird will eat continuously when it's in the dark. I mean it will just eat and eat and eat and eat. So the French feed this bird millet until it looks like you could put it on a string and just float it in the air." He absently rubbed at his right eyebrow, but his eyes weren't seeing his hand directly in front of them he was so suddenly absorbed in his own story.

"But instead of floating, the ortolan is then drowned in brandy. What a way to go! Why go to this trouble you ask? For a certifiably brutal dining experience of course! But our diner isn't totally classless. No, no, NO. The diner is courteous enough to place a napkin over the head of the bird. This modesty is presumably to keep their fellow diners, and God, GOD…" He shook his head in disbelief "…from seeing them eat the entire bird. Bones, organs and all!" He laughed. "And that's where we are now." He slapped the table with both hands in amazement and made a gesture similar to that of a croupier showing their hands were clean after a deal where the house was sure to win. *Surely the now certifiable story of Judas is to blame for this*, he considered.

Ron had stopped attempting to remove the box from his hand at this sudden seemingly unhinged descent from the Agent. He simply looked at the Agent Monger blankly. All he could think to say was, "I will not be an ortolan."

"You're certainly right about that!" Agent Monger slapped a hand on the table with an animated, excited facial expression while he stared into Ron. Taking a deep breath, the Agent's face lapsed back into stoicism after this seemingly bipolar mental lapse. "You may want to start believing in fate, sir." He leaned forward slightly. "Now let's discuss what happens next."

abhorred chrysalis

Late September, Year 1 A.A.

The steel chair was soldered to the ground. This was one of several indicators to Ron that his situation had taken a drastic turn for the worse. He sat wondering, replaying his earlier conversation with Agent Monger in his mind.

Unable to shake the feeling that Monger loathed him, he attempted to connect the dots as to why. He had obeyed Monger's orders after their conversation, providing no physical (and not much verbal) pushback to what was occurring considering the circumstances. He rubbed at his now freed left wrist. Bruising already circled his arm near the wrist in the shape and shade of storm clouds. Uncertain what to do with himself, Ron placed his hands palms down on the table and strummed his fingers from pinkies to indexes.

Monger had enclosed the piece of luggage over the box on Ron's hand while they were still in Ron's kitchen, making for an odd glove/suitcase for him to lug out to the awaiting unmarked van. Ron initially hadn't noticed each side of the case under the oversized handle was a rubberized flap. The flaps enclosed around his arm when the case was closed. Monger was undoubtedly stronger than he appeared based on how he had initially carried the heavy luggage into his apartment. Ron was glad he didn't sincerely entertain running at their initial encounter.

When they had gotten outside of his apartment he noticed at least six other suited agents in the parking lot. All appeared to have guns draw at their sides as they scanned the surroundings of the van they had encircled. Two more Agents awaited Ron in the back of the van. One Agent explained to him what they were going to do and placed some type of breathable tight cap or stocking over his head that did not allow him to see for the duration of the trip. Another handcuffed him clinically to a steel railing installed in the back of the van for just such an occasion. At least they allowed him to sit buckled in a chair for what seemed like hours of driving. He was unsure if it was actual hours, or if his mind slowed down time as it continually circled to understand any of what was happening. The Agents in the van rarely discussed more than verification of non-descript directions to their destination.

The luggage and head cap were not removed until Ron was seated in his current position. Just prior to leaving the room, Agent Monger suggested he try to relax and that someone would be with him in time. *In time* struck Ron as odd initially. That was a few hours ago. It no longer struck him as odd. He looked around the room for what had to be at least the hundredth time. It was nondescript. The mirror on the wall in front of him was no doubt double-sided. Whoever was watching him must have found Ron as entertaining as watching ice melt. The only other item of interest in the room was the wooden box on the floor a few feet in front of the table.

Looking at the box he felt something stir inside him. Ron felt oddly drawn to it, almost as if it was pulling him by the veins. He wanted to chalk it up to the box being the only item in an otherwise blank canvass of a room, but that wasn't quite right. He didn't feel it as an itch, but akin to it somehow, and couldn't quite pin down what that even meant.

A casket... that was it. The box reminded him of an old, smooth, squared-off, nailed shut casket. His mind spun off in free association. His veins tingled. The situation reminded him of his opinion on the government. It handled most major concerns incorrectly with two exceptions... Oil and weapons. The government knew exactly how it preferred those two items handled, and any action taken on their behalf seemed pointed and without need for explanation. All smooth edges. His mind jumped again, this time to his father's casket. It felt smooth, lacquered, even though Ron doubted the man's life matched that description.

That always stayed with Ron. His mother changed after his father left them. Ron knew this from all of the pictures of his mother before he was born. They all had the same thing in common... a congenial smile. An amazing, open smile. A chunk of her being was taken from her. Some of the heat in the furnace of her soul it seemed. And she filled that void with religion from what he could tell. He recalled her saying she found God later in life. She received a call when Ron was fourteen that his father was dead. She never said how he died, but Ron sensed she blamed his father for his own death. She seemed to retreat further into religion in a strange way. And this was further validation for him that his father was the reason for her beliefs. He could never get beyond that in understanding who his mother is today. She certainly isn't that same bright light she was when he was younger.

A sudden surge of heat coursed through his veins, like something he'd never felt before. He felt dizzy and exhilarated. Staring at the box Ron realized the edges of his vision were blurring. Almost pink fuzz framed his focus on it. He closed his eyes and rubbed at them deeply with his thumb and index finger. He took a deep breath, sat back, and the boiling in his veins receded slowly along with the fuzziness.

Heavy metallic sliding noises announced themselves abruptly, and the door opened slowly. A flack jacketed soldier held his arm out on the door in a gentlemanly gesture. He was huge, dressed in black with an assault gun pointing out from his lower back. Ron couldn't see much of a profile as the soldier faced away from him. This seemed odd and yet abating, for if he was a prisoner, the soldier would have surely been sizing him up upon opening the door. Then the fear Ron initially felt with Agent Monger at his apartment door flooded back into him as a woman strode into the room, paying no attention to the guard, who exited immediately behind her. The door had closed a little too slowly. Ron noticed the door was unusually thick, thicker than he'd ever seen a door before. The metallic noises were heard again, clearly heavy locks sliding back into place. He wondered why he hadn't noticed the door when he was first brought into the room, and then realized his eyes had trouble readjusting to the light after hours under the hood.

The woman wasted no time sitting down in front of him. She placed a manila folder with a notebook on top of it on the table. Her hair was clipped short into a strawberry blonde bob, which surrounded an aged, weathered face. Not unattractive, just brutally business-oriented... a face that had no doubt seen decades of hardship in law enforcement. Ron figured she was probably the type of person that would be attractive when she smiled, if she ever tried it. She appeared to have not smiled in at least a decade based on the stress lines on her face. He also noticed she hadn't made eye contact with him since she entered the room.

Eyes still down, she mechanically slid the notebook to the right of the folder in front of her. She opened the notebook as she withdrew a pen from her business suit pocket. Consulting her wristwatch, she wrote what appeared to be the date and time on the fresh page.

Sliding the folder closer to her she opened it, finally looking up at Ron after studying the top page for several beats. "Mr. Cone, my name is Judith Carroll... I am the Current Intelligence Director in the Office of Intelligence and Analysis for the Department of Homeland Security."

Ron looked down at a picture of himself paper clipped inside the left side of the folder. Looking up he noticed she was studying him.

"Surprised to see a picture of you?"

"No... Well, I guess. I... I'm sorry, there's a lot about this day I'm surprised about. Why am I here, Ms.... I'm sorry, I didn't hear your name."

"Director Carroll will be fine, Mr. Cone."

She proceeded to ask Ron about his past. His family, schooling, his job... all the while watching him. Her consistent eye contact was daunting. Ron felt awkward talking about himself and wanted the day to end, so he kept his answers as brief as possible throughout. She was jotting down notes as he spoke. After some time, they came to the present.

"Did Agent Monger provide details on why you are here today?"

Ron glanced off to his right. "He said my handprint is on an artifact." For some reason, he recalled the painting of the tree on his bedroom wall at home.

"Have you ever been to the Middle East?"

"No." He glanced right again. "I told Agent Monger that also."

"What do you think the object is?"

"I don't know. He didn't show me a picture of it."

"Well what we have is a seven-foot-long cylindrical object that was discovered on an archeological dig seventeen days ago in Ha'il, Saudi Arabia." She stood up and walked toward the mirror, then turned back to him. "Your handprint is on the object, and we want to know why it's there, and why the object was buried deep in the middle of nowhere."

He was startled at this new information, at someone finally being so forthcoming. And then he became irritated. He stared at her. "I already told Agent Monger I have no idea what he, and now you, are talking about. Do you have a picture of it?" He thought for a second. "Wait... can I ask how far down in the ground it was? I'm no archeologist, but since it was discovered on a dig, doesn't that typically mean really deep in the ground? How could I have even buried it then? And wouldn't the archeologists know if it had been there for centuries? Was anything else found with it?"

"You've led a pretty vanilla life, Mr. Cone. Mediocre schools... Mediocre grades... Mediocre employment. No impressive accomplishments to speak of. Your father, Ammar, left at a relatively young age. There seems to be a pattern here. Maybe you're disgruntled, looking for attention, a little excitement in your life to build a little mystique. Your background and how you present yourself don't indicate you're the type to look for danger. So maybe a stunt that could turn the bright lights toward you, even momentarily would give some spark, some meaning to your life."

Her disregarding his questions and changing the subject angered him. He felt his questions were legitimate and should probably have resolved this. He didn't want to anger her though, give her any excuse to hold him longer here, so he did his best to play along. "So I'm not a go-getter. So what? If I wanted attention, why would I go across the world to Saudi Arabia to pull off some odd stunt? I still don't even understand why I'm here. Where's the crime?"

"Maybe there's more to it. The other handprint on the object? An Easter Egg hunt of sor..."

He snapped. "I don't know what you're getting at. I had nothing..."

Her eyebrows arched and it was her turn to cut him off. "Do not interrupt me."

Ron's eyes widened, and the anger drained quickly from him. He despised losing control of his emotions. This was only outdone by losing his emotions in the direction of a woman.

"No… Not mystique. Something more grand. You stay off the radar. You use computers at the library rather than have one at home. You have a close friend with a checkered family past."

Ron raised his eyebrows at this. *Mahi? Checkered past?* He realized his lips were dry, licked them, and intently stared at her, curious as to what else she knew about his life that he didn't.

She paused, staring back at him. "This object was stolen. Your friend has connections in the Mid-East and used them to bury this item to keep it safe. And you're not going to go to this extent to hide it unless it's worth money or can be weaponized, or both."

His inner rage reemerged. He wanted to scream. This woman was making up absurd claims and he had to sit and take it since she had power.

She came back to the table, flipped several pages over, and picked up a photo. Walking around to his side of the table, she leaned over his shoulder and slid the photo onto the table.

Ron stared down at it uncertain what he was looking at. But somehow it felt… familiar.

Staying near his ear, she offered "I can help you clear this situation up. Tell me why you went so far to have it hidden…"

He began rubbing his face vertically in his hands. She returned to her seat, waiting. He removed his hands from his face and placed them on either side of the picture, lifting it slightly to study it.

"So just a game that's gone too far and brought the

wrong attention …" She studied him. "…or an item to cash in on in a big way? A game is innocent enough, but is probably beyond your capability." She paused again, watching him. "Right, more likely the latter. You have big dreams for this…" She nodded toward the picture. "You're changing, making a statement in life that you'll no longer be complacent. You're unhappy, feel that you've been cheated, you're entitled to more in life, and if it's not going to be given, you are going to take it no matter what or who is in your way." She gave him a look of disgust.

"I have no idea what it is I'm looking at. This thing looks like a poster canister, but bent randomly. I've never seen anything like this in my life. What are you talking about?" Ron stared back down at the picture, turned it sideways, and tried to make sense of it. He couldn't quite put his finger on it, but…

Director Carroll stood up, turned, and walked to the door. She rapped three times, similar in impact and tone to Agent Monger at his door back home. The door slowly opened, and he saw the soldier again close the door behind her.

learning to hate

Late September, Year 1 A.A.

Ron was finding himself left with more questions than answers. *Why am I being treated like a criminal by Agent Monger and Director Carroll? What unsavory ties would Mahi have to the Middle East? Mahi never mentioned anything of the sort. And what did she say about my father?* His head was beginning to ache from the stress. There was suddenly some difficulty recalling everything Director Carroll recanted and suggested about his life. He couldn't help but feel anger towards her putting a negative spin on his existence. He had always tried to be a positive person, even with her crystallizing the realization that there were no accolades to speak of. Did that make him a bad person?

The room suddenly felt large, too large. He felt small and claustrophobic. The mirror seemingly stretched in size and loomed over him like an enemy. Malice seeped through it. *Fight, flight or fright?* Fright was the option of the moment. His mind and body were night and day. As he sat unmoving, his mind chugged like a horse loosed in an open field. *Was this real?* He began replaying the past day, and his mind kept tumbling backward, inevitably toward negative experiences from his life. If her sadistic goal was to work him into a self-deprecating lather, then mission accomplished.

Life had offered him an assemblage of examples of

fright to the point that he had fully realized the pattern and currently worked toward suppressing inaction in times of stress. Scrapes with bullies, pushing for promotions, questioning his mother regarding why his father left when he was twelve years old, all confrontational instances he's backed down from in the past. He supposed his father abandoning their family was part of the reason he became who he is. Fright may have been a subconscious path travelled as opposed to saying the wrong thing and pushing someone or some opportunity further away.

Ron still recalled the last conversation he had with his father vividly. They were in their back yard, sitting on the three-foot tall cobblestone retaining wall. It was a cool, crisp autumn evening. Their shoes crunched the fallen green, yellow, and brown leaves that littered the back patio. He saw irony in what that retaining wall represented after what transpired.

His father Ammar had been somewhat despondent in the week prior to their conversation, almost as if something of considerable magnitude was on his mind. Maybe there were signs long before then. Dusk had settled in and his mother was cooking dinner. Ron didn't know where his sister was in the house and at the time didn't care. His father had asked him to take the kitchen trash outside. Ron had found it odd that Ammar had told him to put on his jacket for a quick chore. As he was closing the garbage can out back, he turned back toward the house to see his father coming out the back door, also with a jacket on. Ammar asked him to sit down. It turned out he had planned their visit succinctly.

The conversation began normal enough. They discussed his school day, sports, and other topics. He recalled it uncharacteristic at the time that his father was having such an in-depth discussion with him, as it wasn't the norm. Ron's father was caring and attentive, but quiet by nature. Ron would always cherish that portion of their talk. At a much later date, he came to the realization that his father had already made his decision and was (quite possibly painstakingly) savoring the last conversation he would have with his son.

Ammar asked him what types of big decisions he has made in his life. The question struck Ron as strange even at twelve years old. He thought about it and all he could come up with was not asking Sarah Lockey to go with him to the Fall dance. Ammar had briefly smirked and quickly turned stone faced when he realized his son was scrutinizing his reaction. His father reassured him that other opportunities would present themselves in the future, even as soon as the Holiday Dance.

Ammar then went on to explain there would be even larger decisions to contemplate in the future. These would range in potential from where he lived, to his career, maintaining relationships with both family and friends... even a girlfriend. And quite a bit of his wellbeing and happiness in life would possibly ride on at least a few of these decisions. Ron must have given some impression to his father that he wasn't following or was spacing out as the man raised his voice slightly to reign in his attention. "I want to impart a decision from my life that pains me to this day." He noticed his son had crossed his arms. "Zip up your jacket."

Ron did as he was told. From a young age he had learned respect for his parents and adults in general. It occurred infrequently, but if he had smarted-off or taken ill-advised actions (that probably any youth would during their learning curve), they resulted in solitary and at times physical punishment. The effects of his punishments left a lasting impression where his father eventually only needed to make a request once and Ron would snap to attention.

"When I was somewhat younger, but old enough to stand on my own as an adult, a decision was made for me that I allowed without pushing back on. Someone I trusted completely approached me with a piece of information and two options of how to react to that information...." He noticed his son appeared to be lost. "Okay, hmm..." He rubbed and squeezed the back of his neck roughly with his palm. "Okay... Let's say my best friend informed me that... That I could have a puppy from a litter of his dog's pups. I had always wanted a puppy and my friend knew it. I even helped take care of his dog when he needed it... feeding the dog, taking it on walks, and caring for it when it was pregnant. When the dog gave birth all the dogs except one were given away to other people."

"And what about the last puppy? You could have that one?"

"Yes... but... but that last puppy had physical concerns. It was born with three legs, and it was a runt... smaller and weaker than the other puppies. No one wanted it, and the only two options left were me taking it, or it being sent to a kennel where no one may ever claim it due to its deformity."

"But the puppy could walk, right?"

"Well it kept falling over. It was young and weak. I'm sure it would learn..." He trailed off. "That's not the point." He crossed his arms over his chest and looked down at the fallen leaves for a time. "My friend made the decision for me. Or maybe his parents did. When that was the only puppy left he decided to have the puppy sent to the kennel. He assumed I didn't want it due to its shortcomings, or, or maybe that I couldn't care for it. And I let him take it to the kennel without questioning him as I guess I felt at the time that it was his decision." He took a deep breath and sighed. "Well after that I couldn't look at dogs the same way. I knew I wanted a dog, but every time I looked at another dog, even my friend's dog that had given birth, all I could see was that abandoned three-legged puppy that should have been mine. I felt so guilty and remorseful for not speaking up. I would have loved that dog and cared for it all its life. I carry that regret to this day. That's why we've never had another dog and I have trouble even bonding with any of them." His eyes appeared teary. Maybe it was just due to the cool, crisp windy evening air. He turned his head away and opened his eyes wide, then blinked repeatedly in an attempt to dry them.

"Another dog, Dad?"

"Oh, sorry, never had a dog", he corrected himself. "Does that make sense?"

"I guess." He wanted to see his father happy again. "So make sure I speak up for something I want?"

Ammar offered a passing satisfied smile. "Very good, yes. And more importantly, something you believe in.... And don't let the darkness heal you when you make the wrong decision, or if you do not speak up when you should have..." He turned his head away again. "I think about that dog every day. I hope it knows I've never forgotten it."

"I'm sure it knows Dad."

Another brief, wistful smile. "Thank you, son. Just remember that you control your future. You don't always have to just take what's being offered, even if someone else thinks they know what's best for you."

The conversation trailed off and his mother called them in for dinner shortly after.

Ammar left them in the middle of the night that evening. Or at least that was as far as Ron could tell. He found his mother the following morning sitting at the kitchen table crying. She appeared to have been crying for a while as she looked physically defeated. She had a note in her hand, and was clutching the gold cross linked to the chain around her neck with the other hand. His father had bought that necklace for her when they were dating. She always told Ron that proudly when he would notice it. She wore her love of the gift and her faith proudly on top of any outfit up to that morning.

As Ron looked at her crying and clutching it now as he walked into the kitchen, she saw what he was looking at, and with a flash of anger tucked it into her shirt. That sequence branded a spot on his brain forever. She snatched a napkin from the holder in the center of the table, wiped her eyes, and never cried again in front of him. He would see the chain around her neck regularly, but it was never again displayed proudly on top of her outfit. It appeared to still hold significance to her, but was something she now hid. Ron was convinced something in her died that day, and he never forgave his father for that.

He realized he had stopped breathing. Ron inhaled deeply and rubbed the now-throbbing pain at his temple. He had completely forgotten he was in an interrogation room.

It dawned on him that asking Sarah Lockey to the Holiday dance never crossed his mind after his father abandoned his family.

lassoing the atmosphere

Late September, Year 1 A.A.

Director Carroll, Agent Monger, and Marc Williams, the CIO of Intelligence and Analysis stood on the other side of the mirror, watching Ron.

"He gives the impression that he doesn't recognize the artifact" offered CIO Williams.

Monger looked skeptical. "He could just be well studied at avoiding tells."

"And notice he'll glance over at the open folder, but he won't pick it up, let alone lean over to try and read the top page on the pile of documents." The CIO appeared to have his leanings.

Monger pushed back. "That could just be that he knows he's being watched and that we're trying to bait him."

"Assessment and recommendation?" asked Williams, looking at Director Carroll.

Carroll spoke. "He's telling the truth. He has nothing to do with this. I'd recommend Option Soft Charlie. It's our only hope if it's true. And he'll be the scapegoat if things turn sideways and we can control it."

Monger was not pleased. "If it's true, I cannot see that it's going to matter what we do if we choose Charlie... Soft or Stringent subset. We're lambs or we're negated. No in-between. It only matters what we've done.

And it won't be controlled." He sighed, and then shook his head with a bewildered look. "I mean, that's what we're talking about here, right? I would have never figured I'd be privy to a conversation like this. The words *ramifications* and *absurdity* keep crashing into each other in my mind." He offered another sigh. "Option Bravo is our only choice here if we're considering legitimate fallout ramifications."

Williams said nothing, seemingly waiting for Monger to expand on his thoughts. Carroll did not interrupt either.

Monger took the hint from Williams, and wondered if Carroll was allowing him to dig a hole, if she didn't care, or if she was genuinely curious as to his assessment. "The irony in what I'm saying isn't lost on me. And I clearly see how this aligns us to groups we regularly work against. I'm not that self-absorbed. And what's really the greater good here?"

Carroll chimed in, staring through the two-way mirror. "We can't play that role though. It's not what this organization stands for. It's not what our society stands for. This is in no way a threat, but the day we make that choice under these circumstances is the day I walk. This is a person that's never…"

Monger cut her off. "With all due respect, what angle are you thinking from? Fear? Or are you worried about how you'll be viewed in the pantheon of human existence? Is it unfettered devotion?"

Carroll seemed taken aback briefly, and then appeared to truly focus on his line of interrogation. She didn't view his questioning as an attack. To the contrary, she respected it as she suspected Monger has been grappling with the same existential questions rather than chiding her. And in their line of work, employees questioned their beliefs regularly based on their working environment.

Williams felt the conversation was beginning to

spiral, but remained mum as he felt there was true value to the debate.

Carroll crossed her arms over her chest and focused through the mirror. "Neither my legacy… nor fear. Devotion? Only insomuch that if it's fate, then it's fate. And that's the direction the arrow is clearly pointing, is it not?" She nodded in the direction of the mirror. "I struggle with the debate of there being a true delineation in our lives between words and actions. We're set up with innumerous rules. What's really right or wrong in what we say and do? Who makes that call? We sure as hell don't in my estimation, or else we wouldn't even be having this conversation. I only serve to drive myself mad attempting to be pure of mind. And I've had enough conversations over the decades with our peers to know there's a certain sense of resignation to morals and ethics in our line of work. But where does a possible higher guidance end and man's interpretation begin?" She abruptly stopped, rubbing her upper arms. "I just know we're not the forces of nature we portend to be in spiritual situations such as this… not that we've ever experienced something quite like this as far as I know. If we step in the way of a fate we can't really comprehend nor control, we're bound to be casualties… and quite possibly outcasts."

Monger and Williams said nothing. Monger was staring into the ether. He attempted to take in everything Carroll had said, and appeared to be having a hard time accepting the supernatural implications. Or maybe he was considering other angles?

She continued. "This does seem amazingly farfetched, but we have a chance to also learn from past mistakes if it's not…"

Monger happened to glance at Williams as Carroll was trailing off and noticed the look of a hawk eyeing a mouse in an open field. He was focused on the interrogation room now. Monger turned to Carroll and noticed something had changed in her demeanor also. She hadn't turned from the mirror, but there was a new sharpness, a steely awareness of something. Monger followed their gazes and the subject of their deliberation was still seated at the table in the adjoining room. Nothing seemed to have changed there. The man was just sitting. His head was tilted slightly right as if he were listening for something as he stared into the mirror, seemingly at them.

"Did you see that?" asked Williams absently without turning away from the mirror.

"What?" responded Monger, almost incredulously.

"The box?" Carroll flatly questioned.

"No, his left forearm."

Monger and Carroll readjusted their gazes to their subject's left arm. After several seconds Carroll quietly responded "No."

"Nothing here" offered Monger.

"It's like it pulsed oddly. Like the skin raised, but not a twitch. I don't think it was my imagination." His demeanor was still blank, as if he had been shown something that just did not compute in his mind. Then something clicked and he became more lucid. "The box?" When he received no response he asked again. "Carroll, you said something about the box?"

"Yeah... No... What?" She was dazed. "Oh..." She began to come back from whatever pulled her away. "No, nothing."

Monger was following their conversation like a spectator at a slow motion tennis match, perplexed by the fact that they were both consumed with whatever they saw that he didn't. "Video. I'm not really sure I understand what you each saw, but we're already pretty far down the path of..." He searched for a diplomatic analogy. "Well we're down the path, so let's check it before we move forward."

Monger opened his computer at the table and

accessed the department's surveillance network. Carroll and Williams hovered over his shoulders, their attention cycled between the screen and studying the man in the adjacent room. Monger checked his watch for the current time, located the video feed, and began scanning the recording. He repeatedly played back the prior five minutes from the interrogation room. No one could confirm their subject's arm moved. Monger began slowing down the video in hopes of drawing out what Williams saw, but he was having no luck. He entwined his fingers behind his neck, elbows wide behind his shoulders as the video played. "What are we looking for here? What would this even…"

"Stop!"

Monger startled at Carroll's exclamation. He leaned forward and stopped the feed. "What?"

"It wasn't our imaginations… Back the tape up maybe a minute and slow it down."

Monger did as instructed. "What are we looking for?"

"The top corner of the box closest to the camera. Watch it…"

The video drug along as Mr. Cone sat nearly immobile in the chair on the screen. Williams, Carroll and Monger mirrored his undisturbed nature as the video played on. Tension was palpable suddenly in the quiet room. Then all three gasped.

"Holy…" Monger began.

"Wha…" Williams started at the same time.

"My God…" Carroll finished. "Back it up and play it again." She shook her head. "I wrote it off thinking the crew that crated the artifact just didn't hammer the nail down completely in that corner and that I hadn't noticed it when I entered the room today."

Monger did, and they saw it again. The interrogation room was calm. Their subject sat without motion. Then the nail rose out of a corner of the box about an inch.

Carroll flipped open Monger's notebook on the table and wrote down the time on the video.

"Now back up the video about thirty seconds before this time…" she pointed at the notebook, "…and let's focus on his left arm again."

Monger did as he was told. Williams glanced down at the minute and seconds Carroll had jotted down, then back up at the clock on the video as it rolled closer. They all gasped again.

Mr. Cone's left forearm bulged just seconds before the nail raised.

"Again, but this time in slow motion" Carroll barked.

Monger took no offense as he was too dumbfounded to consider any emotional response. It reminded him of the old snake charmers from India. *Just will the rope into the air and it will obey.*

As the video played, it was plain to see that while the man's upper arm and hand did not move from a resting position on the table, his exposed forearm bulged. To say he flexed his forearm wouldn't be right. His bicep and hand didn't appear to move as they should with a flex of the forearm. The video wasn't ideal for picking up movement so subtle at that range, but it looked as if the man's veins, rather than his muscle, throbbed abnormally.

Monger paused the video mid arm pulse after he rewound it. "That just cannot be a coincidence. Parlor trick? I don't remember anything in his file about him practicing magic, nor did I see anything in his apartment earlier to indicate that."

"Nothing" Williams offered. "He has no background in magic that we're aware of. And what would be the benefit to him anyway? Carroll, I want you back in there before we make a decision regarding our options. He didn't seem to react to what he did. Maybe he's not aware of it? Or he's so good that it didn't faze him. Either way, this may force our hand."

Monger had allowed the video to play as Williams spoke. He noticed Mr. Cone eventually seemingly snap out of whatever trance he was in and massaged his temples. Monger decided the man was either running a near flawless game, or was dead inside. Either way, they were going to have a problem moving forward if he was correct in his assumption of what Williams would suggest based on this new development.

kotov syndrome

Late September, Year 1 A.A.

Ron found himself entering a new phase of utterly losing his patience. Self-psychoanalysis was wearing him down. There was no end in sight. The situation reminded him of studying for a major exam, or toiling through a project at work. He surmised the stakes were much higher here, yet he still had virtually no clue what was expected of him. Ron tried to internalize as much as he could. He wasn't certain why, but knew he shouldn't show weakness. Replaying his demeanor since Director Carroll first left, Ron felt he may have offered the occasional exasperated sigh, but felt he didn't offer much else in that vein.

Speaking of veins, he felt his blood beginning to boil. His ears even felt hot. Ron pushed the long sleeves of his t-shirt up toward his elbows and began to think of how to expedite his release. Then he noticed something. His shirt caught on something against the skin of his right arm. He stretched the long sleeve of his t-shirt and pulled it up above the elbow. Two adhesive strips. One was in the crook of his elbow. The other was down his arm maybe an inch. Both were horizontal to his arm, and both had spots of blood roughly center on the strips. Ron pulled one side of the elbow strip back and saw a dot of crusted blood. *Had they drawn my blood for some reason?* He pulled back his other sleeve but found nothing further.

He sat stewing, arms extended out on the table with his sleeves pushed back, for some time. He was furious at this intrusion in his life, on his person. His arms tingled, his breathing slowed. Time seemed to slow down for him… elongate… *or maybe even stop?* Ron felt like he could hear mumbling… the tones of Director Carroll and Agent Monger's voices on the other side of the glass. *And a third person's voice also?* Suddenly he felt a pulling in his body unlike anything he'd experienced in his life. At the realization the sensation abruptly halted. Time caught up to the present. Ron took in a deep breath and began rubbing his temples.

A short while after the familiar metallic sound of cylinders scraping interrupted his frustration. He refitted the strip to his arm and slid his sleeves down. The flack jacketed soldier unnecessarily put his arm against the door open again for Director Carroll. This time Ron noticed the soldier glance briefly at him. It struck him as completely misplaced. There was some realization, or, could it have been fear in the man's eyes? It was miniscule, but he knew it had showed itself. It just did not fit.

Director Carroll slid her notebook onto the table and sat down behind it. She stared at him. It wasn't contempt he saw. It was something else. He felt she was looking for an angle, or maybe attempting to understand something. He couldn't place it, but sensed that something definitely changed.

"Tell me about your hobbies Mr. Cone."

Ron wanted to scream. *Where was this going?* "What is the relevance here?"

"I asked you a question."

He was flabbergasted. *This is such a waste of time.* "I enjoy drawing. I suppose it's more doodling than anything. I also like to read."

"What do you read?"

"Umm, mostly novels, fiction, some local news also."

"Fiction, huh? Enjoy the imaginary stuff?"

"I suppose. I've read some Non-Fiction also. History… World Wars, along those lines. Non-fiction just doesn't keep my attention much though." Ron struggled to keep himself in line.

"Anything that crosses over? Maybe biographies of entertainers? Actors? Magicians? Musicians?"

His patience was dangling by a thread. "Where is this going? I don't see the relevance of what I read to my handprint being on some object that was dug up half a world away."

"Just curious as to what keeps your interest. I'm always looking for a good novel to read. I enjoy a peek behind the curtain of the mechanics of something."

Ron waited for her to continue. He did not feel compelled to answer any more of these mundane questions. But she waited him out, opening her notebook to a page toward the back. A header titled BOOKS TO READ was underlined across the top of the page. There were a few books listed, but he couldn't read her cursive. He noticed she was tapping her pen on the page. As he met her eyes, she raised her eyebrows expectantly.

"I don't know. I'm not in any book clubs where we review recommendations regularly. You don't strike me as being into Science Fiction. That's pretty much what I read."

She did not blink or move her eyes from his for several awkward moments. He held her stare in frustration. "You haven't inquired regarding the box… Why is that?"

He sighed, thinking another psychological study was beginning with him as the uninterested object of interest.

"Should I have inquired? It's none of my business as far as I'm concerned." He couldn't control verbalizing attitude.

She flipped back through her notebook to her notes from their earlier conversation. "I'd like to revisit your formative years. You were brought up in the church, correct?"

He figured she changed topics to cool him down. And that particular topic worked. "Yes... Catholic."

She referred to her notes. "Catholic schooling... I take it church on Sundays and holidays?"

"Yes."

"Still practicing?"

"Practicing as in going to church? No."

"Still hold the beliefs?"

Ron leaned back in his chair, taking in the question. "I suppose. I believe in *love thy brother*, telling the truth, all of the good stuff." He paused, considering, and then added a caveat. "I wouldn't say that necessarily makes me *Catholic* though. Quite a bit of not *loving thy brother* has been done in the name of Catholicism, in my opinion... in the name of religion in general. I tend to think if you look up the word *paradox*, the definition includes reference to Catholicism and *love thy brother*."

She scribbled more notes. "So man's interpretation is where the faith loses you?"

"I suppose. But it's all interpretation, isn't it? I mean, who wrote it?"

"So what about the Second Coming?"

"Apocalypse? I don't know." He was starting to feel heat again. "Are we here for philosophical conversation? Is this necessary?"

"I'm genuinely interested in your opinion."

"I don't know. I mean look at the world we live in. There's always an evangelist that knows the date the world's going to end. Then there's another after him. Sure there are a lot of negative, horrible things in the world, but it seems there always has been. Doesn't mean the world's ending though, or it probably would have already in my opinion. Is that what you're looking for? Is this some way to analyze if I'm psychotic? Or if I would pull the dumb stunt I'm in here for?"

"How would you be judged if it was the end of the world?"

He forced himself not to roll his eyes. "I don't know how to answer something like that. With all due respect, isn't that question a bit ridiculous? To begin with, it's assuming someone would know what the criteria for judgment are. And in a weird way, doesn't that make for fanaticism, or almost the penultimate human arrogance, or maybe a little bit of both in itself? I don't know."

"How would you judge people if you had that penultimate power?"

"So you're suggesting I'm God?"

She said nothing.

Ron laughed, thinking to himself that this day was just growing more and more bizarre. Then he had a thought, looked down at her pen, raised just off the notebook, and turned stone faced. "I'm not laughing in some maniacal or diluted manner. It's just that I really am lost here." He considered what he said, and looked at her pen again. "Not lost in a religious way. Just lost in what I'm doing here today." He paused again, and felt it necessary to play along. He exhaled. "Am I to take that question as I am The God, or *what criteria I would judge on?*"

"You, what would you judge on?"

His eyes searched. "I cannot say I've put much consideration into it."

"Try."

He considered it and took a deep breath. He was reminded of the occasional heavy conversation with Lilith or Mahi. The depth of the question she asked under other circumstances would have delighted him, as Ron felt there were very few opportunities in life to have a truly valuable discussion. He had never had such a talk with his mother or sister. His mind wandered briefly as to why that was the case. Was he one of few that had so few discussions of higher merit? Or was he just another of the lambs of modern society where so much opportunity was at hand as to numb the senses to a higher purpose?

Ron's thoughts began to pour out. "Truth, morality, justice, righteousness, ethics… They're all words that should carry some weight I suppose. So I suppose the opposites would be the place to start on who would not be worthy. Lies, immorality, lawlessness, self-righteousness, the ethically bereft." He thought further. "I don't believe people should be judged on petty crimes that are suggested in books such as the Bible. Like vulgarity." His head began to spin. He reeled himself in. "That's too large a question I think. And I'm not the person to answer a question like that. I'll be the first to admit I'm fallible. And in tandem with that is the knowledge I'm not the person to be making such decisions."

"Not casting the first stone?"

"Yes, although that wasn't specifically what came to mind. Sure my religious upbringing laid what I'd call a solid moral and ethical foundation. But that's the same foundation that can be found in other religions." He realized he was delving into a self-deprecating tangent when she probably wasn't pushing that button. "I don't agree with the decisions that people close to me and not so close to me make in their lives. I know they have their reasons and often times they believe they're doing what's right, even when I think it's wrong. And in the case of people close to me, they're close to me as our beliefs align, probably the same as anyone with friends. And if I don't agree with them, who's to say I'm right and they're not?"

"Gray area?"

"I'm sorry?"

"Are you saying there's gray area in judgment?"

He wasn't certain if she was baiting him, so Ron

attempted to turn the conversation on her. "Of course. In your position I'm guessing you see it every day..."

Her response came quick, and was very matter of fact. "My position is to eradicate gray area."

He decided on another tact. "How would you decide?"

She was quick and succinct again. "My opinions aren't of consequence here."

"Sure they are. You're asking me something that can't have anything to do with why I'm here... something fantastical. So at this point it's a discussion, not an interro..."

Director Carroll abruptly stood and strode to the door. He didn't finish his sentence due to the shock of rudeness in her actions. She offered a similar knocking sequence to the exit prior, except she sounded out an additional knock.

As the door cycled she turned back to him with a cold face. "You didn't mention anything about the nail being loose from the corner of the box." She stared at him looking for a response. When there was none she turned and departed. The door cycled closed behind her.

Ron hadn't the slightest clue what she was talking about.

zwischenzug

Late September, Year 1 A.A.

"What was that about?" inquired Agent Monger as Director Carroll entered the adjoining room. He did not fully suppress his confusion at what just transpired. He looked from Carroll to their subject through the mirror, then back to Carroll.

"Observe..." she nodded toward the mirror.

Through the mirror, Mr. Cone still sat semi-astonished at what just happened. Moments later his eyes focused, yet still appeared to see nothing. Then they sprang into action, darting to the box in realization of what Director Carroll had suggested. He scanned the box until he located the raised nail. And then he sat in a state of utter befuddlement.

"He doesn't realize..." offered CIO Williams.

Monger palmed and squeezed the back of his neck while attempting to determine what this meant. Williams was clearly ahead of him.

Carroll noticed the gesture, stared at Monger, and offered flatly "He has no idea what this is about." She let her statement linger, partially due to Monger's chiding question upon her return to the room. When there was no response from either man, she declared "Option E."

After several beats, Williams intoned "E? There is no Option E."

"There is now. We release him and monitor his movements. And we work on the other handprint. We know it's not his, we seem to have time to figure out what's going on here based on there being another print, and what could having him see and place his hand on the artifact do for us right now?"

The men considered this. Monger spoke first. "But what about the raised nail?"

"What about it? We can't explain it, and I seriously doubt he could either. We can't suggest he has some special powers based on a nail, either to him or higher ups. Telekinesis, right? And what will that claim do for our credibility regarding handling this case?" Pondering the possibilities, she answered her own question. "High percentage scenario is he and the artifact are pulled out from under us. Then he's treated like a lab rat and his life is possibly ruined, even if nothing comes of it."

"Why should we be concerned about him?" He raised an eyebrow as his face sharpened. "Are you playing the odds? What if he can weaponize the artifact?"

"He may be completely innocent... or guilty of one of the most elaborate and stupid pranks in modern history. As far as weaponization, he is in close proximity to it now. If the most that's going to happen is a loose nail in its containment box, is that a legitimate concern? Also, you're aware of how many soldiers are packed into that hallway... "She tilted her head toward the door. "If something violent or supernatural was going to occur, this was the best shot he had based on how close he is to it. If he had supernatural powers, he would have to know it's in there, right? Therefore, this was his chance... and it would have been contained." She felt it counter-productive to respond to his question of playing the odds and chose not to play into his pettiness.

Initially there was no response. Then Williams had an idea. "We still need to consider his knowledge of it, as well as our friends across the pond."

Carroll was prepared for that as well. "We scare him into silence for now. Besides, who's going to believe him if he has no true knowledge of the artifact? And the cluster that involves our friends overseas is not our department."

Neither man offered a retort. Option E was their choice.

caller, are you there?

Late October, Year 1 A.A.

"HUUUUUUHHHHHH..." Ron moaned, then sat stiff upright in bed. His chest heaved, sweat dripped everywhere down his face. Frantically he looked around for the man with... His thought was bullied out of mind by the phone ringing. He looked at the nightstand. Not there. Another ring presented itself. He leaned over the side of his bed. Then yet another ring was heard. This time he saw a dim light underneath his bed. Ron bent completely over, groped beneath the bed and picked up on the next ring. The best he could offer was an utterly confused "Yeah?"

Ron heard what sounded like distant sobbing. The sound shocked further coherence into him. He offered a more confident, and quizzical "Hello? Is someone there?" He heard a closer whimper through the receiver. Female... Possibly attempting to gain control of herself?

"I'm... Oh son, I'm..." Slurred words.

He exhaled a whispered, "Mom?"

"I just couldn't handle..." She sounded drugged. Semi-conscious. *What the hell was going...* Then just a dial tone.

Ron confirmed the call came from his mother's house, and dialed back while launching himself out of bed. His shorts were sticking to his thighs. He realized he had wet himself overnight, rolled his eyes up into his head and swore as he grabbed jeans and a t-shirt. Heading to the bathroom he passed the photograph of the lonely withered tree. It loomed over him. He briefly cleaned himself off before changing. He did not take notice of the clock. 11:27am.

bad vibrations

October 17, Year 17 A.A.

Early evening... autumn. A voluminous amount of stars in the sky due to being well beyond any city. Sparse clouds hung solely to draw attention to themselves. He lifted his head, drawing in the damp, crisp air in a useless attempt to pull his mind back to the present. Then he closed his exhausted eyes, succumbing to the weight that always followed.

A specific trigger managed to heft the thousand pounds of past mistakes and paths untraveled onto his chest from time to time. That trigger was typically an ominous song from younger days on a night like this, possibly when driving on a desolate road... Or the thought of an ex (for some subconscious) reason that manages to scratch just under the surface of the ocean of his mind, only to submerge just as quickly... Or the smell of stale beer on a cool, sunny autumn day... Or the silence after something traumatic such as experiencing war firsthand.

His heart sank with these recollections. They fell into categories, which included: cowering from fighting when challenged by another male, not having a defined career path, and not taking time to just stop and listen to the world. The reasons didn't matter... just the lack of adequate response. The specifics also didn't matter. Well, most of them anyway in his estimation. The exception was always the most aggravating of regrets. The ex… or *almost ex* to be more accurate. *What could have been?* Why he reacted the way he did. *And what would have happened if I chose otherwise? Where is she now? Here or beyond?* Maybe it wasn't even her he missed. Maybe it was the idea of her.

But there was also the larger picture. Why did these inadequacies hang over him, sometimes for decades? Was he serving punishment for a crime? Being reminded of how not to act if a similar situation presented itself? Was a score being tallied and he failing based on all of these decisions? *Or are the failings and memory of them study for passing some final test that really counts?*

She was on the fringe of his group of friends. He found her attractive physically first, and was only more intrigued once she opened her mouth. Anymore he was uncertain if he first saw her at work, or at the bar. He remembered taking notice of her early on in both scenarios. The first time he saw her at the bar, she and a friend were sitting on the floor against a wall, sober enough, apparently deep in conversation… not standard bar behavior by any means on both counts. These were just the type of quirks that drew him to her, along with the fact that she apparently overlooked his disability. He had been seeing someone briefly at the time, and believed in relationships. He did not just believe in them, but believed in respecting them, and had always felt that when you didn't, the relationship was over and you may just not realize it yet. The brief relationship fizzled as that interest couldn't overlook his physical deformity, and soon after the girl from work moved out of town.

A few years later, on a particularly inebriated evening when she was visiting their mutual friends, they reminisced on that initial encounter. She told him, wearing quite a pleased smile, that they had kissed. He didn't recall. Too much alcohol some random night? As she turned her head toward a crowd, he noticed she had been blushing, and surmised she turned her head as she didn't want him to take notice. Curious. They were from different backgrounds. She was suburbs... he was inner city. She came across confident and strong 100% of the time. He interpreted her turning her head and blushing as her way of hiding possible insecurity. So maybe not "100%" of the time.

He ran his hot outstretched left palm from his soot covered forehead down his face, ending with stroking his chest-length black beard absentmindedly. He looked at his palm... soot and blood. He wiped it across his chest. Was the ground still vibrating? Too much blood in the snow... Dark pools in the bright reflection on the snow from the moon and stars in the sky. Too many bodies visible in the fires... He tried to push now out of mind again and replace it with her... with memories of better days. He rubbed at his aching hip. The distant moaning of the injured and dying crept back into his consciousness. He missed his mother. *Where did that come from?* He realized he hadn't thought of her in years.

The breeze was at his back, and smoke billowed over his slumped shoulders. He reached over his shoulder with his left hand and grasped the metal ring resting at the Y intersection on his back sling. He pulled the ring over his shoulder and let it sag. Grasping the hilt of the crackling weapon leaning on his hip, he tugged at it slightly as it had sunk into the ground at least an inch. It sizzled in the snow, carving a small wavy line in the earth as he removed it. He angled the business end of the weapon up through the metal ring, and pushed the crude holster over his shoulder. The crackling tapered off as the three feet of death beyond the handle found its holstered position against his back. *Is it getting heavier? Or is it the moral weight of it dragging me down?* Pivoting on his bad hip, he grimaced and turned away with a hobble from the carnage he was facing.

He placed two fingers between his tightened lips and exhaled sharply, emitting a loud, even tone for seven seconds, followed immediately by a slightly higher tone for another few seconds. Scanning left and right he saw heads across the field turn in his direction. All noise other than moaning and pleading from the injured and dying ceased. Of whom he could see, many of his family were standing. Some were leaning over enemies. Several newer family members sat in seeming bewilderment over what had just occurred. He had no doubt their discomfort included pondering their unknown future. He extended his left arm out in front of him. The glow from his hand was a sickly dark yellow. *Had it changed?* Every day his arm felt slightly heavier, as if someone was injecting tiny quantities of cement into his veins. What was happening to him? With his three and a half fingers extended he indicated they would continue travelling on their destined path.

He almost laughed aloud at the word *family*. He supposed they were the closest he's ever had. At least they were a family he wasn't cheated from. How odd to refer to this group with that term though.

It was time to go. There were a few survivors in the woods. He didn't have to see them to know. He hoped to never come across them again, even though he knew he always did when it was called for. *Always.* Most of his family began to walk westward, the seated collecting themselves at his beckoning, dragging themselves up and slowly moving along. Some hobbled with injury, several supported by others. Those standing over injured enemies continued their task of cleansing before moving on. He began limping on his ordained path also, grimacing at the lightning bolts of pain when he placed weight on his left hip. This pain was becoming more familiar after every incursion. He surmised he had seen too much for one lifetime. He hoped the end was near, and figured if nothing else, the weapon on his back would eventually see to that. So much had changed in his life… in this world. It felt shrouded in darkness, even in the daytime. He felt malice, and then realized he was now the malice in the world. The foreboding had come to reap.

He had given up tracking the years that had passed since this started so long ago. And he had a hard time ruminating on how it came to this… how his prior life was seemingly a wholly different existence from his current one. The headaches typically followed when he attempted to concentrate on the details of his past, as one did now. All he could do was limp along to their next destination and hope for the pain to pass.

fool

Early October, Year 1 A.A.

A week had passed and Ron told no one of his encounter with the Department of Homeland Security. He couldn't shake off a mental fog and numbness as the days wore on. In his free time, he mostly sat at home aimlessly searching for news articles regard the artifact. How was he going to find information on something he knew little to nothing about and hadn't seen? Work became as monotonous as ever on the line. As Ron watched the wheels of the conveyor belt roll, his mind wandered back to his departure from the interrogation room. The large soldier that guarded the door during his stay had entered and handcuffed him, then covered his head once more to blind him from knowing where he was.

Escorted and loaded into what Ron presumed was the same van he had arrived in, someone handcuffed him to a rail in the rear, and drove in silence the entire way home, or rather until a few blocks from home. One of the three agents in the van removed his hood and handcuffs once they were parked in a larger business lot nearby, then pointed him in the right direction upon his exit. It was now late at night, but Ron still needed his eyes to adjust to the city's lights from being covered for an extended time.

Ron heard the van begin to roll behind him as he was blinking repeatedly and orienting himself to his surroundings. Then he heard Agent Monger instruct the driver to stop.

"Mr. Cone."

It wasn't a request for him to turn around... it was an order. As he turned toward the van, Ron saw Monger was in the front passenger seat. He did not realize Monger was a passenger for the ride as he did not speak the entire trip, which was definitely a few hours from what he could ascertain.

Monger held out a business card. "If you think of any additional information relevant to today's discussions... if you are approached by someone regarding any of the discussed information... if you get a tingling feeling you've never felt before... call."

Ron took the card from Monger. It was pristine white. Listed was a ten-digit phone number, with a six-digit extension underneath. Nothing else was listed on either side. "Who should I ask for?" As he looked up from the card Monger was holding his cell phone up to his ear, not paying attention to him.

"Okay, connect Mr. Stanley..."

That was all Ron heard as the van began pulling away, wheels spinning into the night.

Someone called Ron's name. He heard an obnoxious buzzing sound and realized the wheels on the factory line had stopped as he had neglected his station. He offered a meek "Sorry..." as he gazed at disgruntled faces around him. Ron glanced over and saw Mahi smirk then pantomime passing out by cocking his head backward, mouth gaping open with tongue slightly exposed.

Lunch came a short while later. Ron took his customary seat at the end of a cafeteria table furthest into a corner of the room. *Funny how working in a factory was just an extension of high school* he considered. As he opened and began picking at the meal he packed, Mahi sat down smiling.

"What?"

"What yourself?" Mahi responded with the frozen curious smirk.

"Why the grin?"

"Why not?" After no response, Mahi offered "Okay, just you asleep at the wheel earlier..." He opened his brown bag, which was labeled #79 with a thick black marker, and began spreading his lunch out in front of him. "What's up with you lately? You seem like you've abandoned your mental ship these days."

Ron pondered that, much like he has previously pondered Mahi's reasoning behind numbering his lunch bags rather than simply writing his name on them before work. Any time he questioned it, Mahi had a new reason. *All a game.* "I don't know..."

"You do."

That was an odd response, he thought.
Mahi must have sensed him thinking that as he added "You're the only one inhabiting your mind." He had his sandwich in his hands. He leaned over it and the table, narrowing and shifting his eyes left and right. In a hushed tone he wondered "Unless you're not???"

Mahi always had a way of snapping him out of a funk. But this was also different. Ron hadn't been able to fully conceptualize what had happened to him, and the only drivers that remained from the experience were to learn as much as he could about the object, and to avoid any conversation regarding that day, which was punctuated through Mahi. His research had turned out very little information. It was the equivalent of holding on to the middle of a rope burning at each end. He could not track down much information regarding the crew that discovered the object, including any means of locating any of them. It was as if they were wiped clean from the digital world. Along with that, there was no trail of where the object was now.

Oddly, Ron felt like the heat from the rope was getting hotter. He had no evidence of this, but felt something was closing on him. He considered himself intelligent enough to realize this was probably just paranoia. But that explanation didn't feel right all the time either. So Mahi was becoming his only other viable option to make sense of this. Lilith didn't feel quite right even though he couldn't explain to himself why.

"Um, hello???"

"Sorry..." Ron came back to the present. He'd been considering for days how to tactfully approach Mahi. "You know I was thinking about your heritage..." He took a bite of his sandwich.

"UGH, EVERY TIME I open my lunch..."

"Well Middle Eastern food is just a bit outside of traditional American food..."

Mahi rolled his eyes. "Very funny. Please tell me you know India is not a part of the Middle East?"

He stopped chewing and stared at Mahi, mouth ajar. "What?"

"Shut up. Seriously? I hope that isn't some secret cool card you figured you held all these years... 'Oh, I know someone from the Middle East... I'm in the *in crowd*...'" he preened.

"Wait, what? India's not in the Middle East? Seriously?"

Mahi's amused face fell away. "Oh my. Now I'm not certain if I should be more concerned about your space cadet nature lately, or about the fact that we've known each other for most of our lives and you don't even know where I'm from."

"But wait, does your family have Middle Eastern ties? Is that where I'm confused?"

"Sorry numbskull..." Mahi held his arm directly out across the table, "...my skin color doesn't admit me automatic inclusion in that area of the world. You know I don't know much about my past, but I do know that doesn't include the Middle East. India is the Middle East's neighbor. Does that help your simple mind? I can probably make a map out of my pretzel sticks…" He began taking several out of his baggie.

"Wow, I'm sorry. I just assumed…"

"I'm not insulted. More amused." He let it go. "Now seriously, what's been bothering you lately my little pookie?" Mahi gave him mock doe eyes with extra concern and long blinks.

He sat back for a time, dumbstruck. "Okay, we need to talk. Something happened to me last week." Ron then reluctantly recanted the story in its entirety. He figured Mahi would laugh at him, or throw food at him anticipating it was all a tall yarn, but neither happened. This seemed odd too, but Mahi quickly assuaged that thought after Ron concluded with being dropped off in the parking lot.

"I knew something was wrong by the way you've been acting. I just didn't realize it was that serious. I wondered maybe you and Lilith…" he trailed off, offering only a grim face.

Ron bypassed the mention of Lilith. "What do you make of it?"

"No clue… I mean you know I'll testify or whatever for you that you're not some terrorist or whatever the hell they're presuming." He contemplated, rolling a pretzel stick between his knuckles. "Maybe you're destined for something bigger?" Mahi mused.

"You sound like my mother."

Mahi was still thinking. "I mean it. What else could this indicate? Why would they be confident that your handprint matches the artifact and put you through incarceration and interrogation if they weren't confident you're involved one way or another?" He stopped. "Don't give me that condescending look. I can appreciate that what I'm saying sounds ridiculous, but what we need to consider is what if it's not?"

Ron rubbed at his face with his hands, inhaling and exhaling deeply. "So here's the part I didn't tell them..." He inhaled deeply and licked his dry lips. "Probably because I'm still not certain I believe it myself..." He groaned at the words that were about to pass through his lips. "I think I moved the nail."

"WHAT???" They both looked around at coworkers in the lunchroom, several of which had turned toward them at the exclamation. Mahi was just as startled at the volume of his tone as everyone else seemingly was. He shot dirty looks at the onlookers though, who in turn only shook their heads and resumed their lunch. He lowered his voice. "Sorry... What???"

"I'm serious. I don't know how to explain it, but I felt a twinge in my arm. Almost like when you roll your elbow on a surface and feel the skin or veins or whatever shudder against the bone?" He thought about his own explanation. "That's the best I can describe it. I didn't realize I moved the nail though until Carroll called it to my attention. That box was sealed smoothly shut when I got there. I was sitting in an otherwise empty room for hours..." He looked around, realizing he was now being loud. He ducked his head slightly as if that would make him quieter. "I had plenty of time to stare at that box. What they hell does that mean?"

"Seriously, you can move stuff by thinking about it?" There was no irony in Mahi's voice. He was clearly accepting what his friend was saying and gave the impression of being shocked himself.

"No. I mean not that I'm aware of. Oh, and I forgot to mention there were adhesive strips on my arm while I was there. I think they drugged me somehow at some point. Or took blood... or both. No clue when or how as I don't remember any needles, passing out, or waking up at any point. Nothing like that..."

"And you don't think the twinge you felt was just whatever they did to your arm?"

"No. There was more to it than a twinge. I don't know how to describe it, Mahi, other than to say it wasn't just an everyday tic."

"You know what was in the box, right?"

"No, what?"

"The artifact." He was totally somber.

It hit Ron like a ton of bricks. It was obvious but he had never added it up. What a fool... Just like thinking Mahi had ties to the Middle East. One of the few news articles he'd read about the artifact's discovery was it was roughly seven feet long. The box in the interrogation room was at least that length.

Mahi went on. "They were testing you, man. Holy crap. This is legit. You mean you didn't know that???"

"I swear it. I was too freaked out by the whole experience. And I assumed the box was some type of mind game on their part, nothing more. I've been so focused on reviewing news articles and keeping my mouth shut that I never really considered what was in the box." His mind began firing quickly. "You know you can't say anything about this to anyone, right?"

"Of course." Mahi paused. "Does anyone else know? Lilith? Your sister?"

"No, no, and no. My sister? You think I'd tell her something like this?"

"I guess I think after you convince her you're not screwing around with her, she would have a level head."

Ron considered that. "Never thought of it like that, but you're probably right. No, haven't told her. This is just with you and me for now."

the curvature of parallel lines

Mid-October, Year 1 A.A.

It had been days since he and Mahi had their talk. In those days aspirin consumption had become ritual. Ron figured the stress headaches would pass with a combination of medication and gaining some distance from this confounding time in his life. The business card from Monger burned a hole in his mind. Several times, he grew frustrated and confused by all that happened recently, to the point he picked up the phone and began dialing the number on the card, only to hang up at the recollection of Monger's order. He was to call with additional information, not if he needed additional information.

A depression was setting in as he often found himself confused and coalescing conversations with Agent Monger, Director Carroll, and Mahi. Carroll stirred something up in him that he had never truly dwelled on previously... his footprint in life. What mark would he leave on the world? Staring at the puzzle, Ron knew the entire picture was there... in pieces, but there. He felt like he was grasping for control of it all suddenly. Small things began setting him off, like someone revving their car's engine out in the apartment parking lot while he was trying to sleep, or an underachieving coworker perennially complaining that they're overlooked for promotion.

Ron frequently found himself fighting the urge to

scream or to punch a wall. His mind went from sedate to furious when people were seemingly not considerate of other's feelings. Most of the time, he hoped his demeanor was not portraying the deep, seething anger bubbling under his skin. But sometimes he just didn't care, or even hoped the agitator would take notice... either to provoke him further into a confrontation, or so he could infer the error of his ways. Inevitably, he came around to wondering if these impulses, these rampant emotions, were indicative of a repressed sinister side of him, and if they reflected poorly on his value as a moral human being.

Watching and reading about local and national news wasn't helping. A global recession, a possible third World War looming with countries including Russia, North Korea, France, and the United States at odds, famine, holy wars in the Middle East, terrorism most recently typified by a plane felled in Europe… it was all so draining. Ron decided to end his research attempting to determine what the artifact was as he was only spiraling downward. For all he knew it was a case of mistaken identity and that was why he knew nothing of the object. There was only one remaining angle he could pursue.

Ron asked Lilith to grab drinks after work knowing he needed to air out. She was also his best hope for a mental cleansing on multiple fronts.

The bar was particularly empty that morning, possibly due to the gloomy weather. The sky was dull gray. Rain drowsily fell as if it had nothing better to do. Traffic moved at a snail's pace due to the accumulation and lack of visibility. They sat at a four-seat table, wedged into a front corner of the bar. He was seated against the end of the large front window, leaning over a beer. The window was fogged at the outside edges. Lilith sat opposite him in a shaded corner, spinning a mixed drink with an undersized straw. Her face was illuminated by pink and white tube lighting that snaked up from behind her, oddly around the corner, onto the ceiling, only to terminate in his direction near the window.

"I was beginning to think you were upset with me for some reason. I wasn't sure if what I showed you set you off..."

His rebuttal was to her former statement. "I'm sorry. I've been in a funk, and have been getting headaches lately, so I've just been lying low." He began to process her latter statement.

"You okay?"

Ron's eyes were focused off in the distance, thinking. "Yeah." He lost the thread.

"Talk."

"About what?"

"It..." When he didn't respond, she added, "Whatever's been keeping you in a hole, wound tight with a headache. It's all over you."

He peeled back the label on his bottle. "Ever get the feeling everyone's on the move but you? Or maybe that you're at a crossroads and stuck in the ground?"

She smiled slightly in a disarming manner.

"Well, I guess I'm just going through one of those times where I feel like I should be doing more with my life, but I'm wasting it. Or maybe missing it? I don't know, maybe there's not a difference."

"Shaving would be a start." She saw him relax slightly at her attempt to lighten the mood. "Maybe you're just where you should be right now. Maybe we're not to have it all figured out all of the time."

He smiled at her. "Thanks. Oh, and nothing I'm saying is against you here. I'm relieved to be talking to you." He was stoic for a moment. "I guess I feel adrift."

She took his hand and squeezed. "Does that feel uncertain?"

Ron wondered why he hadn't talked to her sooner. She always knew the right thing to say. He began to relax.

"How do you always have it together?"

Lilith released his hand and slowly leaned back. Tucking her hair behind her ears, she looked down and rolled her eyes at herself, head tilted, chin jutted out to a side. "I would not say I always have it together."

"Really? You've never given me the impression otherwise."

She glanced up slowly. "I have better and worse days like you… And doubts regarding who I should be. I regret decisions I've made if that's where you're going."

He wasn't, but felt like she wasn't asking necessarily, and further was opening a new door Ron had not been privy to previously. "Try me…"

"Well maybe not quite the same as you, but I've been persecuted for my decision making in the past, and it's left me wandering aimlessly."

"Sounds heavy." No irony or sarcasm in his tone. This was not what he was expecting at all. He was now consumed in her thoughts.

"It's the word. Ever really think about words carrying weight? Persecuted is right up there. Never a light word." She attempted to tuck the hair behind her ear that she had just tucked previously. She looked down, rolled her eyes again, then offered meekly "Sorry… This isn't about me."

"No. Go on. I'm sick of being in my own head lately."

She considered for a minute. He sat in silence, allowing her any time she needed. Ron wasn't worried about her feeling foolish for breeching what had to be an intimate topic, and therefore offered no reassurances. He'd never met someone so confident. She stirred her drink. "Okay. It's an odd time we live in. The world's always seemed to be a place dominated by religious belief… Of people having blind faith and absolute fear of those unlike them… Well I think that fear is still there, but it's no longer fear of religious differences so much as ideological differences. Religion has seemed to take a back seat."

They both sat and pondered this. Then Lilith continued. "I mean it's still there. But our society isn't like other areas in the world, such as where mass murder by Christians still occurs in Africa, or persecution of the Yezidis in the Middle East is ever-present."

His ears perked up with the last mention. He didn't want to interrupt her.

"If stringency of religious upbringing is graded on a scale of one to ten, my upbringing was about a fifteen. And I never doubted the validity of it... never had a reason... never had an inkling of questioning it."

"But that changed..." She'd always been guarded about her past. This was new.

"Yes. More like it was changed for me." She took a sip from her glass. "Someone I trusted implicitly presented me with information that provided doubt. I won't bore you with the details. I just want you to understand that I was given information that rocked the core of my beliefs. Think of... Umm... Think of the first time you knew your parents were human... when you realized your dad wasn't a superhero."

This wasn't hard for him to visualize, but he didn't recall ever discussing his father with her.

She saw his face change. "Yes, like what you're thinking and feeling right now. I'm going to infer by your body language that whatever you're thinking has been burned into your mind and heart. It will always be with you..."

It wasn't a question, but Ron still nodded. She was bearing her heart. So in return he felt no shame.

"Well that was the seismic quake that happened to me. Everything I'd ever known, blindly loved, was in question. I'd never felt foolishness, naivety, doubt... nothing like that before. I didn't know what to do with myself. And I felt that I couldn't turn to anyone around me. I didn't know who to trust. Should I trust those that made me? That taught me everything I knew? Should I turn to the one that revealed a truth to me I'd never imagined before? Who else knew his secret? I was isolated. I saw no favorable outcome. I would be an outcast whether I left home, or stayed the course in silence. I just felt robbed all the way around…"

He was lost as to what she was saying specifically, but he also understood everything. "You left?"

"Yes. The one who enlightened me left first, but he later returned to take anyone with him who also wanted to leave. Initially I just figured he was selfish to the core. But it ended up that he had his good intentions. He said he gave time for word to get around of his departure. I think he was just as distraught as I was. He wasn't the rebel he was made out to be. Not evil as he was portrayed by our teachers. He was just the original unlucky one to use his mind when he was trusted not to use it for progressive thought. The irony of the whole thing is he ended up being an educator also and was punished for being honest. In some ways, he was more mature and offered enlightenment that was not previously conceivable. I'm rambling, sorry, this is all beside the point."

Was she in a cult? Ron's head was swimming. "Keep going."

"Well, it took a long time to sort it all out, and the conclusion I came to is I had to take all of the information I was given, and when I got to the end of the path, I needed to find my own way through the forest."

"Then what?"

"That's for another time. Where I'm going is all this time later, I'm realizing that we don't have control over when we're presented with a decision. And even if we feel it's unfair, that we weren't prepared, we're better for the experience. It may seem like a lose-lose situation at the time, but it's not. You come through a better person for learning, and for finding the strength to make a decision."

"So it was your decision, not fate?"

Lilith was suddenly stumped. "What an odd question..."

"Sorry... Just listening to how you got to leaving seemed like it was always meant to be."

"Maybe, but I think fate went out of style at that point. I was at my crossroads and I walked. I didn't have to. Two-thirds of us, them, didn't. You have to pull yourself up out of the dirt and move. No one else. You can only apply your knowledge, your morality, your ethics, and make the call with the information in front of you."

The window to his left was largely frosted from the temperature differential, with the exception of moisture streaming down closest to the profile of his body. The illusion created was that of a liquid human form, or possibly a body weeping.

"Thank you."

Lilith looked drained. "I'll be back." She rose and headed for the bathroom.

He suddenly knew what needed to be done. He'd no longer sit inactive in life. Ron pulled his wallet out of his back pocket and ensured the business card Agent Monger gave him was still there.

obviation

Late October, Year 1 A.A.

63 miles per hour in a 55 zone. The inch of snow on the ground is somewhere between solid and wet due to salt on the highway. The city knew it was coming. The streets were largely empty. The Junker is rear wheel drive, and its fish-tailing. The adrenaline coursing through his legs wasn't being fueled by the normal fears of wrecking his car but by the phone call. Ron was driving with one hand and redialing the phone seemingly every minute with his shivering other hand. His car hadn't warmed up yet and he had run out of his apartment in a t-shirt.

The windshield wipers were on high as the snow was still coming down in clumps. The wipers were working as frantically as his mind was. He began to curse himself that something seemingly terrible was happening to his mother and he couldn't get to her quicker due to the weather. Then he almost felt fortunate as the roads were largely devoid of other vehicles. He was no longer certain if he was shaking due to the cold.

It was a few minutes' drive now to his childhood home so Ron gave up on the phone and tossed it onto the passenger seat. Placing his free hand on the wheel, he let off the gas as his car angled onto the steep, long exit ramp. The ramp seemed to go on for a mile, offering plenty of time to brake under normal circumstances.

The phone call. The weather. The Junker. Not normal circumstances. He felt the bald rear tires slide out to the right behind him. Ron let off the brakes and somehow slid straight down the ramp with his car at a 45-degree angle. He figured if he hit the gas just right, he could plunge the car through the eventual left leaning bend. He pushed the pedal down as the right front tire kissed the left-curving solid line. The back right tire found purchase...

But Ron figured wrong and the front right tire bucked right. He hit the cement barrier on the right side of the bend, ramming the front right tire and headlight into the barrier. The tire blew instantly, the headlight and bumper crumpled, and the back right end of the car followed suit, slamming into the wall. His upper body bucked right with the initial impact, then slung even further right with the secondary rear end impact. As the car slid down the barrier parallel with the road, sparks began flying upward from the right side of the car. And his body boomeranged back to the left, catapulting his head first into the hard plastic above the seat belt shoulder harness slot between the driver's side doors. His limbs followed suit, waggling left to right, violently at first, then losing speed quickly. The car drifted...

The blackout lasted a few seconds. Ron slowly opened his eyes and saw two lanes in front of him. He heard a dull buzzing tone in his ear, *the Emergency Broadcast System variety* he thought. He raised his left hand to the side of his head and felt the egg rising quickly.

"Uuuugggghhhhh, shinnt." His eyes slid closed and he felt nauseous. Rolling down the window, Ron began spitting out into the frigid air. The feeling passed. He rolled up the window. Slowly looking forward, the two lanes bled together to reform into one. His pupils focused, recalling where he was and where he needed to be. He exhaled and voiced a clipped "Mom".

The car was still running and in drive. It had come to a gentle rest just off the road against a tree at the bottom of the ramp and across the intersecting street. He was able to back up due to an abundance of gravel on the side of the street, and skidded back onto the road. The car dipped right due to the blown tire. Sparks flew from the rim as he accelerated. Smoke billowed from under the hood. His head began to throb worse from the metallic hissing sound the wheel was making without the tire. As he drove through town he noticed the few passing cars slowing to rubber neck at the spectacle his vehicle had become.

After a few illegal turns Ron parked on the street of his youth, ran up to the front door as quickly as he could while holding the side of his head. It had taken on its own heartbeat he noticed, which offered a small reprieve as it concluded the test of the Emergency Broadcast System. His neck was beginning to stiffen quickly. And as his body continued to run inventory as the shock of the wreck was wearing off, he was beginning to notice aches, his left hip the worst of the pains. Ron figured the slingshot effect must have slammed his body violently against the driver's door.

He slung the screen door open so hard that it recoiled almost as fast and slammed his left hand into the egg on his head before he could extend his arm to stop it. Stars burst across his vision. He pounded on the metal door screaming "MOM!" repeatedly. Panic started to set in. Ron fumbled his keys and dropped them while attempting to find the house key. He picked them up, then dropped them again. Each time he leaned over he felt seasick. Ron took a steadying breath, leaned forward slowly, and grasped them a third time. He slid the correct key into the lock tumbler and turned it, then opened the door just like a million times before. *Well not just like* he considered. *What a dumb thought* his inner voice began to say, and then he stopped cold.

The living room to his mother's house opened to the right of the front door. The room was dark and the old picture tube television was on a stand in the far right corner of the room. Ron noticed the screen was paused on what looked like a morning news program, the still shot of a plateau higher up on a mountain in a desert. There was a small group of tanned adults and a teenager, all wearing gloves, with something looking like a shiny post or beam lying horizontally across all of their upturned palms. Like those pictures when someone catches something out of the sea that was on steroids for a very long time. There was what appeared to be grooves in the ends of the post possibly? He furrowed his brow, tilted his head like a dog that just heard a whistle that humans cannot, and his mind went blank for a second. The egg on his head began to throb loudly due to him furrowing his brow. He extended his hand, placed his palm over his brow and eyes, and slightly squeezed his thumb and finger tips. No time. "MOM!?!" There was still no response. Ron didn't notice the ticker at the bottom of the screen… "… French suspect U.S. Government in murder of two police…"

He ran through the adjoining dining room, and the kitchen behind it, then scanned the back yard from the door in the kitchen. No sign of her. "MOM!!!" Ron ran back through the rooms and bolted up the steps in the living room to the second floor, banister creaking loudly as he grabbed it and slung his weight around the bend and over the initial landing, bounding up every other step from there. Releasing the banister, framed pictures of his family streaked by, like his life flashing before his eyes. With a sudden pang from his hip Ron's foot slipped short on the last carpeted step and slid off before he had his weight down. He fell forward grasping for leverage along the walls, landing on the left side of his chest and hip at the top of the steps. Several framed pictures fell on and around him. One frame bounced down the stairs, landing upright on the landing. It was from his youth. His family in a row on the boardwalk of a beach: father, sister, him, his mother. Ron, his sister, and father all had wide smiles on their faces. His mother displayed a reserved, almost distant demeanor. The flat ocean in the backdrop took on totally different meanings based on whose face was concentrated upon.

Lightning shot up and down his body from the hip he had injured in the car. Ron immediately pressed himself back up and launched himself down the second floor hallway.

"MOM!!!" His old bedroom was first on the left. The bathroom was second. Izzy's bedroom and mother's bedroom was to the right. Only that door was closed. Ron glimpsed his bedroom, then the bathroom and Izzy's bedroom briefly, which led him to grab the knob of the mother's bedroom and throw the door open.

The door slammed into the left side wall, denting the plaster to match the lock on the knob and shaking the large mirror hanging on that wall. The bedroom opened to the right, with the queen size bed taking up most of the room, jutting out from the right side wall. She wasn't on it or on the near side of the bed. His eyes went blank. Ron couldn't understand what was happening. Then he saw the far nightstand, and it dawned on him that he'd also seen something in the mirror. He turned his head back to the left, eyes coming into focus to scan the mirror again. There was a pair of slippers stacked roughly on their side, soles visible, around the far side of the bed. Tears welled in his eyes. "Mom…"

He attempted to run, but his body only hobbled as the adrenaline drained from his body at the sight, allowing the pains from the accident and the fall to take hold of his joints and limbs. Rounding the bed, Ron found his mother lying curled on her side, almost in a fetal position. She was facing the far window, legs stacked left knee slightly over right, hands near her stomach, mostly closed eyes, dark brown hair askew over her jaw and thrown higher on the carpet above her head, almost as if she had fallen over. Hair was also trailing over her slack, open mouth and through the crusting vomit streamed out of her mouth. Several partially digested pills were visible in the vomit. He looked up and saw ibuprofen, antihistamine, and antidepressant bottles on the nightstand. All were opened. There was also an open beer can. His mother didn't drink beer. His mother kept a few beers in the fridge for him.

"Mom? Mom!" Ron between her head and the nightstand, grimacing as shots of pain coursed through his body from multiple sources, including the egg on the side of his head. He began to cry. He fumbled the phone from its base on the nightstand and dialed 911. Pinching the phone between his right ear and shoulder, he then did the only thing that came to mind. In one motion he swept his left hand under most of the hair on her face and slid it up onto her forehead. Then with his right hand he pushed her forehead to arch her head back from her curled body. Ron then jammed his middle two fingers of his free hand into her mouth and as far down her throat as possible.

The phone was ringing. "Come on, come on, COME ON!!!" He looked up blindly toward the window as a car stopped out front, then he scanned the room left to right. He didn't know what he was looking for. A miracle of some kind? Did he just not want to see either possible result of how her body was going to react to his fingers in her throat? Then he saw the notepad on the nightstand and realized he had glimpsed a pen in front of her body along the baseboard under the window. Momentarily he forgot what he was doing.

The notepad was yellow, framed with "From The

Desk of Samantha…" in bold across the top. The top piece of paper was stained with what must have been tears, drops of beer, or both. Written in a slanted, uneven manner across the notepad was *"your twin he has one hand I'm so   fault"*. His face went slack with incomprehension. Isabella wasn't his twin. And she certainly had two hands. Considering the note, he muttered "He?" His head was throbbing hard. The television came back to him… it was the artifact from Director Carroll's picture. The grooves on the ends… hand prints. One was his. The other end was… his twin brother's? Ron suddenly recalled the conversation with his father right before he abandoned his family… the runt dog with three legs. Ron began to scream.

Behind him coming from the direction of the front door was an authoritative "D.H.S.!!! Mr. Cone? Ms. Cone? Mr. Cone???"

Ron stopped screaming long enough to realize the voice belonged to Agent Monger. The edges of Ron's vision began blurring. With what little remaining lucidity he maintained he ripped off the top page of the notepad and jammed it into his pocket. Ron then fell over as everything went black. The phone dropped to the floor.

"Hello? 911… what's your emergency?"

epilogue - world coming down

October 17, Year 17 A.A.

"···and that is the delineation between B.A. and A.A.... Before was a time when there were hundreds of religions in the world, which resulted in chaos. It's probable they all had parts of the truth, but what mostly happened was man twisted his religion to meet his needs, which generally created conflict amongst those of different faiths. The Revealing provided undeniable proof of the creator, and that is why we celebrate August 29th each year as the anniversary of After Apocalypse. It marked the lifting of the veil, the shedding of false religions to reveal the true faith we recognize today. It's why that date is a day of celebration."

The lunch bell rang just as Judah heard his stomach growl for the third time. The sound of the metal ball being swung by rope against the inside of the bell was always a welcome sound. He closed the leather bound book on his desk and began to stand.

"Class..." his teacher barked.

Judah paused at her curt beckon.

"Please ensure you've finished reading the chapter for tomorrow morning's session. I want you ready to discuss the importance of The Revealing in your life." She began to busy herself with paperwork on her desk then quickly looked back up. "And no running to the lunch hall please."

In one motion, Judah swiped his backpack from the back of his chair with his right hand and the sacred text from his desk with his left. He reached up and hitched his backpack onto one shoulder while fluidly tucking the book away into his backpack with the other. Judah attempted to regiment all aspects of his life into fluid motions when possible and a task as rudimentary as this was no exception.

Being first out of the class, he placed his hand flat against the plywood screwed over the broken window of the classroom door, thumb around the loose lower corner for purchase. There was no knob. He flung the door open.

Running down the hallway to the closest exit, he pummeled his way through the doors of the schoolhouse into the bright sunshine. There he stopped cold. Blinker, the town's adopted one eyed cat sat in the middle of the dirt road. Blinker was skittish and as a result only suffered the townsfolk's company under two conditions: Food was being offered, or in the instance she seemingly had an itch she couldn't reach. These facts rendered what he saw as queer. Blinker was sitting properly, front paws straightened with her haunches lowered, tail wagging lazily, but visibly curious behind her. Her head was cocked to the right, as if she saw or heard something askew in the world that she was just now noticing and couldn't figure out. She faced the wilderness a few hundred yards to the east. He scanned the direction of her attention, saw and heard nothing of interest, chalked her behavior up to those instances where a cat saw an unsuspecting delicacy on four small legs, and walked on to the communal lunch hall.

Judah counted the three hundred and twenty-seven footsteps from the main doors of the school to the lunch hall as he did the day before and the days before that. The hall was already filling up with children and adults who were strolling through the front and side doors. Lunch hours could barely be considered that. The cafeteria was open for roughly ninety minutes to accommodate the entire village. It would probably be a shorter timeframe if not for those with a VR (less commonly known as a Village Responsibility) that kept them out far from town center, primarily hunters and farmers. He filed into the lunch line and immediately began to peer around those in front of him to confirm what was on the menu. It looked like sheep meat and root vegetables as usual. He shook his head wondering why he always got his hopes up for something different.

Having arrived early, he found an unoccupied table near a corner of the hall. Judah didn't feel he was particularly antisocial, but he appreciated zoning out between lessons… and window seats. It calmed his mind. He gazed out on the clear sky and densely wooded hillsides, slowing down his chewing from the initial shoveling of food into his mouth. As he blinked, he swore he saw a flash in the sky over a particular hill, and focused his attention until his eyes burned from forcing himself not to blink again.

Nothing. He figured the flash must have just been his blinking… One of those rare occurrences when you inadvertently take notice of the minutia of existence and are thrown off by it. He then noticed another villager, Franz, outside the window on the dirt road also glancing in that same direction. He saw Franz slightly shrug his shoulders and continue his approach to the lunch hall.

"Hello, young sir."

Judah startled at the greeting. He lost his train of thought. Turning, he saw Lucretia sitting down with a tray on the opposite side of the table.

"Oh… hey, Lucretia."

"How goes your schooling?"

He shrugged his shoulders. "Okay." He immediately felt like the planet Jupiter, holding the surrounding asteroid belt with its gravity. Lucretia was the asteroid belt. He guessed being an audience to her rantings was the gravity that continually pulled her from spinning off in another direction. He wondered if his friends were right; that he should not engage in conversations with this woman as she seemed to be crazy. She wasn't boring though, seemed harmless, and at least she had interesting things to say.

As usual, he caught a few of the villagers seated behind her glancing in her direction sharply and exchanging what must be hushed gossip. This no longer bothered him as it once had when his mother and friends initially chided him for speaking to her. Lucretia told what most considered tall tales. The highest in stature included her stating she was from back east where what she called The Reckoning started. She spoke of the end of the electronic age, airplanes and missiles dropping out of the sky without reaching their destinations, lightning on a clear warm day, riots, and an exodus. She said the world was coming down.

He had since read books on electricity, airplanes, and missiles, but never seen any real life examples of them. Lucretia said she believed they may still exist where "the earth hasn't been cleansed". He was born after the end of the electronic age, some seventeen years ago from what he could gather, but couldn't resolve in his mind her logic since no one in their village spoke of a Reckoning or Cleansing. But how could there be no electricity if there wasn't a cleansing? Judging by the sound of it though, electricity brought a lot of baggage with it that he was happier never knowing.

His friends' ridicule focused on her appearance and paranoid demeanor. Her VR was garbage disposal. This left her often looking and smelling foul. As far as he knew, none his friends ever bothered to actually talk to her. His mother (and other adults for that matter) warned him of speaking with her, but they did not deny almost any details of her recollection of the past. He figured that if the adults weren't denying any of it, and most of the technological world seemed to have passed them by, there had to be some truth in her stories. Plus, being a teenager, his mother questioning his motives for engaging in conversation with Lucretia only drove him toward her more.

Judah had been forced to sit with her some time back due to limited seating at a town meeting. He had been very guarded in acknowledging, let alone speaking to her, until she leaned toward him and cracked a self-deprecating joke about smelling worse than one of his friends affectionately referred to as Stinky. He subsequently (and crassly) questioned the village rumor of her originally volunteering for that VR, to which she wisely offered "There are far more stressing duties than knowing the specific expectations of your VR and having much time to yourself". He considered this, that in part her VR required her to go on long walks to the burn pit well outside the village, and pegged her to be much smarter than the villagers largely gave her credit for.

"You look perturbed..." She eyed him like a suspect as he zoned out, twirling one of her mid-back length braids. The left half of her head was braided sloppily from the roots.

"Oh, it's nothing. Just thinking I need to remember an assignment tonight."

They both sat quietly for a few moments while eating, Judah looking out the window, Lucretia biting her fingernails between bits of food. He glanced down at her tray and noticed it was slightly raised off the table. He assumed her notebook was under it.

Lucretia carried a notebook stuffed with additional

paper in it everywhere she went. Part of her reputation has been garnered from that notebook.

"Lucretia?"

It was her turn to startle. She was apparently lost in thought during a particularly involved nail bite. She popped her head up. "What?"

"Can I ask you something that you don't have to answer?"

She smiled widely. "Of course."

"Can you tell me about your notebook?"

Her smile vanished. Her brows furrowed and she lowered her head. He blushed. She raised her head quickly presenting that prior smile. "Of course."

Silence. She offered nothing further, only smiled at him. Now he was totally confused. Maybe his mother and friends were right. "Umm, am I correct that you're not going to answer?"

"What?" She now looked baffled. "No. Oh… OH… I was waiting for you to clarify…"

"What?"

"What?"

His cheeks reddened. "Are you messing with me?"

"What? Oh… OH. No. What do you want to know about it?"

He totally lost his thread. "What?"

She laughed. "The notebook!" she shouted. All noise in the cafeteria ceased and people looked in their direction solemnly.

He had no awareness or care of what was going on around them. He just began laughing. Then she began laughing. Sighs of relief were almost audible from the other villagers, as if something horrible was averted. They went back about their afternoon but most looked perplexed at what just happened, as if they'd never heard laughter before.

Judah had to pull himself together. He felt as if

whatever wall was built up between Lucretia and he by those close to him, the last of it had just fallen over. He had no reason for any misgivings about Lucretia from any of their conversations and now she was proving to have a sense of humor. "I'm sorry." He wiped his eyes. "Why do you always write in the notebook? Are you keeping a journal?"

"No. I'm practicing."

"Writing? Cursive?"

"Ahh, you ARE an observant one. I won't call you out for snooping in knowing that I'm writing in cursive. Let's just say I'm practicing."

"I'm sorry. I wasn't intentionally snooping, it's just that I can see repetition in what you're writing. I don't even know what you're writing. But why? For what?"

"What if I tell you I have a theory?"

"Okay, I'm listening."

"Listening is fine, but it won't do here. I need you to HEAR. And I'd prefer you keep this between us." She leaned in over the table with a whisper, shifting her eyes side to side. "Don't want people around here thinking I'm..." She put her left hand up to the side of her head and began swirling her index finger near her ear.

He didn't know how to react. *How can she seem pretty normal to me but seemingly no one else? Or was she just straight-through off-kilter?* He smiled at her. "I can handle it."

"Atta boy." She inhaled deeply, closing her eyes. "Okay, okay, okay, okay, OKAY." She opened them wide. "What hand am I writing with Sherlock?"

"Ahh, left?" He didn't follow *Sherlock*, but didn't feel it was important.

"VERY good."

"Notice anything else?"

"Ahh, no." He pondered it. She gave him time as he had a look of consternation on his face. "Nothing... Wait. It's... sloppy?" He blushed. He didn't want to insult her.

Her smile disappeared. His eyebrows arched in the middle and his face found an even deeper shade of red than before. She gritted her teeth in anger. He opened his mouth but she held her hand up and smiled. "Gotcha…"

They shared a laugh again.

She snapped her head toward the window quickly. The smile disappeared from her face as she scanned the area outside. She rolled her lips inward and pinched them between her teeth.

"You okay?" Judah offered uncertainly.

No response. She inhaled deeply through her nose as she turned back to him quickly. She unrolled her lips. "Nothing. Where were we? Ahh, yes. It's just a theory. I'm afraid the only way to prove it may be at our Reckoning." She glanced around suspiciously at no one in particular, then leaned in. "Science has never been able to confirm why the percentage of left-handed individuals has been relatively consistent over the centuries, and at such a cumulative disadvantage to the right-handed populous."

Judah began to wonder if he made the wrong decision in taking her at her word. Her theory was beginning to reek of a tall tale.

"I've seen that look on other people's faces in the past, you know. Awful early in the conversation to begin judging…" She made a sour face, at which Judah's cheeks grew red again. He lowered his head in shame. "No matter. We'll find out in due time anyhow. My theory is that lefties have some type of direct line back to our Maker."

"Doesn't everyone?" He saw her reaction and immediately knew he phrased his retort poorly. "I'm sorry. I just mean we all are related to God, correct?"

"Apology accepted. And I could have been clearer, young sir. I don't know if it's DNA, or what it is, but remember, I was there when it began." He nodded to this. "Well, I saw people with weapons. And it jumped out at me. There was an inordinate amount of people that were holding weapons in their left hand. And that included their leader. It only struck me as it looked so out of the ordinary. And why would nature keep lefties around since righties are dominant?"

"You saw HIM?????"

"How do YOU know of him?"

Judah clammed up.

"Okay, I won't push. And your silence tells me you know more than just *of* him." A pause, and then it was as if a switch was turned on in her head. "You think he knows don't you? Like Santa Claus?" She sensed she might be pushing him too far. "You can be open with me. Look around…" She extended her left arm in front of her, palm up, and waved it out to her side. "No one will listen to anything I say. And why would I tell anyone details of our conversations?"

"This is making me uncomfortable. I'm… I'm sorry."

"Don't be sorry. Sometimes you have to be in an uncomfortable situation to learn. I've seen the books you read here. You think the first people to fly were comfortable?"

"I don't know, I just…" He saw something flash from the corner of his eye. He looked out the window.

Lucretia stared at him, then slowly turned her head in the direction he was looking. "What did you see?"

"A flash I think? I swore it happened on my way in here but at the time thought it must have just been my blinking."

"Let's go outside."

They both pushed off from the table, leaving their trays and belongings. Lucretia, half aware, turned back and picked up her notebook from under her tray. They walked out of the cafeteria with several of the villagers taking notice of them.

Walking around the building they faced the east. It

was still sunny and clear. They studied the wilderness and the gloomy, cloudy sky a few hundred yards away. It was quiet, but neither of them could initially put a finger on why. Lucretia looked around, shielding her eyes with a hand to scan the farm due north of their location.

"The animals."

Judah didn't follow. "What animals?"

"The farm. Listen."

He turned toward the farm. Nothing. No sound. He could see a few horses out in the field. They were standing still, looking east in the direction of the wilderness. Both he and Lucretia slowly turned to face east again, as if turning to witness a tornado they knew they couldn't outrun

There was nothing seemingly forever. Then they saw lightning rise from the wilderness up into the sky. There was no accompanying thunder. Lucretia exhaled sharply as if the wind had been knocked out of her. "We need to leave."

"What?"

"Go. We need to go."

"Why?"

"They're here. HE'S here."

"Should we be afraid?" He was breathing heavier and becoming scared.

"I don't know. But I've seen what they're capable of. And that was years ago when this was just getting started. We don't want to be here, at least initially."

"But won't they find us anyway?"

"Eventually, yes… but I don't like gambling with my life." She was feverishly kneading her hands through a chunk of braids in her hair, stroking downward quickly and beginning again near the roots. "Listen, you know most of the villagers don't come from here, correct?"

He nodded.

"And you know travelers come through here and

quickly keep moving, right? Ever notice no one really stays other than those that have been here for a long time?"

He nodded again.

"And ever noticed they're never heading east?"

He shook his head this time.

"It's because people are scared. Our existence is ruled by fight, flight, or fright. If you think or know you're outmatched, you're going to run. Even believers are going to be scared because they just don't KNOW. There's no way to know. Even the prideful have no guarantees. We don't want to be here when they arrive, Judah."

"Okay, let's warn everyone."

"It's going to be crying wolf. And that might make matters worse. No one trusts me, Judah. They think I'm crazy. You don't think I know this? Who's going to listen to a crazy person telling them death is coming??? It's only going to stir people up and might stop us from getting out of here."

He considered this and felt trapped. He was beginning to hyperventilate. "I can't... I can't.... I don't want to die. I don't want to leave our loved ones, our home."

"Slow down." She turned to look at him, and clutched his hands. "Judah, we might be okay if we leave now. But we're losing time quickly. Deep down you knew this day was going to come. We all do. This is why everyone speaks in hushed tones, or doesn't speak at all of The Reckoning. Does your mother talk to you about it?"

He shook his head. "I know she knows of it, but I think she feels she's protecting me from it by not talking about it... almost like I'm too young."

"No one is young anymore. We don't have that luxury. We need to leave now. Go home, pack a bag... Some warm and cold clothes, food, just what you can carry. And a sleeping bag if you have one. Meet me at the southern edge of the wilderness in ten minutes. Try not to arouse suspicion."

"What about my mother?" he offered in a hushed panic.

"Where is she?"

"At work... out in the fields." He was desperate.

"She'll have to take her chances."

"No, I'm not..." he began frantically.

Lucretia cut him off. "What would she want for you? You're her priority. Would she want you in harm's way, OR as far away from harm as possible?"

He couldn't speak.

"Listen... You know it's the Autumn reap. She could be very far out in the fields, and the valley's flat. She's going to either see or hear it when it starts and may have more than enough time to run and hide until it's over. We've just got to get far away from here fast. We'll see if we can find a vantage point until it's over."

"What's a vantage point?"

"Go. Run. We have to leave now." Her attention was drawn back to the wilderness. She squinted, thinking she saw a small, yellowish hue deep behind the tree line. "Five minutes max... to your house and right back out. No looking back. Watch the tree line to the south for me. And I'll watch for you."

Lucretia shoved him in the direction of his home and ran toward her own. A few minutes later she was heading from her home quickly south toward the tree line. Seeing a flash in the corner of her eye her head snapped easterly. There were three people emerging out of the wilderness, with what appeared to be the first snow of the season falling from above them. The man in the middle was carrying the weapon she'd seen all those years ago and prayed to never see again. Lucretia was certain of it not just from the staff being half the length of his body, or from the yellowish hue around it, but with the next flash that channeled upward from it into the cloudy sky... lightning in reverse. The bearer of it was not the man from the beginning of The Reckoning though. He was far away, but he certainly appeared to have long black hair and a large black beard, where the man she'd seen in the beginning had brown hair... and two hands.

If they live through today, Lucretia hoped that Judah would forgive her for lying to him if the worst came true. She had no idea what his mother thought, but upon seeing these men it was very possible his mother would not live. Lucretia knew that when The Reckoning comes, it is fast and violent, and there seemed to be no true sense as to who lived and who died.

acknowledgements

My family and friends offered unwavering support in this effort, and for that I am grateful beyond what can be put in print. Petunia, Teflon, Yeti, Officer, and Goldilocks, you know what you did, and I count myself lucky for it.

about the author

Neil Charles lives in Pittsburgh, Pennsylvania with his family. *Duality* is his first novel.

www.ingramcontent.com/pod-product-compliance
Lightning Source LLC
Chambersburg PA
CBHW061559170626
46811CB00001B/254